LORD OF THE THREE
A.M. DYER

Paperback: 978-0-6454629-8-2

This is the first edtion of this publication

Printed in Australia and Internationally.

Published by Misty House Press

Mistyhousepress@gmail.com

ONE

Olinander was drowning in his mind. This was worse than drowning for real, worse than any dream he'd ever had. The helplessness went beyond lack of breath. If Olin had to describe it, he would say his very soul was suffocating. The void at the end held no semblance to anything he had been through, and the blurriness was quick to fester beyond his vision, overcoming any sliver of comprehension he managed to gain as whatever surrounded him wrapped itself around his mind. That would have done enough harm, even without the voice in his head and what it said.

Killer.

The fallen pitcher lay before him. The chamber was empty, save for himself. He couldn't feel Levyna. Olin split his effort between overcoming the unquenchable thirst and the oddness in his body, but his mind added fuel to the fire, leaving him questioning everything. What others thought of him. What he thought of himself. He struggled against the questions, against wondering why they had returned to his thoughts while his mind and body were consumed.

Olin stepped away from the fallen pitcher and the spilled water, and his eyes snapped open, staring at the floor of the chamber. "How did I get here" he thought to himself. "I must of fallen". His face ached terribly from where he'd hit the ground, but he quickly realized the pain was the least of his problems.

He wasn't in control of his own mind.

Olin's neck cracked from side to side and he peeled himself from the floor, as though he had been yanked up by some invisible hand. It was terrifying. It didn't feel like consciousness; he had no control. He couldn't even tell if his body was upright. It felt like he was standing upside down, with all the blood was rushing to his head. He was left with mere bits and pieces, crumbs of his own awareness, as though it wanted him to know that he was not dead yet.

At every other barraging heartbeat, Olin swung deeper into the blurriness overtaking him in the void, just enough so that there was some sense of movement, even though he had no perception of where he was headed. And all the while he heard the voice in his head curse him again and again. Or was it to remind him?

Killer, it said.

It was his voice, echoing back at him. How could argue with it? He had tried to convince himself it was wrong, but whatever this voice was seemed to know who he was better than he did. It seemed to know that he was cursed to be evil.

Olin failed to recover consciousness enough to know where his legs were taking him, and every heartbeat that reminded him he was still living waned as time passed. This didn't feel like the lack of awareness from drowning in water. If he was drowning, he'd still be able to feel his arms and legs thrash. Here, Olinander was nothing but a simple cloud inside his own body, up until the moment he broke through the fog and opened his eyes to see what was in his hand and who was on the floor, dead in front of him.

He was a killer. A kingkiller.

*

Ranald turned from the window and saw a face that posed no threat. On the contrary, it was a face that kindled the opposite feeling. The king hadn't seen much of the sciff from Ravinshore after the boy had saved his life, but Olin had come anyway, and, even though he couldn't have made himself more valiant, he had brought the palatine's daughter back with him, rescuing from her kidnappers. The king associated Olin's face with bravery. Loyalty. The face of a personal hero.

Ranald waved, signaling the young man to approach. The uncertainty in Ranald's eyes withered momentarily as he watched the distance decrease between him and the man that had saved his life without hesitation. Perhaps it was excitement for company he could trust that made Ranald ignore the blankness on Olin's face as he approached. For a man who had spent a fortnight being cautious and conscious of every single twitch in the muscles and countenance of those around him, Ranald failed to recognize the signs in Olin.

King Ranald moved his had away from the hilt of his sword sheathed at his waist to beckon towards Olin. The Ravinshore lad stepped next to the king, and in the single instant when the king's guard was truly lowered in the past fortnight, Olin attacked. Ranald's hand jerked between reaching for his sword to clasping at the gaping wound at his throat. The knife cut so quick that his brain couldn't register the attack. All he'd seen had been a twitch of Olin's hand before the blade slid across his neck.

Ranald gasped in confusion mixed with fright from the man who had been watchful for so long, only for the end to come by the hands of the same man that had stopped it from happening. Ranald had not seen it; he still could not see it.

As King Ranald gasped for air and his blood spurted from his throat behind the hands clutching at the wound, Olinander blinked open his eyes. And saw what he had done, the way King Ranald's brows twitched and his face contorted in surprise and shock. And then Olin heard the haunting escape of the king's last gasp.

"You."

Him. Olin. He was the one standing over the dead body of the King of Queen's Hill, holding a bloody knife in his hand.

Olin saw the reality of what he had done at the same time he realized there was already a group of witnesses standing behind him. The blood of the king wasn't just on his hand, but had also spurted across his body. He hadn't been dreaming.

Of the faces gawking at him in disbelief and dismay, his eyes sought out only one – Levyna, his pertes. Olin saw more than just shock and confusion in her eyes; he saw the realization that she had been right. He was a killer, like she'd said. Those grey eyes held revulsion. What else would you call a man holding a bloody dagger over the body of a dead king, if not a cold, pitiless killer?

As his heart beat towards an eclipse in his chest, Olin's lips parted in an attempt to plead his case, eyes focused on her, but before he could speak, he was pulled back to the severity of what surrounded him as a voice screamed for the guards. He didn't pay attention to who it belonged to. Levyna stepped back and her mother moved to the side, and around them, Olin saw other movements that were the opposite of a retreat. He didn't bother to see who was approaching before he moved to the open window and jumped.

Barely conscious, Olin hadn't thought to use his magic as he leapt out the window, and he only had a heartbeat in the air to make sure he didn't break his legs as he landed. Olin heard one thing before his feet hit the ground – the sound of someone calling his name.

It was an eerily familiar feeling – jumping out a window to escape trouble, only this time he wasn't simply the innocent wanderer he had been at Walrea. Olin looked left and right briskly, and before he could decide where to run, he heard something else – the bell. The alarm had been sounded to tell the kingdom that the worst had happened – the king had fallen, and a kingkiller was on the run.

The ring of the bell sounded in his head. It was as though it was truly coming from the confines of his skull. Olin felt the vibrations deep in his brain and grabbed his head, letting out a scream as he was crippled where he landed. The longer the bell sounded, the harder it was for him to bear. Olin dropped to his knees as his eyes grew blurry again and he shook his head violently to bring back reality just as a spear landed right in front of him. He scrambled back just in time to miss the arrow that followed, but another came soon after and ripped through his tunic to hit the wall behind him.

"There he is!"

Olinander lifted his head to see the palace guards streaming towards him from every direction. Unprepared to answer for what he had done, Olin turned and ran, away from the palace, leaving the sentries behind as he vanished.

***

Olin landed in Pedina, in the place he had inevitably grown to call home for the past fortnight and a half. He crashed against the mage's table, knocking over an empty bottle as he fell to his knees. The bell from the palace grounds was distant, though he could still hear it if he listened closely. But at least it wasn't affecting him as much. Then the blurriness took over again and the void tugged at his mind. Olin shook his head, trying to shake the feeling loose. He pulled himself up and stumbled towards the shelf. Finally, he looked up, and then turned around the living room, trying to find something to see his own reflection as the blurriness cloaked his periphery yet again.

Olin staggered towards the smaller chamber and found a mirror. He squinted and shook his head again and frowned as his lips twitched as he struggled to see. Finally, he saw what the blurriness looked like from the outside. He dropped the mirror, ignoring the sound of shattering glass as he turned and reached for the wall for support.

Olinander couldn't stay. He knew it was only a matter of time before the guards hunted him here. There was nowhere else in Queen's Hill he could go. He went to the living room, struggling to catch his breath and keep his consciousness. He looked down at his body, the blood on his hands. No one would be stupid enough to risk harboring him. Not in Queen's Hill.

He used his magic again, landing on a small rock in the field north of Hunter's Grove, falling to the ground on his side. Olin rose, and stepped forward. He looked behind, in the distance at the hills of Queen's Hill, then turned ahead again. Black Castle had promised him its door would be open to him no matter what. He was going to find out if that included being a kingkiller of a sister kingdom.

Stumbling, Olin walked in the direction of the haven he had denied twice, each breath harder than the last. Olin couldn't use his magic to travel any further. He could barely recognize where he was and his steps grew weary. The blurriness came again. The accusatory voice followed. And the void beckoned as his raging heart quickened, as though desperate to exit his chest before. Then it suddenly drummed to a stop and Olinander dropped to the ground.

* * *

Thorne thought he would find it a little less uncomfortable here. He had imagined he would be less distracted and have time to put his plan in place from afar. It would, after all, be wise. Safe. But *that* was one of the reasons he couldn't find rest in Edenborough, even though it wasn't the worst place one could seek refuge.

The Lord Watcher of Walrea was hiding. No matter how much he reminded himself that it was sensible, a part of him was very aware that he was cowering.

The Lord Watcher stood by a tree, watching as the last of three people exited the doors of the temple. He didn't care about their purpose at the temple; he had other intentions for his visit.

"Shall I go in and fetch him?" said the younger man next to him.

Thorne shook his head, "No. This is something I must see to myself. It will do me no good if the old wizard takes you apart," he said to the man who had been his accomplice since his arrival in Edenborough. His acquaintance with the man was a result of debt owed. A life debt, like many others Thorne held. It helped that they were aware of what he could do and how easily he could take the life he had spared away. It also helped that the acquaintances were oblivious to the fact that he was the lord watcher of the Order of Walrea. To them, he was no more than a ghost that appeared every now and then.

The lord watcher pulled the hood of his cape further over his face.

"Wait here," he said and headed inside the temple.

Thorne banished memories of a much, much younger time in his life as he passed the front threshold of the temple. The lit torches on the walls brought back images of nights he had been there before. He had no need for sentiment. Walking past the thick columns, twice the girth of the average human, which were holding the roof of the temple in place, Thorne headed to the back of the temple. He entered a passage, blending into the shadows made scarce by the light from the torch in the bracket, but halted as he came face to face with a man – not the one he was seeking. A man in a dark robe stepped out of a room, leaving the door open.

"You don't belong here —"

Thorne waved his hand, throwing the man's body against the wall. It wasn't enough force to kill him, but it would surely leave the man indisposed for a while.

The lord watcher moved on, past a series of hatches to the room at the end of the passageway. He entered the chamber and closed the door. Candles on sticks and an oil lamp on the table lit the room against the coming dusk.

"He's right. You should not be here," a voice said from a chair facing away from the door. The man sitting slowly raised his head.

Thorne knew the voice. "I am only here because I need to be, not because I have any desire to be associated with filth," the lord watcher answered as he walked to face the man.

A moment passed in silence as Thorne stared at the wrinkled and horror-stricken face of the man that had been his master, lit by the candles and the last of daylight streaming through an open window.

A blanket draped across his useless legs and the right side of his face twitched intermittently. "What could you po – possibly want?" he asked.

"I will admit that I didn't think you would still have your senses, let alone still live," Thorne said, watching as the old man's nose flared. "You should be dead."

The old man scoffed, watching Thorne's movements. "And the world would have been much better had you never been born," he said.

Thorne's right hand curled into a fist. "Yet here I am, Father."

His father's face twitched harder at the word; he looked repulsed by it. Thorne didn't feel like dwelling.

"I seem to have gotten myself into a situation."

"Uhn. It must be something serious to drag all of your rotten ego all the way here," his father said, a tinge of pleasure in his voice.

Thorne ground his jaw, knowing there was no untruth to his words. "I lost my threads," he said.

The old man's surprise was immediate, followed quickly by the flash of a grin, "How did you manage that? I must say that is a feat I did not think you would experience."

"It doesn'matter how; I merely need to know how to get them back, quickly."

"Who was it?" His father's thin gray brows pulled together. "Whoever it was must have been extremely powerful; they must have really wanted to end you."

"Forget about who it was or how it happened, just tell me what I need to know!"

"Hm, I never knew hearing anything about you would bring a smile to my face. But this –"

Thorne hadn't missed this. It was his turn for his nose to flare.

"Tell me!" He stepped forward and grabbed his father's throat. The contact only brought a fleeting reaction, hardly the fear Thorne was hoping for.

The old man smiled. "There's nothing to tell you. Though even if I knew, I don't think I would say. But if your threads have been ripped from your hands, there's hardly any chance of getting them back, let alone returning them to their former power. It's the cruelest thing that can be done to a mage – it means you will never be able to do magic on your own without the use of a medium."

Thorne slowly released his hold.

"Had you been a newborn, perhaps there would be hope that they could form again with your essence. But you are hardly human now, let alone one with a soul, are you not?"

Thorne had been denying it for the past six days, hoping all it would take was time. But when nothing had changed, he'd sought answers from someone who knew better, despite how much he hated that he'd had to do it. The ache of the news was interrupted by the sound of the laughter in his father's voice.

"It's over, Thorne. And I won't hide the fact that I am pleased your evil has been butchered at the knees," The old man said, swallowing hard.

Thorne stared at the man and felt the mountain of rage he'd held for all of his life suddenly erupt. He leaned in, towards his father, so his face was next to the old man's ear as though to whisper. Then Thorne wrapped his hand around the man's neck, holding him still and pulling him close as he plunged the dagger he had unsheathed into his old man's heart, slowly, listening to the futile gasp.

"I will savor this," Thorne whispered, pulling the dagger out and placing his hand with the Alzeibier ring over the blood from the wound. Thorne watched the smirk disappear from his father's face as he used the ring to drain the life out of his body, till all that was left was a mere husk.

The lord watcher stepped away from the body. At the threshold to the room, he looked back and waved the lamp and candles off the table and onto his father's shriveled body, watching as it began to burn.

TWO

“Close the palace gates! No one leaves until he's found and captured!” Petr announced as soon as the sentries arrived from their failed attempt to take Olin.

The prince stood with Damiran, next to his brother's body still lying on the floor of the throne room. He looked like his brother, a calmer and matured version, and spoke with the commanding tone of a king, but he didn't sound desperate to be heard.

Prince Petr looked at the faces of everyone who had witnessed what had happened. The shock saturated in the room as the rest of the king's guards filed into the room.

"Search everywhere in this palace – he may not have gone far, find him!" the prince said to some of the guards who had just arrived, causing them to turn on their heels and leave again.

"Shall I ask why *we* must remain?" Gytha said sternly, staring at the man.

"I suppose it is because His Highness the prince believes that we might know something about this," Fiona answered, still holding her daughter's hand.

"That is surely outrageous," William said. "No one here knew this was going to happen."

Levyna sobbed in her mother's hold. She hadn't known for sure where it would lead, but she *had* known something. She had known that someone would die, if not that the king would be the target.

"Three of us have just returned from a trip to the edge of the kingdom. We stumbled upon this just as everyone else did. We know nothing about what happened," Gytha said.

"And that will have to be proven," Petr said.

"And how will that be done, Your Highness?" Fiona asked, taking a step forward but still holding her daughter. "What will prove that we have no explanation, that we are just as lost as you are?"

The bell continued to ring, and the thudding footsteps of the other sentries could be heard outside the castle. The chaos that had ensued was spreading quickly, but hadn't seemed to reach the throne room.

"Because, unlike you, Palatine, there are some here who are merely strangers," the prince said.

"Strangers who wouldn't be unwise enough to have knowledge of the plot for the king's life and still be standing here afterward," Gytha said.

"They had no reason to return here if they knew what was going to happen," the palatine added. "They surely do not lack the means to remove themselves now – they are mages in the palace as guests of I and my daughter."

Damiran stepped towards the prince. "Your Highness, the palatine is right. If they are mages, they remain here at will."

"Who are you to the kingkiller?" Petr asked, looking at Gytha with William standing next to her.

"Olinander is my son," Gytha answered.

"Then you will answer for your son's crimes until he is found!" Petr said.

The guards closest to Gytha moved towards her.

"You don't want to make that mistake, My Lord," Posdel said from where he was barely standing upright on the edge of the room. If anyone doubted what the Gytha could do when she was crossed, Posdel had a more recent memory to testify with.

"Hold!" Fiona ordered and the guards stopped at the command of the palatine. The surprise was instant on the faces of Petr and Damiran, who seemed to have momentarily forgotten what power she wielded.

"I will ask that His Highness acts with reason at this crucial time, and not have the guards waste their time detaining anyone in this room if Olin is to be found and captured, and whatever possible reason he could have for doing what he did is brought to light. The people here are his family. They will know where he might have gone, if he is not in the palace. We cannot turn on everyone, no matter how dire the situation is."

"What other reason could the kingkiller have had, beyond the fact that he has only carried out the mission of the Red Flame. Surely he is a watcher!" Petr said.

"That is harder to believe than you can imagine after he saved King Ranald from Walrea's plot, do you not think?" Fiona said.

"The Red Flame was after the king –"

"Olin is not a watcher!" Levyna shouted, quieting everyone.

"The palatine is not wrong, Your Highness. They can tell us where the lad could have gone so we can find him," Damiran said in the silence.

"And how are we to know they are sincere?" Petr asked. "The king is dead and these are the closest people to the man who has commited the crime. Holding his mother is only the right thing to do."

Gytha's concern about her son's actions kept her from taking offense at the prince's assumption. "I don't know where my son is, Your Highness, but I want to know as much as you. I want to learn why my son di this, and, more importantly, be sure he is well. I would wager my life that something has happened. My son is not a killer, and certainly not one who does the bidding of any Order."

The commander of the palace garrison appeared at the door, "The kingkiller is nowhere in the palace, Your Highness."

Fiona heard her daugher's instant release of breath, one she might not have even been aware that she was holding.

"Olin wouldn't be foolish enough to stay in the palace," Posdel said.

"Spread the search, go door to door around the city if you have to," Petr said.

"Or they could look somewhere with some chance of finding him," Fiona said to the prince. "Perhaps start with his home here in Queen's Hill."

"And where is that?" Damiran asked.

"That would be Pedina," Posdel answered.

*

Fiona could feel her daughter's hands tremble as she took them. More than anyone else, Levyna was shocked at what Olin had done. It was why Fiona wasn't eager to let her daughter out of her grip; she knew that truly Levyna was the one person who could find Olin wherever he was.

Fiona led her daughter to their rooms in the wing of the throne room and ordered the guards that had followed to stay outside, closing the door behind herself and her only child.

It felt as though they could both breathe for the first time all night.

"Levyna?" she said.

Levyna was rubbing her hands over her arms; her breathing, though steady, was growing audible as she paced a few feet back and forth in the room before her mother got a hold of her. Fiona took her daughter's right arm and then raised another hand to her face.

"Levyna, my dear, look at me," Fiona said, and only then did Levyna make eye contact with her mother again.

"Mother, I . . ." The words failed at the first try. Her fine brows grew quivery over her face and her gray eyes turned misty.

Fiona pulled her daughter close and embraced her tightly, much like she had been dying to do since they had walked into the throne room. Fiona had wanted to hold her daughter in her arms and not let go, not just because yet another death had happened in the palace, but because this time the killer had been someone close to her. Fiona couldn't deny, as she felt her daughter's heavy breaths over her shoulder, that she was holding her child to keep her safe from the evil a familiar face could bring.

But as much as she wanted to lock them both away from the rest of the world while they sought answers as to how Olinander had ended up bringing the end that King Ranald had feared all along, Fiona knew something more could put her daughter in danger. She pulled away, leaving her hands on her daughter's shoulders.

"Levyna, listen to me. I know you're confused right now, but what Olin has done is very serious, do you understand me?"

"I know, Mother, I'm not a child."

"I don't mean you are, my dear, but I know how the two of you are. I know that you are more than close to him and you probably know where he is at this very moment. If you do, Levyna, you need to tell me so this doesn't get worse."

"Wh – what?"

"Levyna, now is not the time to hold back because you want to protect him, if Prince Petr or anyone else finds out what you two are, they will assume you are helping him escape."

"So you would have me tell you where he is so you can tell them and have Olin captured?"

"Levyna –"

"You would give him up?" Levyna said, frowning.

"He has murdered the king, Levyna. Be reasonable! I am trying to protect you and stop things from getting worse for him."

"This is not like Olin, and you know it! He had no reason to attack the king, let alone take his life!"

"And yet he did, did he not? We saw it, everyone saw it."

"We saw him standing there, Mother!"

"With the dagger in his hand. My dear, you have to be reasonable!" Fiona said as Levyna moved to plant herself on a chair. "If you know where he is, you have to tell me."

Levyna looked up at her mother's face, fear and disbelief in her eyes. Even for her, Levyna knew it would take some explaining to understand Olin's actions. How could they be different from what they'd all seen? From what they were all thinking? Olin had been standing over the body of King Ranald holding a bloody dagger in his hand. The king's blood had been on him. It hardly got clearer than that. Whatever reasons there might have been, a kingkiller would get nothing less than the wrath of the kingdom. Nothing less than death. And so would his allies.

Fiona stepped closer to her daughter, "Levyna, where is he?" she asked.

"Are you asking as my mother or as the palatine?" Levyna said.

Fiona realized she wasn't prepared to answer that question.

*

William fell a step behind Gytha as the Grand Sorceress approached the door to the palatine's chamber, only to be blocked by the guards outside.

"I need to see them. Move," Gytha said.

"And who do you think you are to demand that? Step away at once!" one of the guards said.

"Someone who is really not in the mood to explain herself to you. If you value those hands, you will move them from the door at once," Gytha answered.

"You must be –" the guard's response was cut short as his hand suddenly twisted and he dropped the spear and fell to the ground. His partner gasped, looked from him to Gytha.

"Move," the Grand Sorceress said again.

The remaining guard stepped aside and Gytha opened the door, stepping in. William followed. As the door closed, the guard on the floor saw that his arm had healed.

"What are you doing here?" Fiona asked.

"I am sorry, Palatine, but I need to speak with your daughter. I need to know where my son is," Gytha said.

"You know what he has done, do you not?"

"And it does not change the fact that he is my son. Now please –"

"I don't know where he is!" Levyna said.

Fiona and Gytha looked at each other before looking back at her. Gytha stepped towards Levyna and crouched in front of her. "Levyna. Everyone in this room knows that you can sense Olinander and I know that can be a blessing and sometimes a curse, but right now I would ask it to be a blessing. Until we know what caused his actions, you are the only connection we have to him. You are the only connection *I* have to him. I must find him, Levyna. I need him to be safe.

"You heard what the seer said. You might be all we have to save him from what is happening." Gytha said.

How could Levyna forget the seer's warning? She remembered well enough, even if she couldn't make proper sense of it. Levyna rubbed her arm again as she slowly shook her head.

"I swear to you, Gytha, it is the truth: I do not know where Olin is. I cannot . . . I cannot sense him now. I don't feel him, and I am terrified, because that never means anything good. It means something bad is about to happen or it already has. The last time I lost him was when I was trapped by the shifter near death." Levyna looked from Gytha to her own mother and then back, voice shaky. "Something is really wrong, that much I can feel."

"You really cannot sense him?" Fiona asked.

"No, Mother, I cannot. Even in the brief moment when we arrived in the palace and saw him in the … It was like he was there and I could see him but I still couldn't *feel* him, and that hardly happens, even when he's upset," Levyna answered.

Fiona could hear the fear in her daughter's voice and felt terrible that this was what it had taken for her to believe that Levyna was telling the truth. Fiona recognized the agony. She had seen a similar one in Olin himself, merely days before when he had been absolutely clueless about where Levyna was after she had been taken by the shifter. Olin had all but pulled his own hair out, and had almost burnt down Posdel's home in frustration. Fiona had witnessed the toll of his anguish, and what it had done to him, and her daughter looked to be on the verge of something similar.

Fiona shifted to place her hand on her daughter's shoulder as Gytha rose. It seemed as though everyone in the room realized the gravity of the situation, and even though finding Olin was the focus, that wouldn't bring peace for those who were close to him.

"What happens now?" Fiona asked, as her daughter rested her head on her arm.

"I am grateful he is not in the palace," Gytha said and met Levyna's eyes. They were both grateful for that. "I hope he isn't found in

Pedina. If Olinander isn't here or at Posdel's house, then I doubt he is in Queen's Hill at all."

* * *

Posdel hadn't had much of a choice. He led the guards to his home. But he was hopeful that they wouldn't find Olin. But as he dismounted the horse and walked towards the front door, Posdel prepared for the chance that he would have to stand between Olinander and the guards. It was the kind of madness he could not have imagined considering a fortnight before, but after everything that had happened, he knew he couldn't stand uselessly by while another apprentice was murdered. Not again.

Posdel knew whose side he was on, even if all the signs pointed to the obvious. Posdel wouldn't believe that Olinander killed the king, even if the sciff told him with his own lips.

The guards streamed past him, and Posdel readied for the worst as the door to his house was ripped open. He held his breath, listening to the sound of crashing and bootsteps as they searched the chambers, and only exhaled to feel the sharp pain of his injury at the announcement that the house was empty.

Not quite so soon, the mage thought.

THREE

Two nights earlier.

Sallen was no colder this night than it had always been. Yet it was hardly suitable for a man to spend out in the open without shelter, warm food in his belly or ale instead. The latter was Hod's favorite; he could live with a belly full of ale if no food ever came. The wool he wore would keep him warm from the outside and the drink would do the same from the inside while helping him forget the troubles he faced, the troubles that had taken him away from the warmth of his shelter in Crow Cave and landed him in the frozen rear of the kingdom of the hills.

Hod sat at a table in the corner of the bar and stared at the plate filled with the leftovers from the last man that had eaten here. A morsel of bread gone dry and stained with mushroom soup; some sort of meat – bird, he could tell that much – picked half to the bone. There was still enough flesh on it for him to know that whoever had eaten hadn't been famished. Or they had been interrupted before they could finish. Hod stared at the plate, first subtly, and then once he noticed a dog shuffling in his direction, whimpering, his brows twitched and he found himself suddenly glancing between the plate and the dog sniffing around.

It belonged to him. The dog got the scraps in the alehouse and it was lurking for its prize of being patient. Hod knew he would have to fend off the animal if he was to get a shot at some semblance of a solid meal tonight. He kicked furtively in the direction of the animal, making sharp and subtle grunting sounds he hoped the dog's ears would pick up as warning.

The dog jerked away at first, looking like he'd gotten the message, but soon came back, to Hod's frustration. He wanted to curse the thing already. He was still glancing between the plate and the animal, and almost didn't see the server approach with a tray in her hand.

"What will you be havin'?" She asked.

Hod's response vanished in his head as he watched her pick up the plate and put it on her tray. It felt as if he'd been punched in the gut.

"Do you speak?" she asked.

He snapped out of it and nodded a blink at her.

"I said what will it be?"

"Ale," he answered, in an almost whispery, hopeless manner.

"Be coming with it," she said, turning around.

Hod watched in despair as she headed towards the counter, picked the plate from her tray, and tipped the food into a bowl on the floor for the dog. Hod was sure the dog smiled as it dipped its head to eat.

Hod's stomach rumbled and he was forced to look away from the dog till the jug of ale was placed on the table in front of him. He reached for the jug, but the server placed her hand over it and tilted her head. She didn't need to use words for him to know what she wanted. Hod sighed as he reached in his pocket and produced a copper.

"I get one more," he said, raising the coin.

"Sure," the server answered as she took the first of the two coppers Hod had, raising her hand from the drink and turning away.

Hod stared at the jug as if it bore life. Picking it up, he drank half at once. When he lowered the jug, leaving it hovering over the table, he saw a face that sent a shock through his body and almost made him choke on the drink.

"So this is where you come to spend my money instead of paying me back?" The man said. He was tall with large arms and a red beard split in two.

"I – I . . ." Hod stuttered.

The man took the jug of ale from Hod and turned it over his head, then grabbed him by his clothes and yanked him from his seat. Hod shouted as he was dragged outside, but none of the faces watching seemed interested in involving themselves. The man took Hod outside and threw him to the street, then picked him up and tossed him against the wall of the tavern. Hod cried out in pain.

"You borrowed money from me and when it was time to pay you thought running away and hiding in Sullen would save you?"

The man landed a punch across Hod's face so hard Hod nearly fell, but the man held him up and began searching for coins. After rummaging through his pockets, the held Hod's last copper in front of his face.

"Where is the rest of my money?" He demanded.

"I don't have it! That's all I got. I swear it!" Hod yelled.

"You don't have my money and yet you're visiting taverns and filling your belly with ale," The man pocketed the copper and slapped Hod hard across the face. Hod dropped to the ground and the man kicked him, aiming for his belly and ignoring Hod's cries as was bashed into the ground by heavy boots.

Hod cowered to protect his body, but it hardly made any difference. He tried to crawl away, but the man got a hold of him. Hod managed a swing, hitting the man in the face with his flailing arm. It took both men by surprise, but his attacker only grew more murderous and Hod realized what he'd done. His hand scrambled on the ground and found a stone. Hod quickly struck again at the man's head as he lunged for Hod. This hit tossed the man backwards, but not enough to fall. Hod had only made things worse.

Hod tried again, this time lunging, but the man grabbed his arm and knocked the stone out of his grip. He punched Hod in the face again, then picked up the stone and did the same thing Hod had done to his bleeding head, only much harder. The man struck so hard that one hit sent Hod to the ground, limp as blood leaked from the wound.

The man spat on the body, dropped the stone, and turned to walk away, but stopped after a few steps when he heard a groan. He turned around. Hod, who he'd thought was dead, was sitting up, unnaturally. Hod cracked his neck and his jaw, and then began to get back on his feet.

The man with the red beard frowned in confusion. "What manner of tough bastard are you?" he asked as he moved back towards Hod, grabbing him by the shirt and cloak again. But this time Hod didn't react, didn't seem scared at all.

The man's face pinched. There was enough light in the street for him to see the cut where Hod's head had been split open. Then Hod's eyes paled, the black of his pupils vanishing almost completely. The man let him go, but wasn't quick enough. Hod, seemingly helpless a moment before, reached up and grabbed him by the scruff of the neck, yanked free the dagger from his scabbard, and plunged it several times into his belly. He didn't stop till the man collapsed.

This time, it was the man with the red beard lying flat on the ground, blood pooling from his gut and mouth as he coughed. Even near death, the horror in the man's eyes wasn't due to his coming end, but what had become of Hod, who should be dead. Hod, who now leaned over him, wiped the bloody dagger on his body, and then raised an arm to brush his own nose, sniffing as he walked away.

* * *

The lord watcher of the Red Flame stood at the edge of the tower in the order's abode. From the wall, the cold breeze ruffled against his neck and the exposed skin of his face. The tower of the Red Flame's den was towards the south border of the kingdom, but it didn't fail to give a view of the hills that could never be obscured.

Gossie wasn't interested in a view of the hills. He turned his palms up, clasped them together, and whispered a word of spell before parting his hands slowly and waving them in the air in front of him. The spell allowed him a closer look at the troops poised a couple hundred yard east towards the forest, waiting for the order of the king.

It was only a matter of time. Any moment now. The lord watcher observed with intent. From this distance they looked barely bigger than ants clustered on the ground.

Gossie snapped his head west, seeing a figure drawing closer. Soon he saw it was a rider fast approaching. Almost at once, he heard a sound. The lord watcher listened carefully to be sure it was indeed what he had been waiting for. The first sound was distant, almost imperceptible and easily missed if he hadn't been paying attention. But then he heard it again. The next toll of the bell was much louder, amplified now for the den to perceive. A small smile crept onto the Lord Watcher's face as he saw the tiny dots positioned east stir. Not long after, steps approached from behind.

Gossie furled his hands into fists and his spell broke.

"The bells, lord watcher," the fifth watcher said.

The lord watcher turned, "Yes, I hear them," he nodded.

"The plan?" The fifth asked.

"Certainly," Gossie answered, stepping away from the edge of the tower.

"I shall admit, though I never doubted the order, I didn't know just how easily it could be accomplished, considering –"

"Sometimes it's good to let your prey run, let it believe that it has shot a freedom, before you snatch the life from it. It not only makes the chase more thrilling, it reminds the rest that you are not a mere hunter," Gossie said as the rest of the circle arrived in the sixth and the fourth watchers. "Ranald the Great has discovered what it feels like to be on the receiving end of the Red Flame's wrath, despite how highly he thought of himself."

The fourth and the sixth glanced at each other, then back at the lord watcher.

"This is what we have been waiting for, is it not?" sixth asked

"Certainly."

"May we ask how it has been managed?" The fourth watcher said. Eden had only told them that Ranald would never see his end coming. The former Lord Watcher hadn't shared anything else with his circle, with the exception of Gossie.

"All you need to know is that Ranald believed he could protect himself by hiding away inside his castle and he was foolish. The same hands that saved him in the past brought him to his end today. Just as we wanted."

"The Ravinshore sciff?" Fifth asked.

"Yes. Perhaps the only person Ranald would never have suspected," Gossie said

"But how did we manage to convince the sciff to turn on Ranald, after everything?" fourth asked.

"He was made to see what he needed to," Gossie answered, not expanding on his answer. The lord watcher didn't owe them details. "Now that Ranald is dead, we will have what we wanted. We merely need to remove a few more pieces."

Gossie towards the steps, where a watcher stood completely masked. It was the rider he had seen approaching.

Gossie looked at the fifth watcher, and Fifth stepped up to the strange watcher, exchanging a few words before returning to the circle.

"He brings news: the king's brother Prince Petr is at the palace."

"That was too quick," sixth said.

"He arrived earlier and witnessed the king's death," said fifth.

Gossie exhaled, "He was certainly not called because Ranald had died. He was there for something else; he *is* there for something else,"

"Is he going to be a problem?" fourth asked.

"The prince can hardly be more of a problem than his brother was. He's there because he wants the throne," the lord watcher answered. "But it appears we have yet another obstacle to deal with."

"And how shall we deal with it?" fifth asked.

Gossie turned to glance towards the city and the tower of the palace castle. "The same way we have with the ones before him. The king has just been assassinated in his own palace. They will be more wary now, we will have to test just how wary. When we learn what we need, Petr will go the way of his brother. There's no room for a monarchy anymore. The Order will take what belongs to it.

"While we wait to reach the hopeful king, leave word for a ghost on the ground. Should those who think they are in charge decide to be ambitious, they shall learn that Queen's Hill is at the mercy of the Order of the Red Flame, and there is no hope for them," the lord watcher finished.

FOUR

Three days ago.

Ilda had experienced many things in her life. Captivity had never been one of them.

Watchers were never meant to ever be seen, let alone captured. A watcher would rather surrender their life rather than be taken alive. A captured watcher could never return to their order. Instead they would live in fear of fear what the order itself would do to make sure the adversary learned nothing from the captured assassin.

It had been over a week. Ilda had barely allowed herself the comfort of slumber. When she did sleep, it was only be for a short while, before her eyes would open and her head would jerk up. The cell in the dungeons was cold and dark, and it seemed as though conditions only grew worse with every day that passed. Though she had been filled with hardness when she'd been first captured, after days of being left alone with her thought, lackin the torture she expected, cut that hardness away.

Ilda moved her leg to kick away the rat squeaking at her feet as she heard a sound she had grown familiar with during her captivity – foot-steps. Ilda hadn't guessed that the sound of foosteps would make her feel relief, even though the footsteps sounded like a group of people, and she couldn't guess their purpose. At least they weren't trying to hid their approach, for worse transpired in subterfuge. The watcher knew well the mischief that accompanied silence and darkness. She had been part of it. She had *been* it. And for a watcher captured by the enemy, one who might have feared nothing, the silence was all too noisy.

But these steps were different. They weren't thudding like those of the guards when they approached. Whoever made them didn't want the sound to herald the pain or torture they would bring. The quiet and almost invincible approach stirred the watcher, and Ilda exhaled and swallowed hard, tugging on her chains for the hundredth time as though it would somehow break this time. But she had to make some kind of effort to give herself an advantage against whatever was coming. But the chains didn't budge.

The faint steps grew closer and the Ilda's eyes locked on the door of her cell. No voice accompanied the steps. A guard opened the door. Ilda watched as he planted the torch in his hand in the bracket on the wall and stepped out, leaving the door open. The watcher's face pulled in a frown as she saw who entered.

It wasn't who she'd expected.

Queen Ariana stood a few steps away from the gate and observed the prisoner. A long moment passed. The two women in contrasting conditions regarded each other. Ilda, in chains nailed several inches deep into the bricks of the wall behind her, wearing the same clothes as when she'd been captured and sitting on the floor next to rats looked up at the queen and her leather shoes and perfectly pressed grey gown. Perhaps it was the silence, or the way the queen was looking at her, but Ilda sought some dignity and rose to her feet a little too quickly, feeling an ache in her feet and her side. She stood before the queen.

Queen Ariana regarded the effort, looking Ilda up and down. "I don't imagine you rose to show me courtesy," Ariana said.

"I merely grew tired of sitting," Ilda answered.

Ariana nodded, "I've heard about you. Of all the watchers that were captured, you were the only woman. I was the one who asked that you be moved here, so you'd be alone."

"I suppose I should be grateful for the company of the rats and the filth, then?"

"You should be grateful that you are still breathing, watcher. Even though every moment that passes I consider making the decision to change that," the queen answered, looking to quench the smugness in the prisoner's expression.

"Why don't you, then? Have my head and have it over with?"

"Because I wanted to meet you. I wanted to see the face of a woman who chose to be part of the order's attack on her own kingdom – on her own king," the queen answered.

Ilda scoffed, "And now that you have?"

"No," Ariana shook her head slowly, unimpressed "I don't believe this is it."

"What?"

"I had thought you would be ...more. Not this, something merely to be pitied – a used tool to be discarded just like every other one."

"I know what you're trying to do, *Your Highness*, and I don't know who told you it would work, but this is pointless," Ilda said.

"No one tells me what to do. Not even my husband, the king. When I said that you are still alive because I am undecided, I meant it. Had I succumbed to the rage I bore after the attack on my husband and the palace, you would be rotting in the ground with the maggots and not just the rats for company, while crows fed on your head on a pike outside the city."

Ilda swallowed at the description and the queen didn't miss it. "I would have swung the blade myself, separating your head from you body. Trust me, I had much more planned," Ariana said. "But after I heard about you, I wanted the rage to simmer so I could see you clearly.

"You should know. Your lord watcher is in the wind. He has abandoned you all, and your order is begging for mercy from the kingdom."

Ilda scoffed, "And if you think this is the end? Then you are far from as wise as you try to pretend,"

"Oh no, I don't think this is over. I know there is more. I know Thorne is out there somewhere, preparing. I know he will return. I am not foolish. And even though no one seems to know where he is, I wanted to hear it from you for myself."

"Hear what?"

"How you were bought. The order's loyalty was to the kingdom. And the truth is that I expected as much from men whose brains can be controlled by a stick between their legs. It has always been true that men claim power, but the true brains come from a woman. I have not been moved any differently by any watcher that has been captured, I feel equal hate for them all. But for you. . . I find myself with an almost equal measure of resentment and curiosity. How did they buy you? What did Thorne promise, for you to ignore the betrayal of your kingdom?"

"The lord watcher sold me nothing, I merely served the Order of Walrea."

"So you are a puppet?" The queen asked, "A brainless doll that moves anywhere it is pointed and draws her dagger at anything and anyone. Even her family?"

"I am no one's puppet."

"You just said you did everything you were told without question. That's what a puppet does, is it not? A puppet doesn't care if it dies, it takes its own life for the cause even if it's against its own kind."

"You waste your breath, *Your Highness,*" Ilda said, pain laced through her voice.

"I probably am. But I wanted to see you with my own eyes and know, if you claim to not be a brainless puppet, why did you attack your king and your kingdom. What was promised you? What did Thorne offer you, to make you do his bidding without question?"

Ilda said nothing.

The queen stepped forward, cutting the distance between them in half. If it hadn't been for the chains, Ilda could have gotten her hand on the queen's throat.

"Was it wealth you were promised? Or was it power?"

Ilda knew it was either sheer stupidity or a bold confidence in the chains that held her that made the queen step even closer. Then Ilda remembered the glint in the queen's eye when she'd spoken about Ilda's death, and knew she wasn't simply confident in the restraints.

"Or can you not answer because you do not know – perhaps he never promised you anything, he never needed to, and you merely followed like a blind dog anyway."

Ilda wouldn't let that pass. "I don't owe you any answer!" she said, unable to keep the emotion from her voice. "But since you're dying of curiosity, you should know that the order has always done the dirty work of the kingdom, since its creation. It has kept the kingdom from war and given it the peace it now enjoys, all the while enduring the resentment while the king and his "true" allies have been the ones taking all of the credit. It was about time things changed! The kingdom needed to know that we were taking what was rightfully ours."

Ariana let out a breath, and the surprise on her face slowly contorted into an expression of disappointment. "Is that all that it took? A vague claim by a deluded master? It sold the men, it sold them all, and it sold you, too?"

"I am a watcher of Walrea, no –"

"Oh enough!"

Ilda ground her teeth at being shut down so easily.

"You cannot have it both ways: you are either a puppet or a master. And it appears that you are nothing after all. Just a filthy little errand thing. You are a watcher, so I suppose that means you have no child, no love, no family. If, for some season of fate, I had been a watcher, I know I would never have been so brainless. Surely, I would have defended my kingdom and the family I thought could never claim, but I would not have been such a fool. But I suppose you don't know what that means beyond blind devotion."

The queen regarded the prisoner with a long glance from head to toe. "I came here to solve a mystery. I had hoped to find a woman who would prove to me that she had a mind of her own, one who would stir me with her own ambition in the order, even if it had come at the expense of my family. Perhaps I would have seen cause to consider her to be the one who helps end all of this. If anything at all mattered to her, and she wasn't merely under the influence of a mad man, then who knows what she could have earned for herself, if never again my trust. Because the order isn't what it was meant to be, and Thorne has corrupted all of its watchers. But it doesn't matter how strong he thinks he is, it only takes the right person to bring it all down from within. I had thought I would perchance find that person here. But I suppose I was wrong, and you deserve nothing more than to rot like the rest of them before I decide I no longer have a need for you."

Ariana stared the watcher in the eyes. "You should enjoy the last of the decency you enjoy, because I promise you it will not get better from here on out."

Ilda scoffed as the queen turned and left the cell. Moments later, the guard removed the torch, leaving the prisoner with the rats at the mercy of the small, distant ray of light shining in from the entrance of the dungeon. Ilda dropped back down to sit on the floor, frowning as the queen's words mixed with the stench of where she was trapped, stabbing sharply at her senses.

* * *

Present day.

Ilda had been expecting it. She'd thought it would come much sooner, but it was happening now nonetheless.

She heard the steps of the guards as they marched towards her cell and she managed to get on her feet before they entered. Ilda attempted a bit of a struggle, even though her strength was dimished after having little to eat than bread and water. A baton knocked her to the ground, quickly followed by a kick to her side and she groaned in pain. A guard stood over her, the tip of his sword inches from her face. The threat kept her still and sensible as the other guards unlocked her chains from the wall, though they kept the ones binding her hands together.

Ilda was hauled to her feet and a sack was thrown over her head, covering her face as she was led out the cell. She could feel the grip of the guards around her arms, bruising her bones as they walked through what she imagined was the passage of the dungeon. She didn't know for sure where she was being taken, but suddenly she saw light through several tiny holes in the woven material over her head, and she knew she was outside.

She heard no jeering, no voices of a crowd, and wasn't being jostled and pelted with stones, so she must not be walking through an enraged mob heading for the gallows just yet. Instead, she smelled and heard horses as she was nudged into the back of what she assumed was a wagon.

If not the gallows just yet, then it was sure where she would rot, the watcher thought.

As they traveled to their unknow destination, Ilda kept her other senses alive, trying to figure out how far away from the city they were. The sack over her head didn't allow for proper visibility, but Ilda could see enough that she was no longer in the dark.

Once enough time had passed on the road, she reached beneath her shirt and pulled out one of the things that had shared the cell with her. The dead rodent lay limp and still warm in her hands. She had been sure to only snap the rat's neck the moment she heard the guards approaching, even though it had been a gamble. Knowing she would most likely never get another chance, Ilda dug into the rat until she broke skin and warm blood soaked her fingers.

The guards heard her scream as she slumped to her side where she sat. Those following behind were able to see her, so she kept still. The wagon ground to a halt at the command of their leader, who also ordered the youngest guard to check the prisoner.

The guard dismounted from his horse and moved towards the wagon.

"You be careful now -- she's a bloody watcher," the leader said.

The guard drew his sword as he reached the wagon. "Hey! You," he said first. Without making any contact, he saw the blood around the prisoner's fingers and wrists, pooling on the wagon bed.

He gasped "By the gods! She's cut herself!"

The young guard didn't hesitate to reach into the wagon to check. The moment he was within reach, Ilda struck silently, and the guard slumped over. The other guard dismounted his horse, calling his comrade's name to no avail. The guards riding in front circled the wagon to see the commander pulling at their comrade's feet, only for the body to fall backwards out of the wagon. A rat bone was impaled in his neck.

Ilda pulled the sack from her head as the guards realized what was happening. Before they could react, she grabbed the sword off the dead guard, and swung at the nearest guard's face before he could block it. The other two dismounted and she wasted no time, blocking an attempted stab by the first guard and kicking him hard in the chest before rolling out of the wagon to escape another swing of the third blade.

Ilda dropped to her knees and swung her sword at the legs of the only guard still standing, aiming for his ankles. The guard screamed and dropped to the ground. The one she had kicked returned, and Ilda blocked his blade as she got to her feet. Then, this time she kicked him between his legs and, as he bent in half in pain, she slashed at his neck. Moving quickly, Ilda stabbed the guard with the slashed ankles, stopping his scream as she buried her blade in his chest.

But she wasn't done, as the commander returned, face covered in blood and swinging his sword widly. Caught unaware, Ilda raised to block, managing to stop the blade from hitting her neck. But this guard wasn't like the others, and he swung again with a reverse strike, slashing Ilda's right shoulder deep and knocking the sword from her grip. Ilda stumbled backward, with no weapon and her hands still cuffed with the chains. The half-blind guard swung again and Ilda had no choice but to use what she had.

Ilda raised her chains to block the swing and, in the same motion, wrapped it around the sword and pulled it away from her face. She fought with the guard only for a moment before yanking the blade forward and pulling the guard with it. This allowed Ilda a chance to get herself behind the guard, throwing the chain over his head and around his neck. Pulling hard and tightening it with all but the last of her strength, she used it to strangle the guard, who flayed uselsessly trying to hit her. But Ilda didn't let go, pulling harder and groaning from pain. The guard dropped his sword and managed to reach for her wounded arm, pressing hard against the cut, but she didn't relent, pulling back until they fell to the ground, the guard on top of her. Soon enough, he stopped flailing, and she waited a full ten counts before she snapped his neck and released her hold, pushing his body away.

Out of breath and sore to the bone, Ilda didn't allow herself to rest on the ground. Instead she reached for the keys on the guard's body and freed her hands, exhaling at being able to feel her wrists for the first time in what felt like forever. Knowing it was only a matter of time before the stagnant wagon and dead guards drew attention, she stripped a guard of his shoes, a belt that could hold a sword, and a cloak before mounting one of the horses and riding north.

FIVE

Gytha knew when the group that had gone to Pedina returned to gatehouse of the palace that her son had not been found, and it was relief that followed a look on her face that only William recognized. Even if Olinander had been captured, even if they had returned with his body, Gytha certainly wouldn't stand by and watch.

Fiona and the rest moved to the throne room to go over what they already knew. The entire palace had been searched, and so had Pedina and just about everywhere Olin had set foot in Queen's Hill. Envoys had been sent to Ravinshore with the news already, but Olin hadn't been see anywhere.

"He cannot hide forever," Petr said after he heard an account of the search's failure.

"No, he cannot. He will be found," Damiran answered.

Posdel didn't look too upset at their failure to find Olin as he Levyna's eyes.

Petr turned his gaze to Gytha, and Fiona could guess what was coming next.

"Your Highness, it would be nothing short of unjust to make the grand sorceress a villain for something she had no knowledge of. Instead, we should consider letting her find her son and bring him back to explain himself," the palatine said, "She can help."

Petr looked to Damiran. Then his gaze moved to Gytha as though thoughtful, but he nodded at the guard standing behind her, and it was obvious that this one hadn't encountered her earlier at the palatine's door, as they eagerly moved towards her.

William merely stood still. The only people who were shocked at what came next were Petr and his cousin, who stepped backwards as all four of the guards suddenly dropped to their knees, screaming.

"It would have been better had you chosen to be understanding, Your Highness. I never wanted your brother dead, and I wouldn't even be here were it not for my son. who I know is no killer. I will go and find him, and I can only promise that I will get to the root of why this has happened, you can know that much," she said as William took her hand and they vanished.

The guards regained control of their bodies and returned to their feet with no permanent damage done. Fiona didn't look sorry Gytha had escaped. The prince turned to stare at her. "The rest of us will remain here, you can rest assured," Fiona said.

* * *

The Order had forced him to abandon the only home he had known, but Gytha hadn't forgotten. This was the first time in years that she had been this close to Wylie's house, but Gytha wouldn't to let memories hold her back as she pushed open the front door and stepped in. Everything she saw pointed to what her son and Wylie had gone through t the hands of the order. It was grounding. She stood in the middle of the living room as uninvited memories still found their way in. The memories she had of him, no bigger than a boy, seemed so long ago that she felt like she was a stranger standing in the house that her son had grown up in.

"Are you alright, Gytha?" William asked.

Gytha nodded, and moved to check the rest of the chambers in the small house. All she found were things that had belonged to Olin, but no sign of her son in any of the rooms.

"If he's not here, then where is he?" William asked.

*

Ella looked up from the bowl of garlic broth in her hand. Her gaze moved from the window towards the door. Sara looked at her, following her glance as the door opened. Old Ron came in, followed by his son.

"How did it go?" Sara asked as she placed a candlestick on the table.

Her son raised a dead rabbit by the feet and Ella's face lit up with a smile as she put the bowl down and stepped to look closer.

"Next time, you come with us," the boy signed as he gave it to her.

"Says who, boy?" Sara asked as she moved a second candle to the top shelf.

"Oh, don't act like you don't know she's old enough to learn to catch her own food," Old Ron said, returning from hanging up the bow and the arrows.

"Not you too," Sara scolded.

"What lie is there? Were you not already skinning rats and gutting doe at her age?" Ron said as he reached for the top shelf and fetched a bottle of ale. Uncorking it, he drank a gulp.

Sara didn't look pleased to have lost the argument, but waved Ella to bring the meat to the kitchen. Before they made it to the fire, Ella looked back at the door again, just as a knock sounded, capturing the attention of everyone in the house.

"Were you expecting a guest?" Sara asked her husband. Old Ron looked like he was holding himself from swallowing the drink in his mouth.

"I havn't grown so old to forget when I invite someone to my home," Old Ron answered. He put the cork back in the bottle and placed it on the table, then nodded at his son, who moved behind the door, to a tall clay pot which hit their sheathed sword.

Old Ron opened the door. The woman pulled the cloak over her head down.The drink he had downed suddenly threatened to choke him as Old Ron coughed and blinked hard at the who was standing outside his home. Of the many faces he had imagined he would find on the other side, this wasn't anywhere close to his expectation.

"Sweet mother of earth . . ." Old Ron said.

"By the gods!" Sara sounded just as shocked.

"Gy – Gytha?" Old Ron said.

Gytha's lips twisted, pulling up at the corners to force an inevitable smile on her face, "Ronolf," she said.

Only Gytha ever called him by his full name. "What are you – how are you –"

"It's good to see you too," the grand sorceress said, "May I come in?"

Old Ron stepped aside to let her in. An unfamiliar man, with his long hair pulled back, followed her inside. He looked out the door, as though to be sure there was no one else, before he closed the door. Ronolf looked to his wife, who seemed just as dumbfounded as he was at their guest.

Sara stepped away from Ella, whom she had instinctively held to the side at the sound of the knock on the door. Inching forward, she picked up the chamberstick closest to her on the table and brought it closer to Gytha's face, as if to be sure it indeed was her.

"It is you," she said.

"Yes, Sara, it is," Gytha answered, taking the candle from Sara's hand and putting it back on the table.

"How long has it been?" said Sara.

"Too bloody long," Old Ron said as the two women embraced.

Coconut with a tinge of bamboo. Gytha was instantly pulled back to the memories of Sara's handy nature as she caught the scent of the woman's hair even after decades. The smile on her face widened so much it pinched her heart. "That's my fault," Gytha said, "I have a lifetime of apologies to give."

"You do, Gytha. I don't even know where to begin with my questions other than: where have you been?" Old Ron said.

"Duken, and around," the grand sorceress answered.

"And you never thought to drop by, even if you didn't see eye-to-eye with Wylie?" Sara asked, unable to keep the acusasion from her voice.

Gytha shook her head, "I didn't hold a grudge against Wylie. Surely you must know that. Things happened and I made decisions that I thought were the best, then. I have realized better since," she said, looking from Sara to Old Ronolf and then to his son.

"Olinander was here not a few days ago, looking for you. He seemed quite upset when we told him we hadn't seen you for well over a decade. At least until you sent us Ella here," Ron said, nodding at the girl.

Gytha looked at Ilda's child, who stood with a dead rabbit in her hand, watching everyone. The thought of her own child took over her senses.

"Ronolf, Sara, though I have missed you both terribly, I am afraid I have not come tonight to merely rekindle old memories."

"I won't deny that I suspected as much," Ron nodded, glancing from her to William. "Bitter to swallow as it may be, if you didn't think to pay us a visit all this while, it would seem very odd that you suddenly choose to do so now without reason."

Gytha was in no place to argue her fault. "This is William, a friend from Duken. He helped me get here. I had hoped to find Olinander here too."

William nodded at their hosts. For a Duken man he seemed quite tall, well-carved and well-groomed.

Sara's brows pulled in a frown, "Is everything alright? Why would you need any help getting here? And would Olin be here?"

"That first question is a bit of a story that can be answered later. What's important now is Olin."

"We haven't seen him since he came looking for you with that friend of his –"

"Levyna was her name. Good on the eyes, that one – the traveler," Sara added.

"Yes," Old Ron nodded, stepping away from the door. "Have you not seen him since? Don't tell me he's still out looking for you."

"No. We have seen each other since then, but something happened," Gytha considered what she was about to say. It would seem absolutely senseless to such old friends. "If you haven't already heard, then you will soon enough – King Ranald of Queen's Hill is dead," she said.

Sara gasped. "What?"

"Was it who we thought– the Red Flame?" Old Ron asked.

"Honestly, Ronolf, I don't know."

"So what does this have to do with Olin?" Sara said.

"It was Olin."

"What was?" asked Ron.

A very brief moment of silence passed before Gytha answered. "Oli-nander was the one holding the knife that killed the king,"

Sara looked from Gytha to her husband and back.

"Surely, you must be joking," Old Ron said.

"I wish I were, but I saw it with my own eyes. So did many others, including the king's brother, Prince Petr."

Sara let out a breath, "Oh. . ."

"So, so –" Old Ron stuttered.

"Olin got away before he could be captured – before anyone could even touch him actually. No one knows what happened. I don't have an explanation and no one knows where he has gone. He's nowhere in Queen's Hill. The search will reach Ravinshore soon, if it hasn't already, but I thought to check where I know he might have come for refuge. Where no one else might think to look."

"Why would . . . why would Olin do – do that?" Sara asked.

"That's what I hope to find out. No doubt all of Queen's Hill is after him, and it's only a matter of time before Ravinshore. Soon, all of the three kingdoms will have his name on their lips. Every moment that passes makes me worry more that something has happened to him." Gytha said.

"Olinander is not a kingkiller," Old Ron said.

"No, he's not. Which is why I must find him before anyone else. They don't know who he is." Gytha didn't sound like a mother who had been absent from her son's life for over two decades and had only just returned. She sounded like she'd known him every moment since he'd been born. "I know in my heart there is an explanation."

"Oh, this is truly terrible," Sara said.

"I know, and I'm sorry it is the news I have brought you after all these years," Gytha said.

Sara shook her head, "Nonsense! Why do you apologize?"

"Because even though he's not here, the mere fact that you know him can be costly," Gyntha looked from Sara and Ronolf to their boy and the little girl in their care. "I cannot imagine how much worse this will be if your family is dragged into it.

"Don't speak that way, Gytha. I'm angered that you think we would ever see Olin as a burden, and truth be told, you would know better had you been around," Old Ron said, not particularly sorry that his words would sting. He had meant them to. "You would know that Olinander is family here, and this house, with us, will always be a refuge, regardless of what trouble he's in."

"I don't mean to offend you, Ronolf. I know what you mean to Olin, and I know that I owe you and your family more than I can ever repay for helping Wylie raise him and keep him safe. You must know that I have misspoken only because I fear what this might mean."

"We know," Sara said, "And we won't shy away from it. Olin is family, and in this house, we stand by ours, no matter what."

"He knows that he can always come here. Now, if he's not here, it's probably because he has thought to go somewhere else first, maybe thought that staying away would keep *us* out of trouble – a foolish thought I would guess he inherited from Wylie." Old Ron said.

SIX

Queen Ariana tried to banish thoughts of the past fortnight. After everything her family had been through and everything she had seen, Ariana would need to purge many things from her mind in order for Ravinshore to approach normalcy once again. Of course, she knew this could all be some illusion, one that would change if the vermin Thorne returned, but the safety of the present moment seemed all too real, and she wouldn't let the persistently lurking panic strangle her her or her family.

One of her greatest fears was that her family would never be able to sit around a table and share a peaceful meal. And yet they were sitting around one right now. Joy blossomed slowly in the bottom of Ariana's heart as she looked from each of her three children around her. Her gaze stopped on her oldest, George, the crown prince of Ravinshore.

Every day that passed, he took more and more after his father. As she watched, the boy looked up from his place to catch his mother's eyes. He smiled.

Ariana hoped that smile was genuine, and he wasn't still cross with her for keeping the truth about what had happened to his father from him until Edmond was healed and safe. Edmond had taken both of their sides on the matter: he had been glad his children were spared the horror of what he had gone through, glad that they hadn't seen what the Egro had done to him, but he had also made it clear that his son should have known. If things had gone differently, if George had had to take the throne, he needed to be prepared for the worst. Edmond had reminded his queen that their, though their son was young, he needed to know who his father's enemies were. Who his own enemies ultimately would be when he sat on the throne.

The argument had lasted for days, and if Ariana was being honest, it hadn't ended. Her first instinct would always be to shield her child from anything the world could throw at him, but she knew she had to realize he wasn't merely a child anymore. The fate of Ravinshore was shifting to his shoulders, whether she liked it or not. And though she certainly dreamt of the day her son would take the throne from his father, she knew, as George's smile teased joy from her fearful heart, that she would never hesitate to do what she needed to do when it came to her child. Even if, in the end, he didn't like it. In the end, he would survive, because she refused to let the world break him so easily.

After the meal, as she and Edmond withdrew to one of the king's private chambers, Ariana was reminded of the fact that they were living an illusion when she saw Ole standing in the passage with his hands behind his back. It was sundown, with dusk on the horizon, and Ariana had been looking forward to an uneventful evening. But the court's counsel waiting for them was a marker of something amiss.

"What is it, Ole?" She asked before her husband could.

"Your Majesty, Your Highness. Apologies for interrupting your evening."

"Since when do y ou apologize for interrupting our evening, Ole, do you not revel in it?" King Edmond asked sarcastically. "What's happened?"

"It is . . . concerning the prisoner, the one being transported to Black Castle dungeons," The court counsel answered, focusing his gaze on the queen.

"The watcher?" Edmond asked.

"Yes, Your Majesty."

"What happened to her?" the queen demanded.

"Your Majesty, I am afraid she has escaped," Ole answered, swallowing hard afterwards.

"What?" Ariana pulled away from her husband and took a step towards Ole, as though warning him to answer differently this time.

"What do you mean she escaped?" the king demanded.

"She broke free of her guards and escaped, Your Majesty."

Ariana growled, "How? How!"

"It's unclear if the convoy was attacked, but all four guards are dead and the prisoner's chains were found by the body of the commander, Your Highness," Ole answered.

"The order, was it?" The king asked.

"I cannot think of anyone else, Your Majesty."

"How did they die?' Ariana asked.

"Different ways. . . Your Majesty, they had cuts from a blade, but one of the guards appeared to have been stabbed in the neck with a rat bone,"

Edmond's bows pinched, "A rat bone?"

"Yes, Your Majesty," Ole nodded, "And a rat's corpse was found in the wagon."

"That convoy was most certainly not attacked by a group of watchers," Queen Ariana said, "It was just one. It was her – she did all of it. She broke free and killed her guards."

"Even for a watcher, that seems far fetched, wouldn't you agree? She was in chains and outnumbered four to one," Edmond said.

"It would have only taken one – one stupid guard to fall for whatever trick she used. A dead rat, of all things," Ariana shook her head as she clenched her fist. She couldn't deny, despite her anger and irritation and the potential danger that could fester because of this, that she was the tiniest bit impressed by how the woman had managed to escape.

Ariana had underestimated the watcher, clearly. At first, she had assumed the woman must have been skilled to thrive in her trade, but then Ariana underestimated what she was capable of after their meeting. She had hoped that time in the dungeons of Black Castle would make the watcher more willing to realize the doom that awaited her. A realization that would lead her to turn on the order.

"I suppose it's pointless to call for a search – where would we sent them?" The king said.

"She is perhaps already behind Walrea's walls," Ariana said.

"I don't think that's true, Your Highness. It's well known that the order doesn't care for a watcher unmasked and captured."

"Still, it doesn't make her any less of a threat," the queen answered, "She is watcher, a killer, and now she is free."

"Make sure you double the guards around the palace tonight. It's doubtful she would be foolish enough to return here, but if we've learned anything, it's that one cannot underestimate the watchers," King Edmond ordered.

Ole bowed and took his leave.

"I should have taken my chance in the dugeon. I should have let my anger lead and taken her head, like I said I would."

"You did nothing wrong. We couldn't have known she would escape."

"Actually, we could have. If we don't fool ourselves, my lord, we must admit there was always a chance that a watcher of the Order of Walrea could easily free themselves from the back of a wagon."

Edmond stepped closer to his wife, "Perhaps, but at least we know that she will never return to Walrea, as Ole has said. The only reason the order would have attacked the convoy would be to kill her themselves. Knowing that, it cuts the odds that she would escape greatly. She was one person against four guards,"

"She's still a watcher, Edmond. I don't like trying to defend our own blunder – my blunder."

"Oh, hush now," the king took her hand, "We answer to no one. And this was not a blunder, certainly not yours."

"Tell that to the family of the guards cut to pieces and stabbed with a rat bone," Ariana said, pulling away from her husband's gaze and turning on her heels to head into the chamber.

King Edmond followed his queen inside, "You're right. Lives were lost, even though they were doing their duties. Our guards are sworn to put their lives on the line for the kingdom, that hasn't changed. I will not berate myself hostage because they underestimate the prisoner, and neither should you."

Ariana sighed as she remembered the look on Ilda's face when she had visited. Her insides churned at the thought that she had played even more part in what had happened – if her conversation, confrontation, and downright condemnation of the watcher had been taken as a dare. But all she'd done was talk, taunt, she hadn't taken action against those who had attacked her husband and her family.

Now she truly wished that she had.

The queen took a seat on a high back leather chair and looked up as Edmond stepped closer, placing his hand on her shoulder. She stared into his green eyes flickering in the fading daylight. The ambiance of the torches in the brackets and the fire in the fireplace reminded her of the illusion she had been enjoying before she set her eyes on Ole and heard his news. King Edmond brushed a loose strand of hair from the side of her face and took her chin in his thumb and first finger, tilting it up gently so he could stare at her even more, and then he leaned down and kissed her. It was soft at first, but quickly grew deeper.

Ariana was pulled back into her illusion.

Edmond inhaled her breath as he kissed her, then he moved his lips to the side of her face, and down to her neck. Ariana's mouth parted as her husband's lips strayed from her neck to her shoulder, his breath rattling against her skin, and his hand cupped her breast through her dress. He slowly massaged it as he lowered himself in front of her, his kisses returned to her lips as he pulled the sleeve of her dress down her shoulder, so he could kiss more of her chest and bosom. Ariana wrapped her hands around his head and gripped his hair as he dropped to his knees in front of her, with his lips around her breast. She left out a soft moan when she felt his hand reach beneath her dress and rest on her inner thigh and her legs instantly parted.

A fire lit inside her and all of her body was ready to burn. Edmond sensed that every movement drove her towards an edge, and it was an edge he was more prepared to share with her as –

A knock sounded at the door and the couple froze. Ariana exhaled and her husband all but snarled.

"You'd better have a good reason for standing there!' The king yelled.

"My complete apologies, my lord."
Ariana sighed.

"Ole, you test my patience. Someone had better be dead, or I will have you sleep naked in the stables tonight!" The king said, still on his knees, hands on his wife.

"It is King Ranald of Queen's Hill, Your Majesty."

"What does he want?"

"He is dead, my lord," Ole said like a man grateful he would not be sleeping naked in the stables.

Edmond and Ariana stared at each other in shock.

*

"What happened?" Edmond asked as he entered the throne room with Ariana a few moments later, to find Ole with the envoy from Queen's Hill. The two men had ridden nonstop for hours till they reached the Black River, where they had found a demican to deliver them to the gatehouse of the palace castle.

"King Ranald was murdered, Your Majesty. His throat was cut right in the throne room of his palace," one of the messengers said after they had bowed in greeting. The one who spoke was bald.

"The Red Flame finally got to him, did they?" King Edmond asked.

"The order has yet to claim responsibility for the deed, but that is our suspicion, Your Majesty," the second messenger said.

Edmond caught his wife's gaze at the mention of a king dying from the hands of his order. A fate he had faced. A fate that may still yet come to pass. "This is terrible news," Edmond said, turning back to the messengers, "Who's in charge of the kingdom now? I know Ranald's son is not yet of age. Is it the palatine?"

"Prince Petr, the king's brother, was at the palace at the time of the incident –"

"One could wonder about the coincidence of his timing," Edmon said.

The messengers looked at each other and then back at the king.

"It is sad to hear about the king's demise. Ravinshore's heart bleeds for Queen's Hill's loss," Queen Ariana said.

"Thank you, Your Highness," the messenger answered.

"But a king's death doesn't often require an envoy to bring the news by way of magic, unless something else calls for such urgency," Ariana noted.

"I was just about to say the same thing," Edmond answered, looking from his wife next to him to the envoy before them.

"Your Majesty, the urgency is in the circumstance of King Ranald's death," the bald messenger said.

"And what circumstance would that be?"

"That it came by the hands of your subject, Your Majesty."

"What?" said Ariana.

Ole's brows rose in shock.

"A Ravinshore murdered the king of Queen's Hill," the messenger said.

"Surely that cannot be. How is that even possible?" Edmond asked.

"We assure you it is true, Your Majesty, as it was witnessed by many eyes including Prince Petr himself, and Palatine Fiona," the second messenger answered.

"What madness came over this subject of mine? How – how are you even certain that they were from Ravinshore?"

"As to what madness took hold of him, we cannot say. We do not know if he was doing the bidding of Red Flame or someone else. All that is certain, my lord, is that a Ravinshore man known as Olin, a guest of the palatine, was found holding the knife over king's Ranald's body," the bald messenger said.

Ariana stepped forward, eyes wide "Olin, you say?"

"Yes, your highness. A sciff from Ravinshore hiding in Queen's Hill," the messenger answered.

"He wouldn't happen to be a curly-haired mage, would he?" the queen asked.

The envoys glanced at each other, no doubt calculating the odds that their kingkiller was known by Ravinshore's very own queen, "The very one."

"That is madness! Olin was here not a few days ago, dined with my family as thanks for saving my life and the kingdom from the order. In fact, did he not also save King Ranald from watchers of the Red

Flame not so long ago?" Edmond asked. "Are you certain you don't have the wrong person? Perhaps a doppelganger or another young man who merely looks like him? Because Olin has always acted to save the kingdoms, not threaten them."

"Your Majesty, this is not a mere accusation. There were witnesses, all of whom saw him. Olin from Ravinshore killed King Ranald," the bald messenger answered.

"What has happened to him now? Has he been captured? Ariana asked.

The second messenger spoke, "No, he has not. He escaped before he could be apprehended – vanished with his magic – and hasn't been found anywhere in Queen's Hill. That is part of the reason for the urgency of our presence here. A Ravinshore has murdered the king of Queen's Hill. You must not give him harbor. Prince Petr has sent us so that Your Majesty and the rest of Ravinshore will be aware: the kingkiller is to be found and delivered to Queen's Hill, if our anger at this crime is ever be a soothed."

It wasn't exactly a threat. But the message was subtle enough for King Edmond to read between the messenger's words. A king was dead and, whether or not it was explicable, it had come from the hand of his subject. It might not be a threat, but it wasn't a message of peace.

SEVEN

The child's head lay on her lap. Isabelle looked down and gently brushed the soft brown hair away from her eyes. There was no need for her to check if the child was awake -- Isabelle could feel every stir as Mary shifted on her leg, even though Isabelle had asked her to go to sleep. Ever since William had left with Gytha, Mary's mood had darkened. She was no longer as cheerful as she had been before, and acted the same as when Isabelle and William had first taken her from Ravinshore.

It didn't take much effort to understand why the girl was seeping back into her shell so soon after the man she had begun to see as a father figure left. Even though Mary knew where he had gone, knew he would come back, unlike her own father. Even though William had promised he would return, it hardly seemed to have made a difference. With each hour that passed, she listened for the sound of footsteps, watching the door or peering out the window looking for his approach.

Isabelle watched, her own heart swelling in her chest at the little girl's anticipation. Isabelle had wondered what it would be like when she'd taken the child following her father's death. But she hadn't hesitated when Mary had been wrapped in her arms after William had found them, and she had never doubted her intentions towards the child. She would protect and care for her, like her father would have wanted. But Isabelle had been unsure of just how well Mary would take to the comfort of a stranger, and when William had asked her to come with him – something she couldn't deny her heart had yearned for, even before she'd appeared at his door – she had wondered how it would affect Mary. To be in the care of one stranger was one thing, two strangers was another matter entirely.

But all of her concerns turned out to be pointless after all, starting from their journey to Duken. Mary, in her grief, had taken to William just as tightly as the strange woman who'd promised to be the mother she'd never had. She hadn't known he was so good with children. His beautiful stories of wild adventures and his crazy jokes took the girl's mind away from what she had happened to her only true family. For Isabelle's part, William's presence had split the burden of having to care for and worry about Mary.

But now he was gone too. Even if it was only to help a friend. But that was the kind of man he was – a man who helped his friends when they came to his door, no matter the grudge they held, her betrayal or how heartbroken she had left him. It was who he was and Isabelle wouldn't change that for anything, even if the friend he had to help was a grand sorceress.

Mary had battered her with questions about Gytha, most of them focused on whether or not the grand sorceress was the kind of person who would protect her friend, and Isabelle had told Mary truthfully what she had seen and what William had told her – that Gytha often used her powers to help strangers, and would do much more to protect a friend. As Isabelle brushed her hopeful daughter's hair and pulled the blanket over her as she stirred again, she hoped that William wasn't proven a liar, and that, for their sake, he returned home.

She hoped this night's arrival, once again without his return, didn't herald another heartbreak on the horizon for the poor child, and for Isabelle, who had just gotten a second chance with him.

* * *

There was a storm in her head borne completely of silence.

Levyna had been helpless, watching everyone decide Olin's fate, while she remained utterly clueless about what had become of her pertes. She had walked through the rest of the day as though living an alternative reality as the chaos of the aftermath of the king's death unfolded around her. She hadn't imagined what his death would mean, not even after they had helped save King Ranald from the Red Flame. Now she didn't have to imagine.

Olinander was a kingkiller. She could not get the words out of her head, even though they felt like a thought that didn't belong. She tried uselessly to figure out where it had gone wrong. Where had she missed the signs?

Of everything he had been accused of, one was all to similar to what she had called him not long before. Levyna sat on the bed in her bedchamber, questions consuming her mind . What if she was right, and that was all he was? What if she had been blind to the truth all along? What if she had simply allowed herself to et carried away by their magic, and ignored the person he was beneath it?

Olinander had taken lives before; she had seen him do it. Posdel had spoken of that night with the shifter. Even he had been worried, and he wouldn't have been worried for nothing. Was it just Olin's magic that had turned on him? Or had the sciff from Ravinshore merely nothing more than a killer?

Or was there a greater ruse? Had Olin been lying about everything -- was he part of the order? Did Walrea even kill his uncle, or was it just.
. .

She shook her head to chase away the abhorrent thoughts her mind had carved from the darkest crevices. It could not be. Every single one of these questions she harbored felt like a betrayal of someone she cared about. Because she still cared about him, even though she had just seen him kill a king.

And now she couldn't see him at all -- she couldn't sense him, couldn't hear him. Levyna felt nothing, as though she were back to before they'd found each other, and it felt completely alien to her. Like half of her consciousness was missing. Eusa's spell had been better in some ways, to this, for at least then she hadn't been conscious enough to feel this terrible.

Something was wrong; she could feel it down to her soul. If Olinander wasn't a kingkiller then what had happened in that throne room? How had he ended up with the knife, covered in blood? Levyna's mind wound back to Kelegro, to the revelations given by the seer.

"He faces a death he cannot escape. A death that will consume him and everything else. Your phoenix faces death."

Olin faces death. Was this where it would come? What did King Ranald's death have to do with it? Why Olin? Or was this the death that would change him? Levyna found no answers to her questions. She wondered if taking the king's life would be the birth of the change that would consume him. What if what came after was her pertes true nature. A . . .

No. It couldn't be. There had to be something she was missing. If only she could sense him. If only she could hear him -- talk to him. Levyna knew this wouldn't be so hard if she simply had a chance to feel what he was feeling, to get answers.

Levyna remembered his eye -- the look on his face when he'd seen her in the throne room. Despite the shock, she hadn't sensed him then, either. He'd been standing there and she had heard nothing. Complete silence. Levyna thought of the last time that had happened.

It had been after he'd rescued her, when he'd lain on the bed recovering. She'd felt it then. She remembered that odd feeling of looking at her pertes and feeling as though he wasn't there. The feeling had made her put her head on his chest till he woke.

Then she remembered what she'd seen flashing in his eyes -- what she'd *thought* she had seen -- but she still could not make sense of it.

None of this was helping her understand, or helping her figure out where he could have gone. If he wasn't in Queen's Hill, then surely he must have found his way to his kingdom. But Gytha hadn't seemed to think she would find him there either.

Levyna knew Olin. Levyna knew her pertes like none ever could. Gytha and her mother had tried to remind her of that earlier. *She* would know where he was. The'd assumed she would be able to tell through their link. But Olin wasn't there in her mind, and it wasn't like he was merely asleep -- his consciousness was entirely unreachable. But if she knew him, like she did, perhaps she could guess where he'd go, even without their link.

He would have spoken of it.

At some point, he would have mentioned it. A haven where he could be safe for a time like this. Somewhere not just anyone could find him.

Levyna gasped as she lifted her head from her hands, eyes wide.

*

Posdel looked up as the knock sounded, and he pulled himself from the chair, opening the door to find Levyna. He wasn't surprised to see her.

"Have you –"

"No," she answered. "But –" she turned to glance at the guard down the passage.

Posdel turned on his heel and returned to his chair, allowing the palatine's daughter to come in.

Levyna entered and closed the door after herself. She still wore the same dress she'd been wearing earlier. Rubbing her arm, she began. "I think I might know where he is," she said, voice quiet.

"Somewhere his mother won't think to look?"

"Somewhere no one would think to look, actually."

"Black Castle."

Levyna's face pinched. "Yes . . ."

"It was the first thing that came to my mind after I realized he wasn't in Queen's Hill. If Olin wanted to hide, after what he has done, the only place he might find protection is the Castle. That is, as long as he doesn't tell them what he has done. They did promise him an open door."

"He would be there, would he not?" Levyna asked, hopeful now that someone agreed with her idea.

"I think Olin knows the consequences of what he's done. I don't think he'd go anywhere he would be found easily -- certainly not where he might put others in danger."

"I only just thought of it now. I have hardly been able to put my thoughts in order with everything that has been running through my head," Levyna said, stepping towards the lit chambersticks.

"It's understandable," Posdel said, "So would have been your decision to keep this revelation to yourself."

Levyna met his eyes, understanding what he meant, "Surely not from Gytha?"

"No. Of course not her. But I will admit that they had been gone before I too remembered," Posdel answered. "Sometimes, chaos does that to the mind – jumbles things up, and all but makes a fool of you."

Levyna was feeling a lot of things alright -- a fool was definitely one of them. "But if he's in Black Castle, is he...is he safe? I know he's meant to be safe there. But if he was safe, I should still be able to sense him, Posdel. I should still sense him, if nothing has happened to him. But right now all I have is silence; I don't even feel his essence enough to know that he is out there somewhere. Something's not right," Levyna said.

Posdel didn't have an answer, not one he truly believed, and not one he thought the other half of a pertes wanted to hear. "If Olin made it to Black Castle, I believe his chances of staying alive are higher than if he tried to make it on his own. They offered their haven, and he will be protected there."

But Olin refused that haven, Levyna thought. Refused it partly because of her.

She rubbed at her arm, and Posdel saw her face pinch as though something had stung her. "What is it?" he asked.

"He refused them. You said I was part of the reason why he decided against going to the Castle. If he hadn't turned down their offer, this might not have happened. King Ranald might still be alive and Olinander would still be safe."

"Don't do that to yourself," Posdel said. "It helps neither you nor him right now. Olin made a choice and I don't think it was a wrong one. As to whether or not the king would still be alive, I don't have an answer to that."

"I have thought about it so much my head's beginning to ache – and still I cannot find a real reason why Olin would do it! Why would he murder the king? Could it have been caused by his magic? Could it have forced him to attack King Ranald? Or maybe he didn't know – confused the king for an enemy who wanted to hurt him?"

"As much as I want to give you answers, I don't possess any for certain," Posdel said. "Especially not concerning the magic you share. There is a reason that pertes are rare, and I have told you of the toll it can take on the mind. I don't believe it could have gotten bad enough that Olin would walk up to the king and attack for no reason. As to whether or not he was confused, I would say it's unlikely, but not necessarily impossible, if he is far more troubled than we thought," Posdel looked away from Levyna to the burning wick of the candle in front of him as the flame danced slowly against the cold breeze that seeped into the room.

"Before I left for Kelegro, when I went to meet him, he was asleep in his bedchamber, and for a moment it felt as though he might not have been there. I couldn't sense him either. Just for a brief moment. He. . ." Levyna shook her head to find the words. "I feel like a fool because I didn't see that my dream had been about him all along. And now I have tried to think about the death the seer spoke of and it's as if I'm still not seeing anything. I don't know if it is *this* death – if killing the king is what will consume him or if there is more. . . I cannot help the panic in my heart that there is more."

"Look, there is only so much you can do, Levyna. Don't forget how quickly all of this has happened. Everything. Some have a lifetime to understand and control their gifts, you have had mere fortnights to realize who you are, and what you are with another human being. I've never said that mastering the magic of a pertes is easy. Rather, I've told you that it can be far more difficult than being a regular mage. I don't think this is the last of the challenges you will face, but blaming yourself every time things become overwhelming won't help," Posdel said.

Levyna knew it was easier for her to listen to his warning than to actually remember his words. "If Gytha doesn't know about Black Castle, she will have no reason to go there. I don't feel right that I'm here doing nothing, Posdel. I want to do something. We should go to Black Castle, if for no reason than to confirm that Olin isn't there and nothing bad has happened to him."

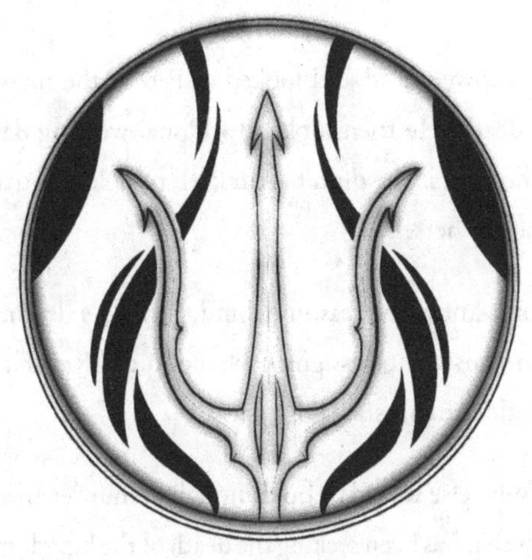

EIGHT

The aldermen arrived within moments of receiving the news of the king's demise. They converged in the throne room with the once elusive prince, Damiran, and the palatine. The body of King Ranald had long been removed and the floor scrubbed clean. The fallen ruler now inched closer to the royal tomb that ensconced his ancestors in the crypts beneath the palace. Even so, the throne room was thick with the heaviness of the horror that it had witnessed, even if it was hardly the first death it had seen. Not even in the last ten days.

Prince Petr sat to the right of the empty throne while the palatine maintained her place to the left. The rest of the counsel took seats flanking the isle.

"This is surely the work of the Red Flame. It must be clear. First Alderman Kon and now this. The order makes no effort to hide what they have done. This cannot be left unanswered," Alderman Simoen said.

Damiran swallowed hard and looked at Petr at the mention of the alderman's death. He then looked to Fiona, wearing dark fox skin across her shoulders. She didn't seem keen to hold the truth of what had happened to herself.

"While I don't know the reason behind the king's death, we should not make the mistake of assigning blame to the Red Flame for the death of the alderman," she said.

"Why not? Who else would be bold enough to murder an alderman, if not the order that has been seeking the death of the kingdom?" Simeon questioned.

"Because I know for a fact that the Red Flame did not do it," the palatine answered.

Damiran looked to the prince, who said nothing. The aldermen's faces twisted at the palatine's statement.

"How can you make such a claim? If it was not the Red Flame, then who?" Benedikt asked.

"The only person who was powerful enough to get away with it," Fiona answered.

"What?" Simoen said as the rest of the aldermen gasped, exchanging a look of disbelief at the realization of what the palatine was insinuating.

"Palatine, do you mean to say that the king . . . that King Ranald had Alderman Kon killed?" Royo asked.

"Yes. That's exactly what I'm saying."

"That's an outrageous claim to make about the king – someone who is not able to deny the accusation, on the account that he has just been murdered!" Simoen said, rising from his seat.

"You will sit down, Alderman Simeon. Remember to whom you are speaking. I may have been chosen by the late king, but I am very much still the palatine of this kingdom and you will remember that," Fiona said, her voice firm as she shut down the alderman's subtle attempt at intimidation.

Simeon dropped back to his seat and she eyed him. "I do not merely make claims. I have no reason to sully King Ranald's name beyond what he proved to be capable of in the last fortnight. I stood here in this very room hours before his death, there by that window with His Majesty, who told me that Alderman Kon's death was at his order, that he didn't trust the man anymore. The king was convinced that the alderman was conspiring against him with the Red Flame," the palatine said.

The aldermen glanced furtively at each other, throwing looks over to Damiran and the prince at the mention of a conspiracy.

"The king confided in me because he believed his advisors were compromised. Now, King Ranald killed the alderman because he couldn't bear the thought of a traitor. It doesn't make what His Majesty did right, but no one was ever going to question him. We all must be aware of this. Even though we don't know for sure if the Red Flame had a hand in the king's death, it doesn't help this kingdom if the order is accused wrongly of the murder of the alderman, when things are already heading towards dunghill, for the lack of a fitting word."

A silence washed over the room after the palatine's speech.

"The answer that's before us now is: Red Flame got what they'd been after all along – the king's death," Prince Petr said.

"I would be the first to agree that is the correct conclusion, if not the baffling fact of how it was accomplished. Olin, the young man –"

"The kingkiller, you mean?" Petr interrupted.

Fiona exhaled. "Yes. Him. Apart from him being from Ravinshore, which means he could not have been part of Queen's Hill order, he was the same young man who helped unravel the order's plans against the throne and the kingdom, and most of all single-handedly stopped the watchers with their daggers at the king's throat, right here in this very room, on the day Palatine Cyrus was killed by the order. Now, I don't know about you, but I fail to see why he would stop the order if he was only going to do the same eventually anyway,"

"Why does it matter? The Red Flame wanted the king dead, and now, he is. Why are we pondering over how they managed it, when all that's important is that they have? It was the order. They could have gotten to whoever they wanted to – perhaps they got the lad as well," Simoen said.

"It matters. Because if we say this is the work of the Red Flame, then we all know what comes after– the war we have been trying to avoid."

"It takes a lot to be a kingkiller," Damiran said. "If the Ravinshore boy did as the order bid, why did they wait so long?"

"One could argue that the order got to him afterwards. A kingkiller must be close to the king. Must be trusted by the king. And from what I've heard, King Ranald appreciated that the young man saved his life. There's hardly a better reason to trust someone than to owe them your life," Prince Petr said. "As to the reason the kingkiller is from Ravinshore, and so could not have been a part of the Red Flame, I believe the order has more than proven already that it's not eager to abide by the rules that bound its foundation."

"I won't deny that I'm saying this from the view of someone who knows this . . . kingkiller. He was, after all, in the palace as my daughter's guest, as he was King Ranald's. He is close to my family. Which is how I know that he was driven to Queen's Hill by the horror of Walrea. Red Flame itself has made attempts on his life many times, one mere days ago."

"And he survived?" Benedikt asked, pointing out how largely unlikely it was.

"Yes, he did. And I know it's hard to believe. But without blinding ourselves to the truth, I will say this. I don't know what explanation there is for what he did, but I know that he didn't follow the Red Flame's bidding," Fiona said.

"Unless he was compelled to," Simeon said.

"And became a watcher less than two days after they tried to kill him?" Fiona asked.

"It's clear you are trying to put your sentiments aside, Palatine Fiona. The king's death makes it crucial for us to question every twist and turn. You say the kingkiller wasn't following the bidding of the Red Flame – and if, for some reason, this is accepted, as a war against the watchers benefits no one – then it leaves room for one assumption:

that the Ravinshore kingkiller acted on his own. And without a reason for those acitons, then we must assume that Ravinshore itself is responsible for the king's death," Petr explained.

A chorus of grunts passed from the side of the aldermen. Fiona's brows rose. "That's a severe accusation, Your Highness. One with severe repercussions," she said.

"As it should, if a Ravinshore kills the king of Queen's Hill on Queen's Hill land, the repercusstions should be severe," Alderman Benedikt said.

Another moment passed as the thought simmered through the minds in the room.

"It won't help if he isn't found and delivered by Ravinshore. They would be indicating support of his actions," the prince said. "They would declare that they are foe to this kingdom."

"Are those our choices then? A war against the order -- our own people -- or war against Ravinshore?"

"The king is dead, palatine. Someone must answer for it. If the kingkiller isn't found, then it makes it a hundred times worse and all of Ravinshore will pay, for that much we can be sure. For the ruler of a kingdom to be killed by the subject of another kingdom is an act of war, and unless Ravinshore is able to offer to us the head of the kingkiller, they must be prepared to answer for it in worse ways.

"We cannot be fooled by who we thought that kingkiller was, and what he has done in the past. If anything, it must be assumed that he merely used his closeness to the palace to achieve is goals. It's true that my brother, King Ranald, had his flaws, and many of you believed he was troubled. But whatever he might have done, it doesn't take away from the fact that he was still king of this kingdom. And no one, absolutely no one, is justified to come into his palace and slit his throat as the kingkiller did. The entire kingdom is waiting for what we will do, who we will hold accountable, whether it's Red Flame or Ravinshore. We must show that Queen's Hill will not be trifled with," The prince said.

"I didn't expect there to be a compromise, Your Highness. I merely hoped that there would be some justice, some effort to spare Queen's Hill a war that will see the lives of more of our people lost," the palatine said.

"You have stated that you don't hold sentiments for the kingkiller. I don't think the palatine of the kingdom should have to state where her loyalties lie," The prince responded. "One must wonder about your proximity to the kingkiller, and your plea for his mother to be allowed to go after him –"

"You should know I merely stated that because I was conscious of who she is – *what she* is – and the consequences of blocking her path. She is a grand sorceress, and what we witnessed was merely a drop in what she is capable of," Fiona said.

"Still, it doesn't mean she won't answer for her son's crime. Who's to say that she's not part of his plan, truly? Even a grand sorceress isn't completely invincible. If her son isn't found, she will be judged an accomplice, as will anyone who continues to take their side. Regardless of what they have done, kingkillers will pay for their crimes," Petr said.

* * *

The urgency that had forced him back to the palace didn't make him forget why it had been so long since the last time he'd been here in the first place.

Prince Petr stood in front of the throne staring at the seat set more than a head above the other two flanking it. He pictured his father sitting there when he'd been just a boy, a boy admiring the king's prestige while dreaming of the day it would be his turn to take the seat and wear the crown. He had done everything right – he had spent almost all of his life since he'd became truly conscious of the mantle he must wear, mirroring his old man in almost everything he did. And he was the oldest, the next in line by birth. All of the signs had pointed to him being the one to take over, and Petr had readied his shoulders for the weight of ruling the kingdom of hills, until that fateful day when Korelius had announced that his younger son was to become the crown prince.

Petr exhaled as he stepped closer to the throne and placed his hand on the golden arm of the seat. Something had broken inside of him that day; he hadn't been the same man since.

Petr remembered the last time he'd stood in this room after his father's decision. It had been the day he'd decided he would no longer loiter around the palace like a purposeless figure, but would carve a life for himself away from everything. He had carried a broken heart into his chamber and wept like a child at the harrowing in his chest. He hadn't let his sadness fester into anger and betrayal.

He had sworn to never return, unless it was a matter of life and death, or the king himself demanded it.

And it was, after all, a matter of death, and here he was with his hand on the throne. The prince looked to the floor by the window, where his brother's blood had been spilled. It had taken death fro him to return.

He'd had many causes to rethink his decision, even before Damiran's visits, but he had remained unyielding. He had wanted to remain buried.

That day, after his father announced that the throne would go to his younger brother, it hadn't ended with only disappointment and a broken heart. Another emotion had latched onto him, reared its head and threatened to consume him, begging that all he had needed to do was let it in. The thirst for maleficence, to make his father pay, and his brother feel the pain he'd felt. The anger had seethed so much it terrified even Petr himself. If he had allowed it, it would have consumed him. There had been many faces in the court who he knew would have taken his side, some who were even expecting the "true prince" to take back his crown. But Petr had buried that urge and anger as far down as he could.

And so he had stayed away, and watched his brother's reign tear at the seams from a distance, until it was too late. He didn't consider himself complacent for this.

The prince walked to the spot where his brother's blood had been scrubbed off the floor, and he stared. Then he stepped, on the spot directly, as he walked to the window. He gazed down at the palace and onto the rest of Queen's Hill through the rims of imminent dusk.

Here he was, after all.

NINE

"What the palatine has said is questionable," Alderman Simoen said, standing in the passageway with the Damiran and the other two aldermen. The four of them had stepped out of the throne room, tearing away from the palatine, who'd headed in the opposite direction. Now they were speaking quietly together away from prying ears.

"That might be, but I am keen to believe she was right," Damiran said.

"You believe her, Lord Damiran? Including the fact that a man has faced the order several times and escaped death?" Alderman Benedikt asked.

"I believe she has no reason to lie to the court."

Simoen grunted as he brushed his full, black beard. "She didn't hide the fact that she and her daughter are close to the kingkiller, conveniently keeping the details of their acquaintance to herself,"

"My understanding is that the kingkiller and Levyna, the palatine's daughter, are the ones with the true acquaintance. The young man went as far as rescuing the girl from the hands of some lunatic, a leihcon that had abducted her recently. It seems the lad isn't ordinary: he has magic, which could explain how he has avoided death at the hands of watchers of the order. It would be understandable that the palatine couldn't see someone like that changing so drastically," Damiran answered.

"Regardless of who he is, the manner with which the palatine spoke of him … one would think it is confidence. There was hardly any remorse in her voice as she spoke of her acquittance with a kingkiller, someone anyone else in the entire three kingdoms would be looking to distance themselves from." Benedikt said.

"The palatine has stated several times that she knows nothing of what the Ravinshore boy has done. She has condemned it, has she not?" Damiran replied.

"And what of her claim that King Ranald had Alderman Kon killed? Surely you must at least question that," Simoen said.

Damiran shook his head, "No, it's not questionable, for it's not a claim: it is the truth."

"What?" Benedikt's voice was loudest.

The king's advisor looked all three men in the eyes, "I overheard it myself as King Ranald told her. I was perched outside the door of the throne room, after I'd asked the palatine to go back in and see if she could change the king's mind, after he made Clemon the commander of the garrison and order an attack on the den of the Red Flame in two days." The aldermen stared in shock, but that was hardly the end of Damiran's revelation. "My curiosity about how the palatine would manage it – or if she would even make an effort -- caused me to lurk nearby. Little did I know, I was putting my life at risk when I heard the king admit the alderman's death was his own doing.

"The shock didn't stop there. The king also said *why* he did it. Aldermen, the palatine was being kind when she said the king had believed Alderman Kon was conspiring against him. King Ranald told her his true reason. Apparently he had seen it in the man's eyes that he belonged to the Red Flame."

Alderman Royo's brows pinched together, "What do you mean the king saw it in his eyes?"

"I mean my cousin merely decided that the alderman was working against him because of the way his eyes had looked. That was what he based his claims of conspiracy on," Damiran answered.

Benedikt's lips parted in shock, Royo took his hand to his mouth, and his fellow aldermen fell quiet.

"And Prince Petr didn't finally return to the palace just because of his brother's death. After I heard the king's confession, I couldn't help but fear that was the last straw – the king had killed a member of his own court, for no reason beyond the fact that the man's eyes had upset him. He hadn't even bothered to question the man, but had simply had him killed on a hunch. The same man I had joined to meet with the king's brother, asking him to take the reins of the kingdom.

I wasn't eager to see what my cousin would find in my own eyes, and so I returned to the prince, riding like a man hunted, to tell him what his brother had done -- the same brother he wasn't willing to declare as unreasonable," Damiran said. "The palatine, of course, is not aware that I know this," he added. He hadn't wanted to admit to her that he'd been eavesdropping on her conversation with the king.

"I thought it had taken the king's death for the prince to finally yield to our appeals," Benedikt said.

"No, it had taken the king ordering someone else's death," Damiran said. "For whatever it's worth, the palatine hasn't kept anything from the court that I believe could make us question her. Until she proves otherwise, she is still the appointed Palatine of Queen's Hill."

"For now, until the next king appoints his own," Benedikt said.

"There's a question that no one has answered: what happens now King Ranald is dead? What becomes of his fight against the Red Flame?" Simeon asked.

"The palatine has sent word to the garrison to hold position outside the den of the Flame. For now, the invasion has been halted until we know for sure who the actual enemy is," Damiran answered.

"And to ask the next obvious question: what happens when it's proven that the order *was* behind the king's assassination?" Benedikt said.

Damiran sighed. "Then I suppose Clemon and his men might not have to wait two days after all."

* * *

The question floated through Damiran's mind only once more before he let it go.

Alderman Royo had asked if anyone had actually seen the kingkiller walk up to King Ranald and put the knife to his throat, or they had merely walked in on him standing over the king's body. At first, it had sounded like a stupid question to ask, considering there had been no one else in the throne room. But Royo, often considered odd by the rest of the court, had blurted the question anyway, due to the seemingly contrasting stories concerning the boy's character and his recent actions.

Damiran had only given it a fleeting thought before casting it aside as a pointless musing from a fairly gormless mind.

Instead, he considered something he didn't feel safe to say out loud in the presence of the rest of the court, especially the aldermen. While Damiran was certainly shocked and befuddled at his cousin's death, he was also relieved he didn't have to worry about his own life anymore. He assumed the same thought would have, even if only fleetingly, crossed the minds of the alderman, once they'd realized what Ranald had done to Alderman Kon.

And while Damiran and Kon might not have been plotting with the Red Flame, they had been talking about bringing the king's brother, a prince with a claim to the throne, to the palace, specifically because they didn't trust the kingdom's fate in Ranald's hands. That had been all but the very definition of conspiring. If the king had killed Kon for it, who was to say that Damiran would have escaped that same fate? Who was to say that Ranald wouldn't learn what they'd had planned, even if they'd thought it for the good of the kingdom? And most importantly: who would have stopped the king from seeing the look of a Red Flame ally in their eyes?

It was hardly something any of them could admit – the feeling of relief that they were no longer doomed. No one could say that a kingdom would be better off with its king gone. But after King Ranald's display of fear, and how he had acted to those who knew him personally, the fact that many didn't find his death abhorrent wasn't completely untrue. Six hundred years after King Mathias of Duken, it was still not completely untrue.

The pain Damiran felt for the death of his cousin was inevitably bated by the knowledge that he wouldn't become victim to the king's madness.

Damiran turned at the sound of steps approaching. A servant informed him the queen called for his presence. Poor Katina. He had hardly thought of her since her husband's death. Damiran turned on his heels and headed in the direction of the palace crypts.

He descended down the large tunnel leading to the basement of the palace and towards the tombs where the past rulers of Queen Hill rested. Torches in brackets and large braziers filled the path with light, highlighting the columns holding statues of the past kings buried in the crypt, beginning with ten generations before Ranald and going back centuries.

The white concrete steps brought back memories of when he'd been much, much younger. Then it had been an adventure to come and see a place considered sacred. Damiran wasn't in the mood for exploration, as he had been as a young lad. The last time he'd been here had been decades ago, when he'd come to see the installation of Korelius's statue after the king had died. Now he walked past the figures of the dead kings, and turned a corner towards the pedestal that now carried the weight of the latest dead ruler.

Damiran halted by a column where he watched Queen Katina standing by the pedestal, resting her hand on her dead husband's head. She already wore a dark dress that flowed down her body to sweep the floor of the crypt carelessly. Damiran hesitated, hands crossed in front of him, as he observed the queen taking in the final moment she would have with her husband, before his body was entombed.

Though the queen's face wasn't caked or battered with tears, Damiran could still see that cheer had been snatched from her eyes. He hadn't thought Katina and Ranald had been the greatest lovers, and the circumstance of their union hadn't stood out in romantic tales – it had been an arranged marriage, and the couple had found each other more than sufferable. Katina's father had been a close friend to Korelius, and their children had been expected to end up together. But, for the short time Damiran had spent in the palace before leaving Queen's Hill, he had seen two people with a good future together, even if their affection wouldn't resurrect the dead.

So far as he knew, Katina hadn't failed in her duties to Ranald and the kingdom. If subterfuges had occurred in the shadows, for each to satisfy a craving the other could not give, Damiran hadn't been back long enough to see it. Despite that, he had been ar too distracted with the chaos hovering at their borders since his return to Queen's Hill.

The Queen lifted her head from her husband's body and looked at Damiran. She remained quiet as she stared at the king's cousin, and it made him suddenly conscious of his lack of tribute to her earlier.

"I heard that you were there," she finally said, "when it happened."

Damiran walked slowly towards her, "I was, Your Grace. Although I didn't witness the act, I was first on the scene, along with Prince Petr," he answered.

She sighed as she placed her hand on her husband's. "Of course – Petr. Of everything that has happened today, somehow I find his presence very hard to make sense of. He doesn't step foot in this palace for decades, and on the day he does, the king dies."

"I assure you, my lady, it was nothing more than a terrible coincidence."

"A coincidence. Is that what you call it?" She turned her gaze to him. "I will need more than that, Lord Damiran. Because right now it seems to me there is something happening in my own palace that I have been blind to."

"Queen Katina, I understand you are going through an immeasurable grief, and I apologize that I haven't offered my condolence sooner."

"I'm not desperate for your sympathies. But I can imagine you had more important things to attend to."

"Not more important, Your Grace, simply more urgent. The kingkiller is yet to be found, and the court has been deciding what to do as regarding who he is and where is he from –"

"He is a watcher, he is from Ravinshore. What else does the court need to know?"

Damiran opened his mouth to respond, but realized they would just rehash the same debate as in court. "A few . . . factors are being considered, one that includes the motive behind the kingkiller's act, when he'd already saved the king's life. The chance that he isn't part of the Red Flame is being considered –"

"So he belongs to the Order of Walrea, then?"

"It is unconfirmed, but is unlikely."

"How do you expect to confirm if he is a watcher? Do you think he will confess to you, or the order will simply tell you that one of theirs carried out the assassination of the king?"

"No, of course not."

"Then why is the court acting clueless, when the answer is right in front of them?" the queen demanded.

"Because, as I said, Your Grace, the circumstance of the kingkiller's presence in Queen's Hill was due to what the orders – Walrea and Red Flame – have done and have tried to do to him –"

Katina scoffed, "And who is making the court believe all of that?"

Damiran considered his answer carefully. "The lad was close to the palatine's family."

"So, Fiona, the woman who found her way to my husband's side by taking advantage of the circumstance that the order created, is the one convincing the court that someone she knows, who happens to have been part of the reason why she became the palatine in the first place, is not a watcher, even after he was caught holding the bloody dagger covered in my husband's blood?" the queen sounded almost bemused. "What kind of spell does this woman have over you men?"

She was grieving, Damiran thought. She was allowed to think whatever she wanted. "Your Grace, the palatine merely made the court realize the consequence of naming the kingkiller a watcher – if we decided he has done the bidding of the Red Flame, it would mean declaring war on the order, and by extension, on Queen's Hill, as that is who will suffer the cost the most. A war against our own people is the very thing we have been trying to avoid.

"It doesn't mean the kingkiller won't face justice. As he is from Ravinshore, if the kingdom cannot produce him and give Queen's Hill an enemy to face, Ravinshore will have effectively accepted that they condone his actions, even if they didn't orchestrate them. And that, by definition, means war."

Queen Katina looked at the pale body of her dead husband. Ranald's eyes were closed and his hands were crossed over his chest. He had been washed; it was almost hard to believe that a man could look this good as a corpse.

"Strange that he looks more peaceful now than he has for a fortnight," Katina said. Ranald had been stripped of the armor and sword he'd worn in life, even when sleeping. He wore a white robe laced with gold, and his slit throat, though exposed, merely looked like a thick pink line across his neck.

"Lord Damiran, I am not ignorant of how my husband had been acting, towards his end. It was very unlike him, the things he'd done, and I know it must have birthed rumors about his mind. But he was still my husband. Hard as it is to admit, this wasn't how I hoped he would find peace." Katina turned to face her dead husband's cousin. "I must ask you now, Lord Damiran."

Damiran's face pinched, "Ask me what, Your Grace?"

"When you said you had a plan to resolve things, you mentioned you would share it with me, and as you still have not and this . . . has happened. I cannot think of what plan could have stopped this."

"Your Grace –"

"I must ask you, Lord Damiran, and you will not lie to me. Did your plan include Ranald dead?" Katina said.

Damiran exhaled. "No. Never. I would hope you knew me better. I'm not someone who would murder his own cousin."

"Even you cannot be so naïve as to think that you know someone completely, Lord Damiran."

"Regardless, just as I had no hand in the palatine's daughter going missing, I assure you I didn't have even the slightest bit of knowledge that this would happen."

A part of him knew that wasn't completely true; he might not have been aware of what Olin had been planning, but deep down, the thought that Ranald's actions would lead to his end had crossed his mind.

"What was your plan then?" the queen demanded. "He is dead now. I should think that the dead don't much care for secrecy."

Damiran glanced at the king's body to momentarily escape the queen's stare. He could feel her eyes burning him as she waited, and he knew there was no way he would escape telling her. "My plan arrived the same time I did to witness what had happened to the king, Your Grace."

"Do not speak in riddles, Lord Damiran."

"I do not. Prince Petr's presence in the palace is my doing," he said. "I had been courting his attention to get him to return to the palace. I believed that his presence would ease the pressure on the king and perhaps even make His Majesty feel less overwhelmed and alone."

Queen Katina's eyes narrowed as she regarded Damiran. "Is that so?"

"Yes, Your Grace."

"So, you merely hoped Petr would return and hold his brother's hand through the chaos, and afterwards return to his old castle content?"

"Prince Petr's presence was the only thing I saw that could help the king and the kingdom, Queen Katina."

"Of course. Yet you saw the need to keep it from me. You didn't have a hand in killing the king -- you were just too busy preparing for his successor," Katina said, face full of disdain as she stared at the man. She looked at her dead husband. "I wondered then, if I would regret cheering for Ranald to bring you back. I let my concerns be shadowed by the thought of the loyalty you shared. I don't wonder any longer now, as I know for a fact I made a grave mistake.

"You should never have returned to Queen's Hill. We were far better off when you were a nobody wasting away on Maedrian lands, counting the grains of sand inside rotten shells and waiting for the day your existence would expire without you ever having made a single memorable mark. You came and all but stood by as everything fell apart; watched as another person took your role, and the best you could do was plot to usurp the very man you were here to protect."

She turned and looked at him again. She took a step closer, and Damiran swallowed at the sight of the literal fire in her eyes as the flames of the torch on the wall reflected in her glassy gaze.

"I promise, Lord Damiran, you will continue to remain irrelevant, as long as I can help it."

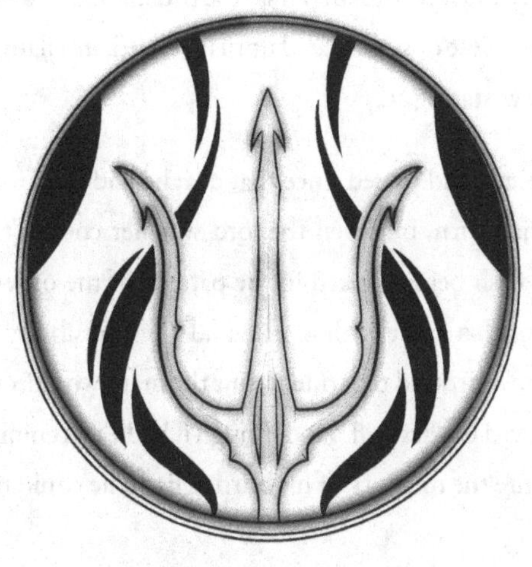

TEN

Otto stared at the fire burning in the center of the room. It pulsed red with life as the kindling burned to coal inside the pit. Tiny red flakes scattered as they were carried in the air before disappearing after a few feet. The breathing heat held the attention of the lord watcher of the Order of the Three.

Many things could be seen in fire, but in this one, the lord watcher saw the very day he'd taken the mantle of lord watcher of Duken's order. It had been in a room much like the one he was in now, only there had been no fire to feed his body with warmth and comfort from the cold.

Otto pulled at the lace of the leather gauntlet of his left hand till he could slide it off. A very faint outline of the hard glove was imprinted around his wrist. He slowly brushed the sleeve of his shirt up his arm to reveal the mark that made him undeniably the lord of the forces of Duken's shadows. Four inches long, some three inches wide, and almost as deep as a layer of skin ran sat the trident that had been pressed onto him by a piece of steel heated until it glowed, in a flame much like the one he was staring at.

Almost a decade had passed since that day; he had long forgotten the feeling of that burn, but even the lord watcher couldn't escape the smell of his flesh being cooked in the pattern of the order's mark. It was an honor that came with a price and a responsibility. Hair grew on his arm now, around the trident, but the mark wouldn't ever leave, even if he carved the flesh off. And though it hadn't left him crippled at the sight of fire the memory of his burned flash, he could never forget entirely.

Thorne of the Order of Walrea was such a flame. Otto wasn't paralyzed by the thought of him, nor did he tremble at the sight, but the Three's lord watcher knew that a man like Thorne wouldn't be quenched so easily. He wasn't the kind to keep silent after he'd been beaten. He was the cockroach that would keep plotting even when you seperated his head from his neck.

Otto had thought about Thorne almost every day since he had disappeared in the aftermath of his failed conquests. He had kept eyes – many eyes – peeled for what would signal the Walrea lord's return, or even an attempt at one. The harbor of Duken was riddled with watchers who knew to send word the moment he was sighted, though Otto knew it would hardly be so easy.

He'd been expecting something, a sign reeking of Thorne's handiwork, and Otto had gotten just that earlier today, in the news of the death of King Ranald of Queen's Hill.

His first thought had been Thorne. He hadn't been seen or heard from since the incident on the ship just off the shore of Edenborough, but Otto could sense the lord watcher's plans sliding into place. Even if Thorne hadn't actually given the order himself, Otto knew the death of the king was indirectly caused by what the lord of Walrea had started almost a moon cycle ago.

It hadn't been his order, it wasn't his kingdom, yet Thorne had his claws in the Red Flame, as though he'd been born of Queen's Hill. Otto would have been impressed, if he wasn't conscious of what that could mean for the three kingdoms.

Otto pulled his shirt up around his flank, reached for the dagger. The tip of its blade was red hot from the fire. He brought it to his skin. He looked down merely to ensure he wouldn't miss. The heat came before the pain as the steel melted into his flesh and the muscles of his belly tensed. He groaned hard as the veins of his cleanly shaven head and neck tensed. Finally he withdrew the dagger and dropped it on the ground. A hard exhale escaped his lips as the burn seeped from his side to the rest of his body.

The lord watcher let go of his shirt, covering the marks patterning his flanks. The thought of Thorne of Walrea didn't make him tremble, but a flame wasn't something he forgot easily.

* * *

Levyna had barely closed her eyes all night. She'd violently stopped herself from sleeping, but her efforts had yielded nothing. She still couldn't sense Olin. She'd been convinced --- partly by her mother – that sleep might give her the chance to sense something, perhaps hear from Olin. Fiona had convinced her that resting her body and her mind might allow her to dream about him. Maybe.

Levyna hadn't told her about what she and Posdel had guessed of Olinander's possible location.

Levyna turned her head towards the window as rays of daylight seeped between the cracks. She pulled the heavy blankets off her body, got to her feet, and opened the window, wanting to feel the cold of the foggy dawn breeze against her face. As much as it should have been a pleasant morning, waking in her own bed, a pit opened inside her at the knowledge that nothing had happened in the quiet that darkness brought, and a new day had formed with still no answers as to Olinander's condition. As her mind began to wake, so did the memory of the day before, and what she had witnessed her pertes do.

He was a kingkiller and she knew him. She *knows* him, Levyna corrected herself.

A knock sounded on the door and a maid entered with a bucket. She bowed, muttering a greeting as she turned to fill Levyna's pitcher. The maid hadn't said a word out of order, but Levyna thought she saw something in her eyes for the brief moment they made contact. It wasn't resentment, neither was it so much judgment or blame, but it was a question, one that Levyna was sure would be echoed in the thoughts of every guard, chambermaid, and servant in the palace. What did it mean, that she was so closely acquainted with the man who had killed their king?

Levyna looked away from her chambermaid, back out the window as the sun chased away the morning. It had been a day since the king's death. Many would wake dispirited, no doubt, and grief would ache in their bones, along with questions as to what this would mean for them; and many will have already passed judgment.

Her chambermaid picked up the bucket left overnight and left. Levyna wondered what it meant that she didn't care about anyone else's opinion, even after what she'd seen with her own eyes. All Levyna cared about, all that burned in her heart -- even more than questions about why he'd done it -- was if Olinander was safe, if he was still even alive.

She rubbed her hand over her arm as she stepped away from the window, then stood still looking down at her bed and remembering the moment days before when it had been Olin, standing in this spot looking at her and asking if she was well after he'd rescued her. And she'd shown her gratitude by calling him a killer. Now, more than ever, that memory stung.

She needed to find him.

Levyna walked to the fresh bowl of water and began washing her face and sponging herself clean. Her heart sang gratitude to the absent maid that the water wasn't ice against her skin.

She thought about the end of her conversation with Posdel the night before. He'd cautioned patience. She'd known it wasn't because the man was worn from the stress or wasn't just as anxious about Olin's fate as she was. He was. Posdel was just as concerned about him as herself. But he'd still advised to wait till daylight.

Daylight was here now, and she wasn't prepared to wait any longer. She began to fasten the laces of her ankle boot. Whether or not Posdel was prepared, she was going to Ravinshore, to Black Castle. She was going to find out if Olin was there.

There was no knock on the door this time before it opened, and Levyna lifted her head to see her mother walking in. Levyna didn't miss the tension in her expression as Fiona closed the door behind herself before approaching.

"Levyna?" said Fiona.

"Mother," Levyna answered, pulling her laces tight.

Fiona regarded her daughter as she put the final piece of her attire in place. The dress, the cloak, the boots, the look on her face. Fiona had seen this before.

"I thought you would still be in bed," she lied. She had *hoped* her daughter would still be in bed, even though she wouldn't have wagered on it. She knew her daughter wasn't simply distraught about the king's demise. Not when they'd still had no word about Olinander.

Levyna shook her head at the suggestion, "No, mother. My body rejects the comfort sleep brings right now. It feels abhorrent," she said.

"Did you at least try to get some rest?" Fiona drew closer, till she was standing in front of her daughter.

"Yes, I did as you asked. I gave it a chance, merely because I hoped I would find something in my unconsciousness, but I received no dream, heard no voices, and found myself nowhere close to Olin," Levyna answered as she got on her feet.

"I'm sorry to hear that. But perhaps you just need to rest a little bit more and clear your head –"

"Mother please, don't tell me to seek answers in my bed or in calmness in my head, because neither of those will bring me anything. It's a hard thing for me to do – simply sitting still and waiting for something to happen and doing nothing else. I have done that and I know for sure that it only brings me closer to breaking down."

"So what are you going to do – what are you dressed for?"

"I am going to see if I can find him, mother."

"And where will you go? Almost all of Queen's Hill has been turned upside down in search of him and yielded nothing. You've said you don't know where he is, that you cannot sense him. What has changed? Don't tell me you plan on walking across the country looking for him," Fiona said.

Levyna didn't respond at once, considering what it would mean if her mother knew what she suspected. She knew her mother cared about her, and her connection with Olin meant that Fiona was bound to care about him, too, but Fiona was also the palatine of the kingdom, in service to the throne. A throne that had just seen its king murdered by her pertes.

"I have to try, mother."

Fiona shook her head, "You haven't answered my question, daughter. Where exactly do you intend to begin your search? And how would it be any different from allowing the king's guardsmen to continue searching Queen's Hill? Unless you lied to me and to Gytha, you still don't know where he is, do you?"

"I didn't lie to you. I still can't sense him. I don't know where he is."

"So?"

Levyna stood, feeling the weight of her mother's eyes fixed on hers. It looked very much like her own eyes peering back at her.

"Levyna?" Fiona prompted.

"I don't know where he is, for sure, but I have a guess," Levyna said.

"You do? Where?"

"In Ravinshore."

"Where in Ravinshore? His mother is there already, surely she would know to look wherever you suspect."

"Not so, mother."

Fiona's brows twitched.

"Not if she doesn't know he would have any reason to go there," Levyna said.

"And where is this place a mother wouldn't think of?"

"Black Castle," Levyna answered, looking away

"Black Castle – *the* Black Castle?"

"Yes, mother. Olin's uncle told him to go there before. And, when we went to Ravinshore earlier, looking for Gytha, King Edmond had the wardens offer Olin an invitation to stay at the castle. But he refused," Levyna looked in her mother's eyes, so Fiona could see what how much the words hurt her. "Olin refused, mother. But they told him the invitation would still stand, and their gates would be open to him if ever he was in need. If he's not in Queen's Hill, and Gytha cannot find him in Ravinshore, the only place I can think of is Black Castle,"

Fiona considered her daughter's words, "But you said nothing about the Castle when Gytha and I questioned you yesterday."

"That was because it wasn't the first place I considered, even when I wasn't already rattled to the bone," Levyna said, "It only came to me much later, and even then, I couldn't be sure."

"So, now your plan is to do what? Storm Black Castle in Ravinshore, demanding to see him?"

"Perhaps not storm, but I would at least ask."

"And you would do this alone? You would face the fortress of Ravinshore by yourself, as a foreigner?" Fiona asked.

"If that's what I need to do. Though Posdel is aware Olin might be in the Castle -- he is of the same opinion, and he was the one who said we should wait till morning before taking action. But it doesn't matter whether or not he chooses to come with me, I will go on my own."

Fiona swallowed hard, hoping to hide the pain in her eyes at the knowledge that her daughter hadn't thought to confide in her first. "You told Posdel, but you didn't think to come to me, Levyna?" her voice almost betrayed her.

"I wanted to. I want to at once, but I . . . You have a responsibility to the throne and the kingdom, mother, I know that. And I know what it could mean if you learnt something about the man that had killed the king – you would be compelled to share."

Fiona took her daughter's hands and held them tight, "It is true that I have a responsibility to Queen's Hill, but first of all, before everything else in this world, I have a duty as your mother. To protect you, to be there for you. To do all that I can to make sure your path is better than mine, wherever it may take you. I haven't lost sight of my priorities, Levyna, I would never. And it breaks my heart to think that you wouldn't trust me enough to share something with me."

Levyna looked down at their hands and back up at her mother's eyes. "It's not that I don't trust you, mother, it's –"

"Whatever it is, it cannot be anymore. I am first *your* mother," she squeezed Levyna's hands a little tighter. A brief moment passed before Fiona continued. "Even with everything that has happened, know that I would rather have Olin be safe, where we can hear what he has to say before taking any action. I do not wish him harm. Because most of all, I don't wish any hurt to come to you, and I know what he means to you, which is something I am grateful for.

"Now, I cannot pretend to comprehend fully the kind of connection you have, but I know it is deep, so I understand your need to find him. But you have to listen to me when I say this is not the right way."

"Mother –"

"Listen, Levyna, just listen," Fiona hoped she could persuade her daughter towards caution. "What you plan – going to the Castle either alone or with Posdel – isn't the best way. But it doesn't mean it's the only way."

ELEVEN

Sara opened the door to see Gytha standing outside staring at nothing. Ronolf had gone with William last night to check where Olin might have gone, if not Wylie's or Old Ron's, but they'd had no luck. It had taken all of Sara and Old Ron's efforts to get Gytha to stay the night and resume her search in the morning. Being a mother herself, Sara knew Gytha's pain. She could imagine the thoughts running through Gytha's head with every moment that passed that she hadn't found him. She knew sleeplessness would be the least of the things that plagued the grand sorceress.

Gytha turned to see her old friend join her in watching the road, and, just as she had last night, she tried to control her expression, tried not to show how much the company meant to her.

"William is still asleep," Sara said.

"Yes. He needs the rest."

"He seems to be a good man."

"He is. He has been a true friend -- left his own family to help find mine. I don't know how I always seem to find myself surrounded by people like him, despite all of the horrible choices I have made and things I have done."

"Because he sees what the rest of us see in you – that you are a good person. A selfless one."

Gytha scoffed and shook her head, "Clearly you mock me, Sara."

"Of course not."

"It's fine if you do, I know I deserve it. A selfless woman doesn't abandon her child and hide away for a decade and a half. A selfless person does the opposite. Ronolf was right – if I had been here, in Olinander's life, then I would have known more. I wouldn't be clueless about the details of his life. I would know where my son is right now. If I'd been around, paid attention to him, I could have stopped this from happening in the first place."

Sara placed her hand on Gytha's shoulder, "This isn't a blame you should carry. I don't mock you when I call you selfless, because I have imagined what it would feel like if I had been the one in your shoes. After what happened with his father, I don't think any mother could blame you for what you did – you wanted to keep your child safe at the expense of everything. It doesn't get more selfless than that. Because you gave up everything so your son could grow, and he did. And it's you, Gytha. I know *we* haven't seen you in a decade, but I don't believe for a moment that in all of that time, you knew nothing of your son's wellbeing.

"And hunting Thorne was hardly for your own pleasure, was it? Only a selfless person would hunt a monster across the sea to stop him from ever returning to hurt the one she loves. Only a mother would be willing to sacrifice everything the way you nearly did. And you know what? I know you would do it again."

"In a heartbeat, Sara," Gytha said.

"Then don't torture yourself. Ronolf was hurt when he said those things to you, and you know it – it was his way of telling you that your absence ached. He missed you, as Wylie did, and it was hard for all of us when you weren't here. Ilda's disappearance was already enough for Wylie to break and then you . . . But you are here now, when it mattered, and that's the important thing. And you *will* find your son," Sara said, squeezing Gytha's shoulder.

Gytha, feeling the shift in the air and sensing a presence, turned her head sharply to the left to find a figure standing. Her breath steeled as she saw who it was, "Levyna."

Sara's eyes widened at the sight of the young woman. "Oh, Levyna!" Gytha and Sara stepped towards the traveler.

"Gytha, Sara – nice to see you again," Levyna said.

"I shall say the same. How are you here – are you here?" Sara asked, voice awed at seeing a spectre for the first time.

"I am, in part," Levyna said.

"Has something happened? Have you found him?" Gytha asked.

"Nothing new has happened in Queen's Hill and Olin hasn't been seen, but I have come because I think I know where he might be."

"You do? Did you sense him?" Gytha asked, anxious.

"No, I haven't yet," Levyna said, disappointment in her voice, "But I remembered something last night. I didn't think of it before because it was – it's Black Castle," Levyna stopped herself from rambling.

Sara's face pulled into a frown. Just then, the front door opened and William stepped out.

"Black Castle?" Gytha asked.

"Olin was invited by the wardens when we visited the palace in Ravinshore – looking for you. They offered him shelter in the Castle, and though he refused, he was told that he would always be welcome. I have thought about it, and, if you haven't found him here, then there's no other place I know where he could have disappeared assuming he's still –" she couldn't bring herself to finish the thought.

"Then by all means, we shall head to Black Castle at once," William said.

"I wanted to go myself, I was prepared to, but my mother thought it best that I come to you instead, since you are already in Ravinshore. And, considering I would be a foreigner at the gates. Also there are eyes on us. Mother thought it would make things difficult if it the court learned I had gone looking for Olin, after I said I didn't know where he was."

"Of course," Gytha said, stepping forward to touch the specter's arm. "You did the right thing. Thank you for coming to tell me."

Levyna looked between Gytha and Sara, who still had awe on her face. "Please, find him," she said.

Gytha nodded, "I will, I promise," she answered. She let go of Levyna's arm, and the specter vanished.

Sara recovered enough to meet Gytha's hopeful eyes and said, "We have horses you can take,"

* * *

Gytha wouldn't have thought to head in the direction of the fortress, perhaps not until it was too late. Gytha's heart thudded in her chest at the fact that she would have written him off as dead, before she considered that he could have gone to the castle. It was indeed a last resort, and not one many chose if there were other options.

"You should stop thinking about it," William interrupted her thoughts.

Gytha turned to look at him. Their horses had slowed to a trot midway from Hunter's Grove.

"What?"

"The thoughts in your head right now."

"You cannot read minds," Gytha said.

"I don't require telepathy to know what thoughts are giving you that look on your face."

Gytha exhaled and turned to look ahead.

"You should stop."

"She cannot sense him, William. The one person who might as well be half his essence can sense nothing."

"That's not –"

"And worse. I, too, have the feeling that something terrible is happening. It's as though my gut is twisted in my belly."

"We will find him."

"If –" Gytha thought to rephrase her words. "Walrea is here. What if he walked right back into their arms? I know Black Castle would never deliver him to Walrea, but should they find out what he did, I don't think they would protect him, William. And if they did, I fear it won't be peaceful. What if the castle has taken him for an enemy and turned on him? What if they have passed their own judgement?"

"No."

"No?"

"I choose to believe that you will find Olin and he will be alive and safe. I have heard of the things he has done, all hardly with any help. His magic –"

"The same magic that could very well be consuming him!" Gytha said sharply. She sighed upon realizing her error. "I am sorry, William, that wasn't right of me. I know this is hardly your fault."

William scoffed, "It baffles me how a grand sorceress can appear so clueless at times," he said. "Did your friend Old Ronolf not warn you against the very thing you are doing now? Is it so hard to believe that there are people who would share your problems?" He asked.

Gytha had no response for him.

"There are. We have all made bad choices. I would know, I'm a master of terrible decisions. At least I was. But I still found the way to making better choices, and you were there to help me when it mattered. You and Isabelle, even if it was at different times. My father used to say: if someone offers you a hand when you are flat on your arse on the ground, when it's their turn, offer them two hands. You have offered me help more times than I can count or repay, the least I can do is help you find your son. And you *will* find him," William said.

Gytha didn't say out loud her main fear: that what was happening to Olin could have been inherited from her. She had been lost when her own magic had taken over. She had killed a man – the love of her life, and Olin's father. In the midst of the fear in her chest was a tightness at the chance that her son could be lost as well. She had left him to seek answers and control, and she had found it after years of work. Olin's magic wasn't quite like hers. Being a pertes meant it was stronger, for him.

If Olin didn't control his magic, it would consume him.

If he was consumed by his magic, it would be her fault, for failing to see the signs.

"At Kelegro," Gytha said. "The seer. She was talking about this, about his magic."

"Maybe, but you must do your son a favor and take your mind off the worst possibilities. He's your son, and you are Gytha the grand sorceress of the fifth realm. You are Gytha the great no matter how many times you want to reject the title. Whatever your son is facing, if he shares even a drop of your blood, I wouldn't wager against him – and I would pray for the man that does. I believe your son is alive, Gytha, and hasn't been captured by Walrea or harmed by the Castle. And today might be the day Ravinshore knows what it feels like to wrong the mother of flames."

Gytha took a breath and nodded, kicking the horse into a trot as they drew within sight of the fortress Black Castle. Gytha felt the fire she had quieted for so long burst to life inside of her.

*

Gytha could feel the energy of the shield ensconcing the castle as they dismounted their horses and led them the last ten yards up to the gates of the fortress. Regardless of the urgency for their visit, one should never make the mistake of approaching the Black Castle gates on the back of a horse or with weapons in the open, as that would translate to a challenge.

"You must remain quiet until you are allowed to speak," Gytha reminded her foreigner friend and William nodded his understanding. Crows cawed as they flew above the giant wall cutting off the castle from the rest of the land, a wall which hadn't been conquered by any man or force since it had been built.

The gates of the castle were made of the thickest raised grain wood, and were well over a century old. The black, forty-feet slabs, reinforced with steels bars and pins, would not budge, no matter what was thrown at them. Gytha could see hardly any signs of decay or weakness as they approached the gatehouse.

If the look of the wall wasn't enough to discourage visitors, the silence would. William and Gytha weren't spared the utter quiet that greeted them outside the gatehouse, once the birds had passed. It gave the eeriness of the fortress even more weight. Gytha couldn't hear a single sound from her surroundings, nor from inside the castle; she didn't even know if there was any life at all within. It was as if the air stood still in a pocket of space in front of the castle gates.

"State your business! For you halt at these gates with two fates!" a faceless voice announced.

William looked up, trying to see where the voice was coming from. On the roof of the gatehouse, there were tiny windows barely human-sized set into the towers that flanked the gate; they were shut. There was no one to be seen. It was as if the voice was coming from the gatehouse itself.

"I seek to find one!" Gytha answered.

"There are none who enter this fortress with a wish to be found afterwards," the voice said.

"And I have come regardless because I must know if he has marched through your gate and into your halls!"

"Know that whomever you seek is not here! Now, turn around and leave at once, or meet your end for trespassing!"

"I am Gytha, grand sorceress of the Fifth Realm. I simply desire to meet with the wardens, to ensure in person that whom I seek has not been through your gates, and I shall be on my way after,"

A moment passed without a response, and not long after, a loud screeching that mimicked the growl of a giant beast sounded through thee air as the large gates parted. Gytha was only a step ahead of William as they walked through. The silence outside the gates fell away once they passed inside, and men in dark cloaks stood by and scrutinized them as they approached. Gytha saw man houses and faces within the wall of the castle, but not the one she sought.

"Let them through!" A different voice called. This time it was one Gytha recognized. She looked up towards a balcony in the distance, spotting a familiar figure.

The horses were taken from them and so was their single weapon – the dagger William carried. They walked up a set of stairs, that led to the balcony where the figure waited.

Gytha locked eyes with a woman warden, one standing next to a man of the same rank. Both of them were dressed in all black.

"Abeni," Gytha said.

"Gytha," the warden answered, before stepping forward. "It's indeed you. I thought my eyes were deceiving me."

"It's me, Abeni. I should thank you for letting us through. This is William."

"A foreigner!" The man said sharply.

"He reeks of the land of the sea," Abeni said.

William didn't bother to ask how they had known he didn't belong and where he was from.

"I assure you, the man means no harm. He is with me."

"Then he shall stand in the street or outside the gates, his very presence in this room is a violation."

William made to move but caught sight of Gytha's slow blink. "But I, too, might as well be a foreigner."

"You have Ravinshore in your blood, Gytha, you can never be a foreigner on this land," Abeni said.

"Let him stay, please. I shall vouch for him."

"And who vouches for you, Gytha of the fifth realm?" the man demanded, his face steeled.

An exhale passed before the words followed. "I do," Abeni said. She met her fellow warden's gaze as she turned. "I shall vouch for her, and she for him," she turned back to the visitors, "What brings you to Black Castle, Gytha?"

"I'm hoping to find out if my son has found his way here," Gytha answered.

"And who is your son?" the man asked.

"Olinander of Hunter's Grove."

The wardens looked at each other. "Wylie's nephew is your son?" Abeni asked.

"Yes, yes he is," Gytha answered. "You know him. Is he here?"

"No, he's not."

"He is not?" Gytha asked.

"Your son is not here, Gytha," Abeni repeated.

"I was told he was offered a place in the castle, that your gates would always be open to him."

"And that is the truth," the man confirmed. "A truth that existed until your son became a kingkiller."

Of course, news had reached Black Castle. That was the least of the things Gytha had been worried about. "He hasn't been sentenced as one," she objected.

"But he was found holding his dagger over a king's dead body. What else shall you call him?" the man asked.

Gytha wasn't here to debate. She would stand and argue with anyone about her son's innocence on any day once she knew where he was. All she wanted now was to know where he son had gone.

"Do you have him? Have you captured him?" Gytha said, staring Abeni in the eyes.

"We don't have your son, Gytha. If we did, we would tell you. He didn't reach the gates of this castle, lest we aid or judge him," Abeni said.

"We haven't set our eyes on him since we met at King Edmond's palace," her partner added.

TWELVE

"Swear," Gytha said.

The warden chuckled. "What?"

The grand sorceress stepped forward, "You say that you haven't seen my son, that you don't have him. So will you swear it – by the gods?"

"We are wardens of Black Castle, sorceress, we gain nothing from deceiving you and we do not swear," he answered.

"I promise you," Abeni said, ignoring the tightness on the face of her counterpart, "Not as a warden of the castle but as someone you know from another life, I promise you that your son is not here,"

It wasn't exaxtly what she'd asked, but it seem to have garnered the same effect from Gytha. Her face twisted with anxiousness at the realization that they really didn't have her son. She turned sharply away from wardens and towards the door, as though looking for an exit.

William saw the look in her eyes as worry gripped her a little tighter than she would care to be seen. The answer they had was a relief – at least the wardens hadn't hurt him -- but it didn't mean her son had been spared doom. If he wasn't inside the fortress, then he hadn't had to face the wardens, and he still stood a chance at survival. But, on the other hand, Black Castle could have held him instead of damning him to death. And the other options she'd considered were worse – the Order of Walrea. If they'd gotten ahold of him, now more than ever, he wouldn't fare as well as he had in the past.

In their confrontations before, Olinander had been an innocent boy, saving kings against treacherous plots. Before, he'd been the valiant victim who'd lost all but his life in a quest to get the truth against the watchers out. They had wanted him dead for being the bane to their plans. But now, the Order of Walrea could claim to act against him for a far greater reason, one the whole three kingdoms will believe: ending a kingkiller, whose actions incited war against another kingdom. Though their very actions of claiming responisibility would discourage war. Delivering a kingkiller's head would be seen as anything but a dutiful act.

"We keep looking, Gytha. We don't stop. This is but one more place," William whispered to his friend.

Gytha met his eyes and he nodded.

"I am curious what you intend to do when you find him," the man said. "After what he has done, the very least he will become is an outlaw and a fugitive. I know you're aware of that. So what do you plan to do if you find him?"

"It's *when* I find my son, warden. And I shall do whatever I must to make sure that his story does not end here," Gytha said as she turned on her heels.

"He has taken the life of the ruler of a kingdom, and if he isn't held accountable, he will have all but plunged Ravinshore into war against Queen's Hill. What will you do to stop that, sorceress?"

"You don't understand. I don't expect you to."

"You wouldn't be here, standing in this castle unharmed, if we didn't understand, Gytha," Abeni said. "You must know that the situation isn't in your son's favor, and he won't be the only one who pays for what he's done."

"And what will you have me do with my own child!" Gytha shouted, her suddenly thunderous voice trembling through the room. The walls began to shake as all of the windows flung open. Gytha blinked and settled her own breath, then exhaled slowly to calm herself.

William didn't flinch at the show of power, but he looked between Gytha and the wardens, both of whose faces were steeled with displeasure at the grand sorceress' display inside the walls of the Black Castle. Gytha had told William they couldn't use magic in the castle as guests, lest it be taken as an attack. William readied himself for what their response would be to the possible provocation. Whatever came afterwards, he wouldn't be the first to use magic. But if the woman knew the grand sorceress, as she had said, William hoped she knew her enough to know better than to do something foolish towards an already displeased Gytha.

The man reached for a wand on his gauntlet, but Abeni quickly reached out, placing her own arm in front of her counterpart's even as both of their faces were locked on Gytha.

"I apologize, wardens. That was not meant as a threat," she said.

William knew if it had been a threat, neither of the wardens would still be standing.

"You enjoy far too much grace, Gytha. Much more than anyone else would have survived, regardless of who they are," Abeni said, her voice turning grim from her previously homely tone.

"I am aware of that, and I don't take it for granted," Gytha answered.

"Our memory of Wylie, and what your son did before he became a kingkiller, are the only reasons we hesitate," the other warden said.

Silence filled the air for a moment as Gytha took another slow breath, regaining her composure before she spoke. William's eyes didn't stray from the wardens for even a heartbeat.

"I said you don't understand, because even though I have been away from my son for so long, in my bones I know he is nothing but good. Wylie did more than raise him, he was his father, and if you don't trust me, then you must trust Wylie, for he raised a young man who would choose to risk his life to defend others. So you don't understand that killing the king, this . . . is not my son, this is not what he would do. Not without reason."

"What reason could there be to kill a king?" Abeni asked.

"Perhaps I misspoke. I simply mean there is a chance he might not be the one in control of his magic. It could be consuming him."

Abeni frowned. The wand in her counterpart's hand retreated. "But he didn't kill King Ranald with magic, he used a dagger."

"It would hardly matter if his mind is compromised by his magic. The weapon would only be a means to an end," the man said.

Gytha stared at the wardens. "It doesn't help that I know the feeling of lacking control. If that is what has happened, then . . ." she swallowed. "I am not oblivious to what my son has done, but I would rather find him and ensure he is not lost to his magic. You asked me what my plan is. I indent for my son to live."

*

Abeni couldn't Gytha's pain. Or the look in her eyes. Despite what she knew Gytha was capable of, it was clear as day that the sorceress despaired at the task before her.

"She asks for too much. We have been more than fair, allowing her into these walls and hearing what she has to say, even condoning her expression."

"I know," Abeni said.

"Then you must agree that this is not something we can do. It's not something the castle should do," the warden said.

"No, I don't agree," Abeni answered, "It *is* something we can do. Whether we will is another question."

Her counterpart shook his head, "The castle doesn't grant such privileges, Abeni. It does not."

"The Castle serves as a haven for any threatened unjustly by the Order of Walrca," she said.

"The Castle holds fast on its purpose, its principles, and its role as the true shield for the subjects of Ravinshore."

"*All* subjects of Ravinshore," Abeni noted.

"So far as they are not guilty of crimes against the kingdom, which the young man in question is guilty, by being the kingkiller of a sister kingdom," the warden said.

"Did we not tell King Edmond and his queen that Black Castle believes in justice. That is all Gytha is asking for," Abeni said. "No one argues that the boy has done good, far from it, and no one would argue if we delivered his corpse to the palace and his head to Queen's Hill. But on this one occasion I ask that we consider. Not long ago you and I stood across from the lad in the palace, agreeing he would be welcome in the castle. That's not something we do often, no?"

He stared at her, letting out a sharp breath. "No, it certainly is not."

"And we agreed to the King's request because of what the young man had done for the throne, against the order no less, and even as a stranger in another land where he saved their king. I know at the time, a part of you felt proud for the sciff, and it wasn't just because of his relation to Wylie, a man we both respected. It's that reverence we use to make this decision. Because I know you've questioned the sense behind a king's hero becoming a kingkiller."

"The castle doesn't make such promises, Abeni. Not even if a king himself dares ask us."

"Then it's good that it's not a king asking it of us," she looked him right in the eyes.

"There is a chance, you know, that the boy could already be dead at the hands of the order – of Walrea."

"That is a possibility, though from what we know, the order could never seem to grip him long enough."

"And if this is the one time they're successful, and he's actually dead? This could turn sour."

"More than it already is?"

"Unless King Edmond makes a decision on our proposal," the man said.

Abeni's gaze straightened. "Then the wrath would be ours to inherit," she agreed.

*

"What will you do if they don't agree?" William asked. Gytha stood by the window and looked down at the recluse life those in the fortress were destined for. It wasn't a choice anyone made when they had another. All but a cage, with no interaction with the world outside.

Gytha exhaled, "Truthfully, I don't know. Maybe nothing, just move on and hope that my return here, if ever there is one, won't be to raise that hell you mentioned.

William didn't think Gytha would raise hell if her son came to harm. She would simply become the hell itself.

They turned at the sound of soft steps from the adjoining chamber.

The wardens appeared. They walked to a mirror standing against the wall, with Abeni to her counterpart's left and Gytha to the right of William.

"We have considered what you have asked, Gytha, and we have agreed," the man said.

"For whatever it's worth, grand sorceress, the very least the castle can do is not doom your son any further if he does seek sanctuary."

"So I have your word, then?" Gytha asked. She needed them to say it.

"Yes, you do. If Olinander finds his way to Black Castle, he will not face death, only so long as he isn't a threat to the peace and safety bred within these walls, as it has been for centuries," Abeni said.

Gytha nodded, the worry that had permanently creased her face diluted by a little bit of content. At least there as one more avenue of safety for her son. At least her visit to the fortress hadn't been in vain, and she could tell Levyna the good news, to soften the ache of the disappointment that she hadn't yet found Olin in the only place they'd thought he would turn, if the roads that led home signaled danger.

"Thank you, wardens," Gytha said.

"I know it's not our place to ask, and believe me when I say that I do so only considering the gravity of the situation. Since you didn't find him here, and indeed you haven't found him anywhere you've looked, where will you turn?" Abeni asked.

Gytha's shoulder lowered as she thought. She looked at William, but turned back just as quickly. "A part of me is prepared to go knocking on every door in the rest of the kingdom, as I believe a friend is likely doing so in Hunter's Grove as we speak. But first I will turn to the palace," she said.

"The Ravinshore Palace?"

"Yes," Gytha answered Abeni's partner. "I would ask the same of the king as I have asked you, and if they don't have him, I would hope that my . . . assistance in keeping the king alive and able at least allows me to ask that my son is given a fair trial."

She didn't mention William's hope that the king would remember that the only person in the three kingdoms who'd been able to save him from the Egro spell was asking him for a favor, one that would hardly be considered too high a price for his own life.

"Of course we don't know what the king will say, but, based on our last encounter with him and how he talked of Olin, we have hope it would be favorable," Abeni said.

"Though we should mention that you shouldn't be confused if the palace castle is still a little distracted," the other warden added.

William's brow raised, "Why would the palace be distracted?"

"A prisoner recently escaped from the king's guards," the warden answered.

"What kind of prisoner? Why would his escape have the palace rattled?" William asked.

"She was not an ordinary prisoner, and she left behind quite the scene after she escaped. She killed four men, including a commanding officer. She was a watcher," Abeni said.

Gytha's breath caught in her throat. There weren't many watchers left. Even less that had been captured. She had faced a watcher that day at the palace, and had chosen to capture her, instead of crushing her heart. She hadn't been able to bring herself to kill, hating the thought of once again having someone she used to care about die at her hands, even if this one would have come about from a choice she couldn't help. Gytha hadn't been eager to face the decision in the midst of the attack on the palace, with the poison of the dagger burning through her own arm.

It wasn't impossible that there could be another watcher of whom the wardens were speaking; another woman watcher could have been captured that night. But, as there were probably only a handful of women watchers in the order, there was only one Gytha knew. The only one who could have been capable of an escape like this, taking on four men while bound in chains.

"Do you know the name of this watcher?" the grand sorceress asked.

"I believe she was called Ilda," Abeni said.

THIRTEEN

As Ilda stared at the boy; the crease on her face wouldn't fade.

Why had she done this? she thought to herself once more.

Time had been passing slowly and torturously. It had been a little less than a day, and she still didn't know what her plan was -- all she knew was that she was stuck in a cave with the boy.

When she'd mounted the horse, after killing the guards, and fled north, Ilda'd had no intention of stopping until she was as far away as she could be from what she had done, and the path it led to. North was the opposite direction form where the guards had been taking her: Black Castle. They were still a far distance from gates, enough that she wouldn't easily be spotted. But as Ilda had looked to widen that distance even further, she had caught sight of him, the boy. He appeared quite literally out of thin air. At first she'd kept on riding, only looking back three times. The final time she'd looked back, she'd realized he was on the ground.

It was as though she'd been possessed. There was no reason for her to even consider it, other than the curiosity that had stabbed at her the moment his figure had appeared in the distance. Especially not when she direly needed to put a world between herself and her captors. The king's garrison would be on her heels any moment – there had been no reason she could comprehend as to why, while her entire body ached with the sourness of being kept in a dungeon for almost a fortnight, and she'd only just managed to pry her freedom from the lives of king's guards, she had still pulled on the reins and steered the horse towards the body. It led her back in the direction of Black Castle, something she had just killed four men to avoid, but against all the common sense in her head, and the pain her body had suffered, she'd headed west for a hundred or so yards to the boy's side.

Ilda stopped the horse at his side, scanning the surroundings to be sure they were alone before she called out. Having no time to question herself, she had dismounted her horse, pulled the dagger that had been part of her parting gift from the guards, and kicked at the body before kneeling to turn him over.

At the sight of his face, she'd unhanded him at once and stepped back, then slowly bent to see if he lived. She'd felt his life faintly. It had probably been the reason she went further, and why she'd found herself lifting him from the ground, looking around wildly to be sure they were alone. That, and the fact that he looked like a man she'd once known, and a woman she'd seen just recently.

If it hadn't been someone she'd recognized, her curiosity would have withered quickly and she wouldn't have bothered slinging the body over the back of her horse like a sack of wheat, horse despite the excruciating pain of her injured arm and the wreck of the rest of her body. But that face, the face of this boy who was little more than a pup, saved him. Because she'd known at once who he was.

Bathlom'd had a striking face, and it hadn't been lost when mixed with the strong features of his wife's blood. The jaw and ears had been Bathlom's, bringing back a bit of Wylie's features. But the rest of it – the nose and brows and the thinness of the bridge of the eyes – resembled the lad's mother, the same woman who had almost killed Ilda and was the reason she'd ended up in the dungeons.

Ilda'd seen Gytha in the face of her son lying lifeless on the ground, and it had almost crashed her heart into the wall of her chest with shock. The shock had stayed with her as she'd ridden, in a plethora of distress, both from the ache consuming her bones and the discomfort and hassle of being slowed down by another body slumped behind her. Soon they'd reached north, as she had intended.

She'd endured hours of traveling through the shadowed the woods, obscured by the trees, and had only stopped once by the Black River so the horse wouldn't fail the rest of the journey. She'd slapped the boy's so many times that she feared another hit would leave the mark of her hand on his skin, but he didn't wake up as they rode the haggard path through the trees. Even the cold ground hadn't stirred him, as she'd pulled him from the saddle so the horse could rest. The only reason she'd know he wasn't dead was the deathly slow thump of his chest. His breath had been barely enough to rattle a feather and his eyes. . . his eyes were why she'd rested a hand on her dagger every time she drew near. They'd made her question if she was even alive, or if she'd dreamt her escape, and met Gytha's son in purgatory.

Now, sitting in the cave she'd dragged him into, Ilda stared at the boy, and still the questions wouldn't leave her head. There had to be more reason than mere curiosity and coincidence that'd made her take him with her. Surely she hadn't merely been foolish. The fire before them crackled with warmth, fighting back the chill of the night.

Ilda bit at the hem of her tunic and ripped a clean strip, so she could change the bandage she'd wrapped around her injured arm. It was healing well, after she'd burned the wound closed with a hot dagger to keep it from bleeding. If she wasn't so concerned with keeping him alive, she could stop using pieces of her own clothes to wrap her injuries, and take his instead. No one would question her if he froze to death. She wasn't even sure if he *could* freeze to death, as the last time she'd checked him, his body had been as warm as if a fire burned inside him.

She could be long gone by now -- she could have kept going north, crossed into villages and settlements where she could get herself fed and out of the rags she wore, yet here she was, spending the first moments of her freedom watching him.

He wouldn't wake. And even if he did, there was the matter of who and what she was, what she was sworn to do, and who he was. It wasn't the fear of murder that troubled Ilda, as it had been murder that had set her free onto the path that had allowed for her to find him. And itt was hardly because she was too weak, as he would possibly be the easiest kill she'd made. She was a watcher, and he was the elusive bane to the existence of her order. He was also one of the reasons she'd ended up in the dungeons. Him and his mother.

His mother. Ilda couldn't shake the memory of Gytha's face the last time she'd seen her. That conversion still burnt in Ilda's head.

This was Olinander, Gytha's son and Wiley's blood. That was the only reason he was still alive. If this boy had been any other person in the world, there would have been no inkling of hesitation in her mind. But if he didn't wake soon, what use could she have of him? If she waited any longer, whatever wrong wrong with him could spread to her.

Ilda stared at the lad. He was but a boy who had barely stopped suckling. If she remembered what he was like the last time she'd seen him, he couldn't stop his curiosity. With every moment he lay there, unmoving, she felt more and more curious herself. Every time she glanced at him to find that he hadn't so much as moved a hair out of place, a little more of the memories crept back to her. Memories of the time before she'd been sworn to the Order, to do as she was told and serve her kingdom. No matter the cost.

Ilda looked away to banish the thoughts. It wouldn't do either of them any good if she was crippled by the past. She pulled the cloak she'd taken from the dead guard back over her injured arm and stared at the daylight entering the cave. She could only do this for so long – especially with no food in her belly. Ilda got on her feet, every part of her body screaming in pain. If she had the magic, she could heal herself, or even leave this body behind and find one not broken by chains and torment of the dungeons. But as the only other body nearby was unconscious and barely alive, it would be easier to stay in hers.

The watcher stepped towards the opening of the cave and walked a few paces, seeing a house in the distance. She wondered if whoever lived there had more to eat than bony birds. She'd noticed a fire late in the evening before, one that told her that someone else was around. They were a long way from Black Castle, and even longer from the palace. Ilda wagered she had a good chance of spinning a story to whoever she found there -- at least getting some food before she figured out what she'd do next.

Her ankle twinged as she turned back to look into the cave. The mystery that surrounded the boy wrapped itself around her thoughts for a moment. To approach strangers by herself was one thing, to approach them with an unconscious boy was another. And leaving him behind wasn't up for debate. Just as well she was going to leave the horse at the bottom of the hill.

Ilda stepped closer and nudged again, as though this time her touch would yield a different reaction to all the previous times she'd done it before. But he still didn't move. She had never seen anything like this before. She gently placed her hand on his chest; there was hardly any movement. Kneeling down further, keeping a hand on the dagger on her side, she slowly placed her ear to his chest, hearing a slow thud after a moment.

Ilda checked his eyes again; they were still the same. The blackness hadn't waned. And for once, worry rattled the watcher's heart.

* * *

They had survived the night, though neither of them had really slept. Isabelle brushed dirt the blanket and folded it slowly, placing it at the head of the bed. They'd slept together, only because she had promised she would wake Mary the very instant William arrived. She hadn't had to disturb the child, Mary had stirred on her own long before she finally fell asleep, and William hadn't returned.

Isabelle left the bedchamber to find Mary standing by the window. She had resumed her watch, much like the day before. Isabelle stared at her for a moment before she spoke. "How about we make some breakfast?"

Mary turned, and Isabelle saw she wasn't totally disinterested, but Isabelle knew she wanted William more than she wanted food. But Mary joined her. As Isabelle was about to light a fire, both of their attentions were captured by a knock on the door. The girl's eyes widened and she darted to the door, unlatched, and opened it.

Isabelle felt Mary's cheer vanish when she saw the unkown face at the door. It was a boy carrying a pitcher.

"I'm Alkin. I have some milk for the house," the lad said, "A gift from my father's farm. The goats have been very swell and we thought to share."

Mary simply looked at him, and Isabelle walked up to the young man, scanning the boy, from his brown hair to his chipped teeth and the dirt from uncallused hands. He looked like he was indeed from a farm.

Isabelle took the pitcher from the boy. "Thank you,"

"Of course, my father says to tell Master William that he's still very grateful for what he did for him," the boy said.

Isabelle nodded slowly, like someone who understood what the favor was, "And do tell your father that Master William is grateful for his gift," she lifted the pitcher a little.

The boy nodded and looked from Isabelle to Mary, who still stared in silence. Then he turned and hurried away a few stepps before he returned, scratching his head, "Sorry, mistress, but I would need to bring back the pitcher," he said.

"Oh, of course," Isabelle made eye contact with Mary as she went to turn the milk over in another container before she returned it to the boy, "Here," she said.

"Thank you," The boy nodded again before he turned one more time and hurried towards his father's house, a property not so far from William's. Isabelle watched the boy until he disappeared. This was the first time she'd seen any of William's neighbors at their door since she and Mary had arrived, but it was far from the last.

Finally Isabelle turned to find Mary standing a few steps out of the house, her eyes in the same direction. "It looks like we have a nice neighbor," Isabelle said.

Mary looked up at her, "The gift wasn't for us, it was for William,"

"Maybe, but it's good to know that kind people live around, don't you agree?"

Mary shrugged and looked back.

"And the boy – Alkin – looks like a kind one too." Mary looked down at her hands and back up at Isabelle. "Maybe we can go and pay a visit sometime."

"We don't have goats to give milk."

"No, we don't. But we can still find something to take with us when we go," Isabelle said. "Would you like that?"

Mary shrugged again and then nodded, "Maybe."

That was all Isabelle needed, to know there was a chance the child would welcome it. Despite what had happened, prying her away from her home to protect her wasn't where it ended. Mary'd had friends back in Ravinshore, as well as family to look after her when Alden was away – and Isabelle hadn't even thought to inform them she was taking the child away. Her father's death wasn't the only loss Mary had suffered, and Isabelle knew this. If the child was going to have the kind of life Isabelle hoped for her, it would be filled with more than just her and William. Mary would no doubt need the company of people her age as she grew out of her grief and began experiencing more of life.

Mary looked at her hand, at the bracelet Isabelle had given her that day. She fiddled gently with the stones before she turned to look west, in the direction of Queen's Hill.

"He'll be back, Mary," Isabelle said.

"I know. It's only been a day," the girl answered.

Mary was no stranger to waiting. Isabelle couldn't have forgotten that. Her father, Alden, had been a king's guard and had often been called away on tasks for the king. Mary had no doubt grown up watching for his return. While the ache of Alden's death still had her and William was now away to Queen's Hill, it had been the fear of not seeing him again so soon that had led the way earlier. It was what Isabelle had seen and what had worried her too. The sorceress had not quite had the privilege of seeing Mary, the king's guard's jewel, in her state of anticipation that would be too mature for her age; she had only heard of it from her father when Alden spoke of his fantastic daughter.

"He'll be alright," Isabelle said.

"Of course, he will. He has no choice, he swore to me he would return," Mary said.

Isabelle smiled, "That he did," she said as she placed her hand on the little girl's shoulder, "Come on, let's go in and prepare breakfast, and you can tell me what you'd like to give Alkin when we visit him

"It is not him we're visiting – it's his family!'

"Of course," Isabelle chuckled, "His family."

* * *

"The king is dead, I don't see any reason why we're still waiting in camp," the first man said as he lifted the cup to his lips.

"We should have attacked by now," the second man said.

"Have you both forgotten where we are, and who we're attacking?" the third man, Clemon, answered. "It's the Den of the Flame. It's the watchers themselves we're talking about."

"The king is dead!" The second man said again, "The entire kingdom knows it was the order that wanted him dead. We know they tried once already, and now he is dead. And we still wait here because we're afraid of the order?"

"You're not foolish enough to think this is going to be like any other battle, are you? If that's what you think, then you might as well take yourself to the front of the line, if and when we attack."

"So they kill the king, and they don't even have to answer for it?" the second man said.

"No one said they won't answer for it, but I can wager that half the men in this camp are far from eager to be this close to Red's Flame's den, let alone invade it, even if the king is dead. Tell me something," Clemon said, "Have either of you ever seen a man killed by a watcher before?"

"I have not," the second man answered.

"No," said the first.

"How about a watcher killing a man?"

The other men shared a glance.

"Of course, you haven't. There's a reason the watchers beget terror, and the den of the Red Flame, just like Walrea in Ravinshore, is off limits. You don't see them – they are so fast that there have been rumors that watchers might not even be human. You won't see a watcher's blade coming until it has slit your throat, or impaled your heart –"

Clemon rose from his chair and walked out his tent to gaze at the fortress that was home to the Red Flame, sitting on the hill. He was of no illusion that their presence in the forest was anything but common knowledge for every watcher inside that fortress. Surely they had eyes on them, and would know the very moment the army advanced even an inch in that direction? He hated the thought that they were all but sitting ducks out here. The Red Flame might not have reason to attack … but then again, no one had thought they'd have reason to kill the king, yet Ranald was dead.

"— you wouldn't feel the presence of a watcher next to you until the very moment they were close enough to snuff the life out of you –"

This was a madness Queen's Hill hadn't seen before – the king's army attacking the Red Flame – and he was to be the head of the spear that led the way. Clemon would be foolish if he said that there was no fear in his heart about his mission. This wasn't a war that their kingdom had seen before. The king's army had never faced watchers in battle, ever. Wars were fought against warriors of different armies, not against assassins who thrived in the shadows.

"— anyway you can imagine a man dying, without so much as a breath of scream from his mouth, a watcher is capable of it. They move with air, they move in darkness, they move as shadows –"

A score of men kept watch every night. And every man kept his eyes peeled during the day. It would only take one moment for everything to change. Even as Clemon lay in his tent, sleep seldom found him, as every creak and sound was magnified in his head. He was alert, conscious of the reason for his promotion to the head of this spear -- the previous commander of this army had died very far from a battlefield, and with no sword in his hand.

"– you are the king's guards. You are trained to fight and defend your kingdom against a drawn sword. You are skilled, when you can see what to attack. A battle is fair when you know what the enemy looks like, when you know where he is, when you can see him –"

Clemon would never cower from defending his kingdom, and as they waited for word from the palace, Clemon knew what threat the Red Flame was to Queen's Hill and what treachery they had committed, but it didn't mean that a part of him didn't hate that he was standing here, vulnerable and waiting. The wait had a tendency to soak the hearts of the men with more uncertainty, and battles were hardly won with doubting warriors.

"— so when you ask why we are still waiting, think about that for a moment, and ask yourself if you are in a hurry to learn what it feels like to fight a watcher," Clemon finished, before he walked away.

Every day that passed brought another disadvantage to this battle, and Clemon knew it, but that didn't show on his face. Suddenly he heard steps approaching. Clemon turned in time to feel the stiletto pinch into his throat, then again into his heart. He grabbed his neck, thoughts torn between finding breath and wondering why the man who'd stabbed him wore the uniform of the king's guard.

FOURTEEN

Jankin shifted in bed, snorting like a bovine in the dirt. The red-headed demican's lips moved, as if feasting in his sleep.

"Jankin."

He groaned and shifted towards the wall.

"Jankin!" she called again, shaking him hard.

"What . . ."

"Wake up!"

"Leave me alone . . ."

"Jankin, there are men here!" she said.

"Tell them to go away," Jankin answered, still not opening his eyes. A moment passed, long enough that he hoped she'd listened, but then he was yanked out of his slumber. It felt like the bed had jolted into the air, but Jankin quickly realized that it was he was the one suspended in air.

"Unhand me!" he yelled, thrashing till he was dropped to the ground. He landed on his feet, meeting the gaze of one of the two men standing in his bed chamber, both of whom naturally towered over his diminutive stature.

"Who are you and what do you want?" He demanded.

"Are you the demican?"

"Why is it that ordinary men choose to use their strength to intimidate, even when they are begging for help? Was the plucking me out of bed necessary at all?" he asked.

"Are you the mover?" Elstan asked again.

"Yes, I am, but I'm currently not offering any services," Jankin said. His hands folded across his chest as he stared the man in the eyes. The second man turned to him and Jankin's arms instinctively unfurled.

"And how much would it cost for you to rethink?" Thorne asked.

The second man wasn't familiar, but what little Jankin could see of his face and demeanor beneath his hoodwas saturated with an aura that sent chills down the demican's spine. This was a man he wanted to be far away from.

"I . . ." He glanced at the door where his woman stood -- the panic on her face told him that she also felt nothing good would come if the men weren't pleased when they departed. "Look, perhaps I can make an exception, but you truly should learn to knock on a man's door and not make demands of him like savages," he said.

Elstan glanced at Thorne, who said nothing.

"Now, where do you need to go so much that you needed to disturb my precious sleep?" Jankin asked.

"Queen's Hill," Elstan answered.

Jankin snorted, "What's happening in Queen's Hill that suddenly everybody wants to go there? Why not just board a ship and sail like the rest of them?" He asked, but the lack of response from either of the men told him he needed to move on. "Well, like I told the ones that came before you, I cannot take anyone to Queen's Hill, as I myself cannot be there."

"We're willing to pay," Elstan said, holding a pouch that looked substantially filled with coins.

Jankin stared at the pouch for a moment before he shook his head, "No. Look, I like silver more than the next man, but this isn't something I'm going to risk my life for. I'm sworn to never return to that place, and I wouldn't break that. I can take you as far as Duken and no further."

Thorne glanced at Elstan, who instantly moved towards the door and grabbed the woman standing there.

"What – no!" Jankin protested.

Elstan dragged the woman to Thorne, and he grabbed her by the scruff of her neck.

"Let her go!" Jankin tried to hit Thorne but was held back by Elstan. The demican struggled to free himself, but Elstan held him tightly by the arms. "Let her go, she has nothing to do with this!"

Thorne squeezed harder, without so much as looking at her face as she choked as the air thinned in her narrowed airway. Her own attempts at breaking his hold were just as futile as her partner's. Thorne said nothing, simply held her as she began to slump and her thrashing quieted.

Jankin looked on in horror as she died, but his pleas were ignored. There was no sympathy in Thorne, Jankin could see. He had sensed it from the moment he'd seen the man's eyes.

"Okay – okay! I'll take you to Queen's Hill. I'll go!" He yelled. But it seemed he wasn't convincing enough, as Thorne only gripped tighter, even as the woman's hands fell to her sides. "Please, I beg you! I will take you!"

Thorne let her go and she dropped to the ground, gasping and coughing violently as her color quickly turned gray.

"She willn't catch her breath until we land in Queen's Hill," The lord watcher said.

* * *

Sitting in the room was driving Levyna out of her mind, trying to keep herself under control and not hound Gytha yet again about what had come of her visit to Black Castle. There was nothing else she could do, unless she wanted to break the promise she'd made to her mother to wait a little longer, till she knew what Gytha had found, before she did anything else. Every moment that passed, every moment she couldn't sense Olin, all but told her that Gytha hadn't found him. Or worse, that she had and he was simply –

Levyna stopped short at the sight of Aldith, King's Ranald's daughter, talking to a servant. After the servant left, Levyna walked up to the princess, whom she hadn't seen in days.

"Aldith –"

"It's Lady Aldith to you, is it not?"

It hadn't been, not since they'd become friends over three years ago. Levyna didn't imagine the sudden demand for formality was borne of a renewed fondness. "Of course, lady. I didn't know you were back."

"My father is dead, Levyna. Naturally that would be a reason for anyone to return home."

"I'm sorry about the king," Levyna said.

"Are you, now?" Aldith asked.

Levyna frowned, "What?"

The princess stepped forward, staring Levyna in the face, "I said, are you really sad about my father's death?"

"Of course, I am. Why would you say such a thing?"

"Because I've heard the Ravinshore spy you've been running around with is the one that did it. I've heard they still haven't found him, because you won't give him up."

Levyna's brows pinched, "Lady Aldith, I don't know what you've heard, but I had nothing to do with what happened. King Ranald was the king of *my* kingdom and a dear friend of my family, how could you think I would have had a hand in his death?"

"You call his killer by name, as though he has done nothing. And you don't look very remorseful of your connection to him. Tell me, if you knew nothing of my father's death, why has your kingkiller friend not been found?"

"Because no one knows where he is!"

Aldith scoffed and regarded Levyna with derision in her eyes, "You had better hope that he is, or else you and your mother will pay for his crime!" the princess said before she turned and walked away.

In the passage parallel to the yard, a maid dropped a bucket of water as it suddenly began to boil in her hand as a furious Levyna watched the princess leave.

* * *

Without his threads, Thorne would need to use the Alzeibier for whatever magic he needed, and to use the Alzeiber at its peak, he would need to continue to feed the ring, or it would feed on his own blood with every spell he cast. Until there was nothing else to feed on. Another sorcerer would have been consumed by the ring already, but he had tamed it, now that he knew his magic depended on it. At least if he believed a word of what his wretch of a father had said.

Elstan held on tight to the demican, even as the force of the travel changed his color a little, as it did even the strongest of men. They appeared behind a house in the middle of Pedina. Thorne looked around, and very quickly realized they were indeed in the kingdom of the hills.

The lord watcher looked down at Jankin, whose eyes were flushed with a mixture of rage and terror. The rage was for Thorne, for making him come here; the terror was for what might come after – both fear of what would happen if he was found here, and fear for the woman he had been forced to leave behind under the lord watcher's suffocation spell.

"I've done what you asked, now tell me how to release her from the spell so I can leave this place before I'm seen," Jankin said.

"You shouldn't bother, your whore is cold by now," Thorne said.

"Wh – what?" Jankin's face pulled into a frown as he looked from Elstan, who'd released him, to Thorne. "What do you mean 'cold'? You promised! You promised, you bastard!"

Jankin moved to strike the lord watcher, but Thorne grabbed him by the throat. Jankin refused to not suffer the same fate as his woman, and vanished from Thorne's hold, then appeared next to Elstan, grabbing a dagger from his belt. Then he vanished and appeared again behind Thorne in a blink. He aimed for Thorne's back, but the lord watcher turned swiftly and caught the man's hand, this time with the finger wearing the Alzeibier. Jankin tried to vanish again, but was shocked when he couldn't.

Thorne snatched the dagger from his hand and stabbed Jankin through his eye. The demican let out a whimper. Thorne pulled out the blade a wrapped his ringed hand around the wound. He felt the Alzeibier begin to feed on the blood. The power and essence of the demican seeped into the ring, allowing him to access the magic of the mover. Now Thorne had the gift of travel across a continent and back in a heartbeat without breaking a sweat. As the Alzeibier consumed Jankin, the dwarf's ginger hair turned completely white, and his skin shriveled into ghostly paleness. Finally, the lord watcher released him and the dwarf's body dropped to the ground.

The lord watcher sighed deeply and handed the bloody dagger back to his man. "His foolishness means he doesn't have to worry about whatever terrified him in Queen's Hill," Thorne said.

Elstan slid his dagger back in the scabbard. "Where to, now, lord?" he asked.

Knowing he could go wherever it was he wanted, at least until the Alzeibier had used up all of the demican's essence, there was only really one place the lord watcher of Walrea wanted to go.

* * *

"Lord, we've recieved word from the ground. The commander of the king's guard is dead," The fourth watcher of the circle said.

Gossie exhaled deeply, "And I believe the ghost in the camp didn't face any difficulty?" he asked.

"He remains undercover," Sixth answered.

"Good, we –"

Gossie fell quiet as the fifth watcher turned sharply, knives raised and ready. The other watchers reached for their weapons, and the lord watcher gasped at the sight of the intruder. When he recognized the figure, his eyes widened and he aborted his own spell.

"Stand down, watchers, this is a friend," Gossie said.

"No friend invades the circle of the Red Flame!" fifth said.

"This one does," Gossie answered.

Thorne stepped forward, lowering the hood of his cloak and removing the mask that covered half of his face. He said nothing as he stared at Gossie, noting he was clearly the one in charge. "You are the lord watcher of the Red Flame, now."

"Yes, I am, lord Thorne," Gossie answered.

The rest of the circle glanced at each other at the name. It wasn't one they was easily forgotten. Not in this kind of setting. Not with the reputation that preceded it.

"Watchers, this is Lord Thorne, the lord watcher of the Order of Walrea," Gossie announced and the rest of watchers bowed at once.

*

"I didn't know you had returned," Gossie said, once he'd dismissed the rest of the circle, and they stood alone in the room.

"I only just returned. I was expecting to find Eden, but I'm not surprised it's you instead."

"Yes, things have happened since the last time you were in Queen's Hill," Gossie said.

"So I've heard. Ranald is gone, finally," Thorne said.

"Yes, and those in charge haven't a clue what to do with the country. They have an army camped on the edge of the den, but we managed to cut off the head and will replace it with one of ours," Gossie answered.

Thorne nodded, "You have achieved something many before you have failed at, Gossie. The order all but has what it needs now."

"That praise feels like an honor coming from you, Lord Thorne. Might I ask – Walrea?"

"I have no doubt Walrea remains on the mission. I will return, in time, and will have Edmond's life, as I've long dreamt. But there is something I desire first," Thorne said.

"And what might that be?" the lord watcher of the Red Flame asked.

"The head of a traitor – Otto Rago."

FIFTEEN

Ariana hadn't rested easy since she'd learned of the escaped prisoner. She knew it was slim odds that the watcher would find her way back to the palace to bring harm to her or her family, but it also hadn't been likely that one watcher besting four king's guards. Just as it hadn't been likely that a watcher could slither his way into the palace and poison the king. Just as it wasn't likely that Ravinshore and the three kingdoms would be forced to fight against the same orders that had been sworn to protect. None of this would have seemed possible a moon cycle ago.

When Ariana closed her eyes, she thought of the prisoner's face. She hadn't done anything worth vengeance, as much as she wished she had, but she had still damned the watcher to the gaols and sent her to the dungeons of Black Castle. She'd played through her conversation with the watcher, and though there had been no point where Ilda had seemed as though she'd given Ariana's offer genuine thought, Ariana hoped deep down that she had struck something in the woman. That her taunts about Ilda succumbing to a tyrant's delusiun would make her question her choice even only a little. It had been unlikely. But Ariana couldn't deny that she'd hoped. Now, that hope seemed like utter foolishness and failure, regardless of what her husband had said. The woman was free and could be anywhere. Planning anything.

She could be north, across the sea already ... or she could be right here in Ravinshore. She could be within the very walls of the palace, and no one would know. She was a watcher, after all.

Though Queen Ariana had taunted Ilda, she had done so carefully hiding the fact that she knew it wasn't an ordinary person who became a watcher, and certainly no ordinary woman, regardless of how she had used her skills. For all of the fear watchers carried, there would always be something more in a female watcher, an edge that would make it even easier for her to achieve whatever she needed to. That edge made her poisonous, in a way that men would never need to be, and Ariana had gone ahead and poked at that poison, perhaps even inspiring it against herself. She didn't want to imagine what it would mean to find out.

So Ariana had woken several times in the night to check on her children while they slept, with guards she trusted watching their doors. Because even though it was highly unlikely that a prisoner would break free from captivity only to return to the palace swarming with guards, Ariana couldn't help but prepare for the worst happening.

Her family had survived the night, and there hadn't been any incident reported, but that didn't mean she was eager to take her eyes off them. She watched George spar with his tutor; Ole stood a few yards away, eyes on the atheling.

"Nothing is going to happen to him, or his siblings," King Edmon said, coming to her side.

"I know you believe so, lord king, but even you cannot be certain."

"They have been fine in the past and they will continue to be. No harm will come to our children, Ariana."

"They were fine in the past because the Order of Walrea wasn't trying to kill you – more than once. You know I'm right."

"They can hardly be safer anywhere than in the palace now, can they?" the king said.

Ariana turned to him, her face full of worry, "You know the answer to that, Edmond, you do. Had it not been for Gytha's intervention, this could have been a different story, and yes, I know this castle isn't the same as it was a fortnight ago, but it doesn't mean I am any less concerned. My worry hasn't faded, not with Thorne out there somewhere. I was concerned even before a potentially vengefull escaped, before Ranald of Queens Hill was killed, by the hands of someone he trusted. Someone we trusted."

Edmond looked away from his wife, down the balcony to his son in the yard. Whether he liked it or not, Ariana had a point, like always. The search for Olin had yielded nothing. Aafter the message from Queen's Hill, the king had sent the emissaries back with no particular declaration, beyond an assurance that Ravinshore had nothing to do with King Ranald's death and if Olinander was back in his kingdom, he would be found and Queen's Hill would receive word. Perhaps he should have added that they would deliver his head, as the kingdom of hills had required, but he'd held back. He was aware of what that could mean, as Ole had reminded him.

But Edmond was also aware of the gravity of what Olin had done. Hence, there might have been some truth in what he'd said to the emissaries from Queen's Hill when he'd called them back and told them Ravinshore would deliver the kingkiller, should he be found.

"We need to send our children away" the queen said

"We are close to them, Ariana. We see them everyday, and I know you all but spend the night guarding their rooms. I know your heart would be wherever they are."

"And so would yours, my lord. I know that, too," she placed her hand on his arm. "But if we must sacrifice seeing them every moment of every day to be sure that they would be safer, then would you not agree that we should?" the queen asked.

Edmond sighed, "And where would be safer than the palace?"

"Snetaya in Maedro."

"That's all the way across the sea," the king said, forehead creasing as he frowned.

"I know, but the farther away they are, the harder it would be for anyone to reach them. And they will have their grandfather to watch them," Ariana said.

"And that would also see them traveling for days, and across the sea, no less. Can't we find someplace in the three kingdoms for them to stay, somewhere perhaps a little closer where they would just be as safe?"

"There is a chance we might go to war with Queen's Hill," Ariana answered.

"But not with Duken," Edmond said.

"You want us to send our children to Duken?"

"My sister is there. She will care for them, you know that."

"But Duken has an order, my lord. Thorne can reach Duken."

"Then we shall make certain that no one knows they are there. I agree that the younger ones must be safe, but he has to stay," Edmon nodded at his heir in the yard.

Ariana opened her mouth to protest, "My lord –"

"No, Ariana. He needs to. No matter what happens, if our son is going to be the king we want him to be, he cannot hide away. He is all but a man now. He should be here to see it all with his own eyes. And we can easily protect him. He will be safe, if for no other reason than because I know you will watch him closely enough to annoy him. He must stay, Ariana," Edmond said again, placing his hand over hers.

Ariana's eyes were filled with a mother's uncertainty as she looked from her husband back to her son. Just then, he looked up at them both with reverence in his eyes. She could hardly argue with Edmond – one, they could watch more closely. He was the heir to the Ravinshore throne and, as she was beginning to realize, there was only so much she could hide him from, no matter what she feared. Ariana only wished that he didn't have to face a rebellious order.

"It would certainly make me feel much if I knew we didn't have to be so concerned about Walrea," she said.

"Thorne is gone. They've been quiet ever since."

"My lord, of course you know we cannot possibly rely on either of those things as fact. If anything, we should be more concerned about what their silence could mean – what they could be plotting in the shadows they so fondly dwell in."

"That's true. Though I'm not under any illusions that their silence means this is over. I've been considering the correct course to take."

"Do we not already have it?"

Edmond looked to his wife.

"Black Castle," she said.

"You agree that I should give the castle charge of the Order of Walrea?"

"The wardens might just make things right. We know they haven't once cared for the order's way of things. They will seek to change it. Even more so, we know that the only people who might hate Thorne more than we do are the wardens themselves. At worst, the wardens will change the way the order's priorities have darkened, and at best they will erase Thorne's legacy and make it so that he never has influence there again. And should he ever show his face in Ravinshore, he will die," Ariana said.

"There will be many who will disagree with this – the crown does not influence the affairs of Walrea."

"And none of them are the king, who the last I checked ruled over the whole of the kingdom, with every man, woman and child as his subject, my lord. The last I checked, none of those people survived the order's attempted murder. If anything, I believe they would agree you have changed the law to quench Walrea's recklessness. Walrea began this, and if you would save your people from a civil war, you must finish it. You are merciful, but far from weak," Ariana took her husband's face and looked into his eyes.

Edmond smiled, took his wife's hand and kissed it. Then he met Ole's waiting gaze with a nod. The court's counsel ended the atheling's spar with the guard and led them up the stairs to meet the king. A message was to be delivered to Black Castle.

* * *

Prince Petr stood with Fiona and Damiran before the rest of the aldermen. They all turned as a guard walked into the throne room, leaving two others who had accompanied him behind at the door.

"What news do you bring from the camp, Kenric?" Damiran asked.

"I am afraid it's ill news, Lord Damiran. The commander is dead," the guard said.

"What?" Damiran said as the rest of the court echoed his shock. "Clemon is dead?"

"He is, my lord."

"What happened? Was the camp attacked?" Petr asked.

"We weren't attacked. The commander was stabbed in his tent at dawn. No one saw anything. No one even as much as heard a sound," Kenric answered.

"How is that possible? Was he not behind our defenses? Protected by warriors like himself? How did no one see anything?" Alderman Simoen asked.

"I don't know, alderman, but none did. The entire camp was awake. There was no breach, and afterwards we searched the entire camp, and found nothing," the king's guard said.

"The killer didn't just appear inside the tent now, did he?" Benedikt said, frowning.

"My lord, we talked to each of the men. All one hundred of them were confirmed members of the guard. There was no intruder."

"We speak of the order. This could very well have been a watcher who infiltrated the camp from within," Alderman Simeon said.

Kenric's face turned grim, "Commander Clemon handpicked those men himself. To say we have a watcher hidden in the ranks of the king's guards isn't only incorrect, it also isn't something you should say out loud. If the soldiers believe they've been compromised it will be impossible to get anything done."

"That doesn't mean it might not be true," Prince Petr said.

"My lord, I believe Kenric is saying it would be hard ask any army to go to war, let alone war against the order of the Red Flame, if they believe one of them might be a watcher. They would achieve nothing with such distrust seeded in their ranks," Fiona said. "Which is why we must not allow the notion to spread," she turned back the guard. "This was no doubt the work of the order, and we can't ignore the possibility that they have watchers who possess magic," Fiona knew everyone was thinking of Olin as she said the words, "We know they are capable. Whoever killed Clemon could have appeared inside his tent. It's the more reasonable explanation."

Kenric nodded at the palatine's words.

"I agree with the palatine, we must be careful how rumours spread," Damiran said.

"But what if we are merely denying the actual truth?" Alderman Simoen asked.

"For the sake of the kingdom, alderman, we should hope that it's not," Prince Petr said.

"My lord, there's no better time to say this, but the men are growing weary. It has been days, and we haven't received orders," Kenric said.

"Why are they weary? Are they not warriors – king's guards?" Benedikt asked.

Kenric frowned, "They are warriors, alderman, but it's not the cold or the lack of sleep that worries any of them, it's the fact that we are camped on the ass of the order's den. It's that we have an enemy we will never see coming, and we have to way to stop them if they continue to pick us off one at a time, the way they've started," the guard said, looking to the prince and then the palatine.

"Surely they understand that the king's death has put things in a very delicate state, for everyone," Damiran said.

"We all know, Lord Damiran, but forgive me when I say things are a little more delicate when you are that close to the enemy. The men want orders, they want to know when we will be attacking, and, if there is still indecision, they want to know if we should consider moving camp," Kenric said.

"The king's murder cannot go unanswered!" Simoen said. "Queen's Hill cannot be portrayed as weak."

"It's not weak, alderman. We are not weak. The court is merely taking the time to make the right decision, instead of an emotional one. Making a mistake will favour no one, least of all the common folk," Fiona said. "We cannot order our men to attack the den of the Flame when there is a chance that another kingdom could have been responsible for the assassination of the king. And should we declare war against Ravinshore with the fox in our bloody pen, then we could be facing enemies on two fronts," Fiona said.

"But a decision must be made, and for the sake of the men of the king's guards, I should like to plead that it is done while we still have a number that can fight. And if I may suggest: while it is well-known that the order had targeted the king, shall it be ignored that a Ravinshore wielded the knife? If the kingkiller hasn't been discovered, then perhaps making Ravinshore feel our wrath would be a good place to start."

"They shall have to answer for it," Alderman Simeon said.

"That might be the beginning of something worse," Damiran said.

"Someone has to answer for the king's death," said Alderman Benedikt.

"And neither of those answers come easy or without bloodshed," Palatine Fiona looked from Damiran to the prince; both met her gaze. She looked back to the guard, "Kenric, you know the men well, do you not?"

"Yes, Lady Palatine, I do."

"Then I should think that it is right that you take charge of the army," she said, looking over at the prince.

"I agree, you shall take command," Prince Petr said.

"And it will be an honor," Kenric bowed curtly. "But my lords and lady, I should like to give the men news of some progress."

The prince and the palatine glanced at each other and Petr nodded.

"Tell them they are warriors of Queen's Hill and their bravery does not wither, it grows strong even in the face of the worst odds," Fiona said.

"And tell them they will have an enemy to fight, very soon," Prince Petr added.

Kenric sighed, uncrossed his hands and bowed before he exited the throne room.

* * *

"Remain where you are! Don't come any closer!"

Ilda halted and raised her hands – at least the one that she could lift. She watched as the man who'd spoken put himself between her and who she assumed was his family – a woman and two children. They looked scared. The man was holding a knife and standing a few yards away from her.

"I mean you no harm," she announced. "I swear it!"

"Who're you and what're you doing here? What do you want?" the man demanded.

"My name is Rena, I'm just a traveler. I faced a misadventure with bandits and a weakened horse. I've been walking for days and met no one, but I saw the fire from your house last night. I was too weak to approach. I only wish for some food and water, whatever you can spare," she said.

The man regarded her thoughtfully, looking her up and down. She knew she looked as though she'd been through something – she made no effort to hide the wretched look on her face.

"You say you're a traveller, where from?" he asked.

"East, Féden, heading to Duken. I lost my possessions – and my part-ner – with bandits at the Black River. I barely got away with the horse and just kept riding."

"How long?"

"What?"

"How long have you been lost?" The man asked.

"About a day and a half, if I'm not mistaken. Though I wouldn't be surprised if I lost track of time. Please, I don't mean you or your family any trouble, I swear it. All I hope for is a meal, even a cold one. It has been days. I promise to be on my way afterwards," the watcher said.

The man looked from Ilda to his wife who hesitated before nodding in agreement. Ilda was glad her display had been enough and she hadn't had to show the man the many ways in which she could use the knife he thought he was holding so valiantly in his hand.

"You can have food and water, but you must be on your way after that," the man said as he lowered the knife.

"That's all I ask," Ilda said as she lowered her hand and walked slowly towards them. She had spent so long hungry that she could tell at once there was food on fire nearby. If she hadn't been trying not to make herself any more of a spectacle, she would have hounded it down. But she merely stood as a young boy brought her a stool to sit on, and moments later the girl came with a pitcher filled with water. Ilda downed it while the man watched closely.

She had heard about families that lived this far north, but she had never really encountered one. All she had to do was get what she wanted from them. So far none of them suspected her to be an escaped watcher.

SIXTEEN

"I know we share his ideals, but there's something I can't shake about Lord Thorne's presence here, in the Den of The Flame, instead of Walrea. Since when were watchers allowed to simply walk into the circle of the Red Flame? Let alone a watcher from another kingdom?" the fifth watcher said, staring firmly into the distance.

"This is Lord Thorne we speak of," fourth said.

"I haven't forgotten who he is."

"Then don't forget the order is striving for what it deserves largely because of his influence," sixth said.

"Again, I don't deny who the lord watcher is, and what he has done for the cause. But for him to invade Red Flame the way he has – what does that say of us and what the order used to be? Since when do we allow a foreigner to walk into our home?" fifth asked.

"But he's not a foreigner, Fifth, he's Lord Throne," fourth said.

"Don't tell me who he is, I heard you the first two times!" fifth snapped. "I'm not arguing his name, watchers. I ask: what remains of the Order of the Red Flame if a watcher of Walrea walks into our circle like our defenses mean nothing. The Red Flame intends to reach our goals – take the power of the throne – and we all but have that now. Why is it that we have to listen to Walrea anymore?

"We don't owe Walrea anything. The Red Flame might share a dream with the order in Ravinshore, but it does not depend on it."

"No, it does not," sixth concurred.

"Then why does it feel like we are – why does it suddenly seem like we only following the plans of one man? Why does it feel like we are serving Lord Thorne's mission?" Fifth asked.

"We don't serve the mission of anyone but the Red Flame, watcher," fourth stepped aside to face his comrade. "It's clear to see that Lord Gossie has merely allowed Lord Thorne here due to who he is, and how much of our goals come from his inspiration. It doesn't mean, in any way, that he is to be lord over this order. That will never be. And to say that out loud is to imply that our lord watcher is weak."

fifth let out a breath and said nothing.

"Lord Thorne is a great mastermind, but the Red Flame does not bow to Walrea!" fourth said.

"You believe that too?" the fifth watcher turned to sixth, who stared for a moment.

"I was there the last time a watcher in the circle implied the lord watcher of the Red Flame might be straying. I believe you were there too, and we all saw what came of those words," sixth answered. "I would suggest you keep the idea out of your head completely."

"And sit by and watch, even when it seems –"

"Fifth watcher!" fourth cautioned in a hush tone so as not to draw attention. "If you value your service to this order, a service that *is* your life, you won't speak of this again and we will forget that we heard you utter these words." he turned and walked away.

The fifth and the sixth watchers watched him leave. "He's right. You don't want to be seen as doubtful, Fifth, not when the Lord of Walrea is back," sixth said before he too walked away.

They weren't wrong. He had been there at table when Eden had slit the second watcher's throat for suggesting the same thing he spoke of. Doubt wasn't a word that was supposed to exist in the heart of a watcher whose life was service to the order. But this watcher, though cautioned, couldn't completely banish the thoughts. The seemingly casual presence of Thorne of Walrea in the den of the Flame didn't merely go against the order's right to rule, but could very well be a bad omen.

The Red Flame had upended tradition to make the kingdom right. He believed this -- he was loyal to the order and to the kingdom of Queen's Hill, and the order of the Red Flame served the kingdom and the people more than anyone else did. Without them, the kingdom would have fallen a long time ago. But they served *one* kingdom.

They served Queen's Hill.

A watcher from a different land who doesn't know his place, ambling into the order's circle as though it was his ... it felt wrong deep into the fifth watcher's bones. It felt so wrong he imagined what Liaton would do, had he still been the lord watcher. But as Liaton was dead, and all watchers of the Red Flame were sworn loyalty to their lord watcher -- whoever it may be -- he could not allow doubt.

He couldn't even doubt how much of Walrea Thorne was still the lord of.

* * *

Ilda had half expected she would be handed stale bread and cold soup, despite what she'd smelled form the fire, but instead she had been given fresh bread while she waited for more. Ilda hadn't thought she would eat the same thing the family made for themselves, and she certainly hadn't expected the mother of the house to bring it to her.

"Thank you," Ilda said as she took the bowl of cabbage and mushroom soup. She had eaten half of the food before she even bothered to look up, which was when she realized she had an audience. The children watching didn't look away, even when she caught them staring -- they didn't even seem interested in the food in their own hands.

"Don't mind them – they don't know it's rude to stare," the woman said.

Ilda shrugged, "Oh, I don't mind," she lied. Not long ago, she would have had reason to take their eyes, at the very least. "You've offered me help, they can stare all they want," she said.

"It's because they don't get to see strangers very often," the woman answered.

Ilda nodded slowly, then glanced over at the man, who had shifted a little further away from a guard-like stance. He now sat with his own meal at a table, eyeing the stranger.

"That's very understandable," Ilda said. Ilda took another bite of soup before she realized the woman sat with empty hands -- she wasn't eating. Ilda slowly lowered her spoon, looking at her bowl. "Oh, I'm terribly sorry."

"What for?"

"I – I have mindlessly taken your meal, have I not?" Ilda asked.

The woman chuckled, "No, no. You haven't."

"But you're not eating. If you won't be offended, you can have the rest of this," Ilda tried to offer to the woman her own food but was swiftly rejected.

"Nonsense. Don't do that. It's your food to eat. I don't have a bowl because I don't have the stomach for morning food. It turns me dizzy very quickly. There is enough should I want to eat, and should you want more even," the woman said.

"Are you sure?"

"Eat, Rena," the woman said.

Ilda admitted it would have been hard to watch the soup go away, after what she'd had to stomach for days on end in captivity.

"My name is Ildawad, by the way," the woman said.

Ilda spilled her next bit of soup.

"Is everything okay?" Ildawad asked.

Ilda blinked hard as she looked at the woman who shared her name. Ildawad. Ilda. The watcher nodded, "Yes, I apologize. I must have been –" she put her hand to her throat "– a sore in my throat."

"Oh, sorry. The soup should help," Ildawad said.

Ilda ate till she was full. As she did, she noticed the demeanor and appearance of the woman sitting next to her. Ildawad wore a woven bracelet on her left wrist, her honey-coloured hair was twisted in very a unique braid, and she wore no shoes, despite the cold. All of that, combined with the lack of affinity for meals so early in the morning, made Ilda suspect. "Do you mind if I ask?"

"Ask what?"

"Are you a healer?"

"I know a few spells, if that's what you mean. I'm a lower mage," Ildawad confessed.

"Oh,"

"Don't sound so disappointed."

"Oh, I'm not. I merely meant it's interesting."

"What gave it away?"

"I should say everything. I have a habit of staring too; I pay attention," Ilda said. *And I'm a watcher*, she didn't add.

"I see," Ildawad said with a keen nod. "I would say that I'd like to know more about how you came to be here alone, but I don't seek to pry. I shall only ask if you need help."

Ilda swallowed the food in her mouth and looked down at her ragged clothes, then back to the woman. "I appreciate that you don't pry, but if you perhaps have clothes that you can spare, it would be most helpful," Ilda said.

"Of course, I'm sure we can find you some."

"I know, I promised your husband that I would be off after my meal –"

"Don't worry about Alec, he's only being cautious. He won't mind offering a little more help," Ildawad said, rising to her feet.

Ilda looked away from the woman, tensing as she caught sight of a single-horse wagon approaching. They were clearly following the path that was led to the house. Ilda slowly set down her food and glanced at Alec, who seemed to have seen the wagon. The little girl was still staring at Ilda.

The calm of the meal was thumped out of the watcher's heart as she began to plan – what were the chances that whoever was on that wagon knew of a missing prisoner, a female watcher? Would they be able to recognize her – the Ilda that owned the alehouse, the mistress that was never to be crossed? Her mind raced to calculate the odds, hating the possibility that she would have to do something unkind to this family that had fed her.

The wagon's drew closer. Time wasn't on her side, but a dagger was. Ilda turned quickly to Ildawad and grasped her hand.

"Perhaps I can have somewhere to get out these clothes now," Ilda said.

* * *

Queen Ariana walked to the throne room, her husband and son trailing a few yards. The guards opened the door and a rare delight filled her, as she set her eyes on the woman that had saved her husband and her family.

"Grand Sorceress Gytha," Ariana said as she approached.

Gytha turned towards the queen, with that weighty smile on her face again, "Your Highness," she bowed, only for Ariana's hands to pull her into an unsuspecting embrace.

"It's so good to see you again, under better circumstances," The queen said.

Gytha nodded as she broke from the embrace and bowed as King Edmond walked in.

"Grand sorceress," Edmond didn't diminish his wife's cheer as he saw the woman. "My wife doesn't lie – your face is forever a reminder of life," he said. "It's a pleasure to have you in this palace."

"And it's an honor to be here," Gytha said, as it went without saying, "And I'm glad to see you are well."

"This is my son, Prince George," Edmond said.

"My lord," Gytha bowed, "An honor to meet you. And Your Highness, this is my friend, William," she introduced, "He allowed Isabelle to find me,"

"And we are all grateful to you, William," Edmond said as William bowed.

With the pleasentries over, the weight of the recent news slowly descended on the room. "Grand sorceress, as much as we wish this was a courtesy visit, we understand that it most likely isn't," Edmond said as he walked towards his throne. He didn't sit, but merelry rested a hand across its back.

Gytha expected nothing less. "You're right, Your Majesty, I'm here in regards to my son, Olinander," she said.

Arian looked between Gytha and Edmond and her son.

"We received the news of what happened from Queen's Hill. It's indeed terrible. While there are many questions to be asked, I suppose *we* –" the king emphasized himself and his queen as he glanced at Ariana "— were hoping to hear it from the horse's mouth," Edmond said. "Is it true: did Olin really kill King Ranald?"

Gytha exhaled, "My lord, I cannot say that it is untrue, but neither can I say that it's truth either."

"But only one can be true, surely," the king said.

"Yes, but the reason is that I – *we* – merely walked into the room to find Olin holding the bloody knife and standing over the king's dead body.

Neither I, nor anyone else, actually saw him slit the king's throat. But I know what it looks like, and it seems there is no other answer –"

"Are you saying that he may not have done it?" Ariana asked.

"I'm saying I know my son, and he would never do such a thing with no just reason. At least not if he was in his right mind," Gytha answered.

"What do you mean by that?" Ariana asked.

"I mean, just before we caught Olin, William and Levyna and went to a seer. She told us his magic is consuming him."

"It could have caused him to do it without his knowledge?" Edmond asked.

"That is the possibility that terrifies me. So I have come to ask, to beg of you, Your Majesty. I have looked for him everywhere, and have found nothing. He is nowhere, and I know what he has done is unforgivable, but if you have captured him –"

"Captured?" Ariana said with a frown. "Do you believe we have captured your son, Gytha?"

"I – I don't know, my lady, which is why I'm here. I would understand if you have him, if he's locked away in the dungeons. The magnitude of his crime is greater than he alone can pay for, but –"

"Grand sorceress, you are greatly mistaken. Your son isn't here. I sent men to his uncle's home, but when they failed, we gave up the search," The king said.

"Absolutely," Ariana affirmed, "Gytha, we haven't seen your son since he visited the palace with his friend days ago, looking for you, in fact. Hearing Queen's Hill's news came as a shock to us, mainly because Olin was the one who gave us the knowledge of the Order's plan for the king and kingdom. Your son isn't here, Grand Sorceress."

Yet again, the words brought relief, along with the agony of still not knowing where he was, of the uncertainty of what could have happened to him. And yet they had no reason to lie. Gytha stared at Ariana, who had begged her to save her husband, and Edmond, whom she had snatched from the clutches of death in the oblivion of Egro. They wouldn't lie to her, they weren't that type of person, to lie so boldly, not in front of their son.

The grand sorceress felt her hands grow cold.

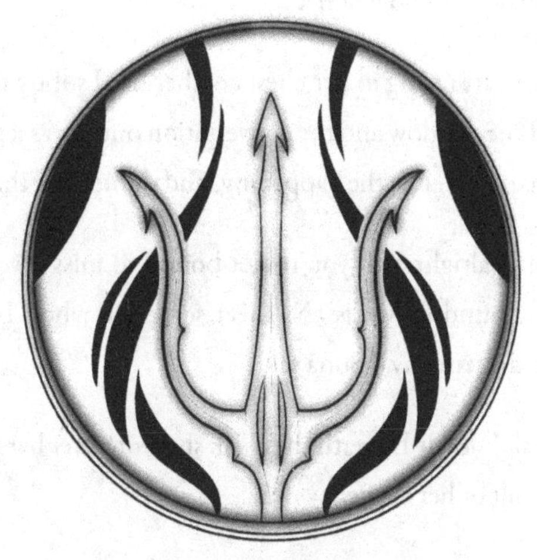

SEVENTEEN

Ilda was well inside the house by the time the wagon arrived. She stood by a chair, away from the door but near the window so she could hear whatever the business the wagon had. Even though she might have been overacting, there was always the chance that this would be where her luck turned. She was poised for action as she watched the little girl go out to fetch a bucket of water. As she watched the girl, just like the very first moment she'd seen her, Ilda was reminded of her own daughter.

Alec welcomed the wagon driver, a man called Bona, and they shared pleasantries. They didn't sound so much like old friends who hadn't seen each other in a long time and more like ones who hadn't seen each other in a week. Judging by the mention of 'the last time', Ilda learned that the Bona's path came to the house very often. It also told her this visit was far from random, but there was still the chance he might know her, or know of her.

Ilda waited, heart racing in her chest and her head subtly tilted in the direction of the window and the conversation outside as it grew closer towards what she feared: the happenings and the news of the kingdom.

"There's news alright, and you're not bound to miss if you'd decide to journey a hundred yards and meet someone who's been in the Ravinshore the past day," Bona said.

Ilda's hand slid slowly beneath the cloak she wore over her filthy shirt, finding the hilt of her dagger.

"What is it?" Alec asked curiously as he unloaded a bag from the back of the wagon and handed it to his son, who carried it gallantly to the front of the house.

The dagger warmed in her hand, and her lip suddenly grew so weary she had to bite it.

"King Ranald of Queen's Hill is dead, and word is that a Ravinshore lad killed him," Bona said.

"You jest!" Alec said.

"I do not. I swear it. It's spreading all across the kingdom now. A Ravinshore sciff, I hear, got in the palace and slit the king's throat, then disappeared,"

Ilda's face pinched as she let out a breath. The little girl approached from the inner chamber and she quickly unhanded the dagger beneath her cloak. As she did -- whether it was from her time in the dungeoun or weakness from the journey – her right hand trembled. She looked down at it and clenched it into a fist.

"Rena?"

Ilda looked up to see Ildawad beckoning to her. She blinked back into the reality she had created as he looked from the mother to her daughter before pulling away from the window and approaching them.

"A Ravinshore kills a Hillander king. That's war, is it not?" Alec asked.

"That is why the news has the entire kingdom concerned. And it's even worse because he hasn't been found, and now regular folk are wary of their fate, all because a turd called Alin or Olin or something spilled the blood of the ruler of another kingdom."

Ilda stopped short at the threshold of the inner chamber and blinked. That wasn't a name she could miss. Olin. Olinander. The sciff. What were the odds? Gytha's very own son was a fugitive just like she was, and a kingkiller no less.

And she had him.

"Are you alright?" Ildawad asked.

Ilda nodded as she stepped inside the chamber.

Ildawad handed the dress to Ilda. "This is very nice," she said, "But if you would prefer something different, the tunic and the breeches are mine as well," she said.

Ilda looked at the clothes set over the back of a chair and nodded.

"There's a rag to help you wash. You'll have to manage the water," Ildawad said.

"It's more than enough, Ildawad. I cannot thank you enough."

The woman smiled and nudged her daughter out the door to give her privacy, Ildawad paused after her daughter stepped out. "Rena," she said.

Ilda looked at her.

"I only ask one thing in return for all of this."

"What is it?"

"That you please not use your dagger on me or my family," Ildawad said, her eyes lowering to the knife that was perfectly hidden in the watcher's cloak.

Ilda was hardly ever taken by surprise, but this woman had surprised her. She opened her mouth to speak, but Ildawad quickly stopped her.

"Like I told you earlier: I don't want to pry. You must have your reasons for the knife and having a clean cloak over filthy clothes. Whatever those reasons, it's not our business and we don't make a habit of making other people's business our own, as you might have guessed. If you want silver –"

"I don't, I swear it. I meant it when I said I mean your family no harm. I really only wanted some food and to hopefully get out of this filth," Ilda said. "I won't harm your family or take anything more from you. I swear on my life. You have shown me nothing but kindness."

Ildawad pressed her lips together like a woman who hoped what she had heard was the truth. She turned to leave, but it was Ilda's turn to stop her.

"If I may ask you one more thing, however."

"Yes."

"You say you're a mage, would you know I could reach someone far away to convey a message? It's the last I will ask of you, believe me,"

Ildawad stared at her, as Ilda spoke. She'd sworn more times to this woman than she could remember ever.

* * *

Ariana knew what Gytha was feeling.

"I've searched everywhere I can think of, everywhere I know that he might have stepped foot. And not just so I may find him before anyone else does, but just so I may find him," Gytha said.

She glanced at William, who stood steadfast beside her, and at the queen before she looked at the king. "Lord, I know, as your subject, Olinander has put you in an impossible situation and all of Ravinshore is at risk, but if I may ask just one thing of you."

Edmond met his wife's glance but nodded anyway, "Speak, grand sorceress."

"I know it's an impossible thing ask of you. I know you must keep your kingdom safe, and the life of one young man might be nothing compared to the rest of your people. But please, Your Majesty, all I ask is if your men find my son, command that he not been killed on sight.

And, if he is captured, you will consider all he has done, and all I have done, and extend the kindness by granting him a fair trial," Gytha said.

Edmond exhaled. He reached over to rest a hand on his wife's. Then he glanced at his son, who stood t his right hand, and to Ole, who stood next to the boy. A moment passed as he pondered his response.

Then he spoke. "Grand sorceress, you have my word that your son will not be killed by the hands of my king's guards, if he is found in Ravinshore, and if captured he will not be harmed. As to his trial: it's not a crime he has committed in Ravinshore, hence, I shall only have a part in it, but know I shall do all I can to make sure that he gets a chance to defend himself," Edmond said.

Gytha nodded, "Thank you, Your Majesty. That's all I ask."

*

Ariana had asked for Gytha's company and left William in the presence of the king and his court's counsel. The sorcerer stood like a soldier waiting on his commander's return.

"Where are you from, William?" the king asked.

"Maedro, my lord," William answered. "But I have since found a home in Duken."

"I see. You're a sorcerer as well?"

"Yes, my lord. But not anything like Gytha, and I say that without an ounce of pride lost."

"I'm not surprised. When it mattered most for me, it was she who managed to drag me away from death. As a sorceress and as a warrior."

William nodded, "That sounds very much like her."

"And you sound like a loyal friend," the king said.

"If only half as loyal as the grand sorceress has been to me, then I should like to think myself a devoted friend,"

"If she's so powerful, why can she not use her magic to find her son?" George, the king's heir quieted the hall for a moment.

Edmond looked to his son, at first to caution him from speaking, until he realized the sense in the question. He turned to William, who was looking at George.

"I believe the atheling has a point," Ole said.

William looked between Ole and the king, "That would have made things easier and certainly spared the trouble of the search, but believe me when I say that is one of the reasons why the grand sorceress is so troubled."

"What do you mean?" Edmond asked.

"If anyone goes missing, it takes a few breaths for someone as powerful as Gytha to find them, so long as she has something that belongs to them – that comes from them: blood or hair or something more. And that's for a stranger. As Olin's mother, Gytha should be able to find him easily, with very little strength, but she cannot."

"Why?"

"Because every time she has performed the spell, it has led nowhere. Which is terrifying, and isn't something any mother wants to face, regardless of what their child has done."

"What does it mean?" George asked.

"On the right day, with the right material, a sorceress like Gytha can find where a dead man is buried with a drop of their blood. But when she does the spell for her son, it leads nowhere. Literally nowhere. It shouldn't be possible, whether he's dead or alive. It means that something terrible has befallen Olinander, wherever he is, something so strong that his essence cannot be traced, as though he doesn't exist. Which is why we must search like she knows nothing at all."

*

There's no greater advocate than a child's mother. Queen Ariana didn't need to be told that as she walked side by side with Gytha down the same passageway she had walked with the grand sorceress's son not days before.

"I hate that our meeting is due to yet another troubling experience," Ariana said.

"I hoped, really hoped, that I would finally find him here and that . . ." Gytha trailed off as the words failed her. "Every moment that passes and I don't find him, I fear the absolute worst. I know what he may have done is terrible, but he's still my son. And you might not know this, but I've failed him a lifetime already. I wasn't there when he needed a mother, and though I've attempted reconciliation now, I've still failed. I cannot shake the feeling that I am partly to blame for what has happened to him,"

"I told him, when he came here, that I believed he was never far from your heart wherever you were. A child never stops needing a mother, no matter how old he is, and no one can blame you for wanting to find and protect him, certainly not me," Ariana said.

"I've thought about it, about the fate that brought me back into his life, and I want to believe that it's not as cruel to end in heartbreak, because I don't think I will be able to bear it," Gytha said. "Olin doesn't belong to any order -- he would never agree with them, after what they've done, what they've taken from him. He hasn't done their bidding, but I don't know what reason could have led to the king's death."

"For whatever it's worth, grand sorceress, you should know you have a friend here, if not for anything else you've done, than for saving my family."

Gytha sighed as she looked at the queen, seeing the sincerity in her eyes. Then Gytha turned away, hearing a voice calling her, one she recognized.

"Gytha, it's me. I know where your son is," Ilda's voice said.

EIGHTEEN

"**Y**ou won't be able to see whoever you wish to talk to," Ildawad said.

"I don't need to see them, merely to convey a message. My voice shall be enough," Ilda said, hope in her eyes as she stared at the woman.

Ildawad regarded her for a moment. "There's something I can triy. Although I haven't had to do it in a while."

"A simple effort shall be enough, Ildawad," Ilda reassured.

Ildawad nodded, "Very well, clean yourself as you intended. I shall be waiting for you."

Ilda watched as the woman exit the room, closing the door behind her and leaving her alone in the chamber. She could still hear the voices of the men chatting away in outside. She looked at the clothes in her hands, thinking. What manner of fate was this? What were the odds? That Olinander had become a kingkiller, and she had rescued him. Not a fortnight before, she had been following the Order's bidding as they sought to kill that very boy. And she hadn't ever recognized him. Not days ago, she would have been forced to take his life so the order could achieve victory. Without the boy disrupting their plans, Walrea's plot would have succeeded. Without his mother's interruption, the order would be ruling Ravinshore now.

Yet she had slung him half-dead across the back of her horse, not knowing that he was now a kingkiller.

But how? Ilda thought. And why?

She could answer none of those questions now -- she neither had the time nor the luxury of presence to wonder. She dropped the clothes on the bed and pulled the cape around her shoulders. Then she stared at the filthy clothes that had seen her in the dungeons. She'd thought several times she would die in them. She had been prepared to. Taking off her belt and dagger, she dropp them on the cape. Being careful of the injury on her arm, she took off the tunic, whimpering as the tattered clothes brushed against the wound. The cloth reeked so much she hardly believed it had been her garment. She did the same for her boots and trousers.

Standing naked, she stared at herself. Her arms and legs were covered in minor scratches, and her belly and shoulders were bruised. Her hands were red from the cold and her feet marked with sores. But she was still alive. Taking the washrag, she dipped it in the bucket and cleaned her face and the rest of her body. Finally, she put on the fresh clothes provided for her.

When she was finished, Ilda opened the door to find Ildawad sitting on a chair with her daughter standing next to her.

"You look better," Ildawad said.

"I owe it to your kindness," Ilda said.

Ildawad picked up a small bowl with a strange liquid and handed it to Ilda. "You'll have to sit to drink it, so you don't fall from dizziness."

Ilda did as she was told even, as her first instinct was to reach for the dagger at her side when being asked to consume something unknown in a stranger's house. It could very well be her undoing. This liquid could be more than just a means to reach who she needed to -- it could lead to her opening her eyes in the dungeons yet again, or worse. But if she was ever to reach Gytha in time without the risk of dicovering, she needed to take the risk. Besides, she didn't really thinkg that the woman who had helped her so much till now would see her perish after so much effort.

Ilda turned the tasteless drink into her mouth and handed Ildawad the empty bowl.

"It's to keep your mind narrow for a moment, to help you focus."

Ilda nodded. Then to her surprise the little girl came to her, hands outstretched and twined with blue threads.

"Think of who you wish to speak with – only them and nothing else – and once you can *feel* where they are, say what you wish to, quickly," Ildawad said.

"How will I know it's not just memory?"

"You will know."

Ilda blinked at the little girl's face as the child placed her small hands on her head. Ilda hardly needed to dig deep to think of Gytha, with the memories of the times they had been friends, when life had been much simpler and less heart-breaking. Ilda clung to the memories as hard as she could, without the pieces that had succumbed to time and faded away in her mind. She held on till she could suddenly hear Gytha's voice; she felt as though she was standing next to the grand sorceress.

"Gytha. Gytha it's me. I know where your son is. Reach Leigesdom and I shall be there. Hurry," Ilda said.

It seemed as though she was yanked out of a dream. She opened her eyes and the little girl took her hands off her head. Ilda's eyelids fluttered and she reached up to clutch her forehead at the sudden headache.

"It should pass," Ildawad said.

Ilda nodded, "Thank you," she looked to the child. "I never knew."

"Not everything is as it seems, and sometimes the more we stare, the less there is to see. We all have reasons for the choices we make," Ildawad took her daughter's hand and held it in both of hers, "They just have to matter enough."

"I have a daughter just like her," Ilda said, the words coming out of her even before she realized it.

"What's her name?" the little girl spoke for the first time.

Ilda stared; she found herself unable to think of a reason to lie. "Ella," she said. "And she is just as beautiful as you are."

The child smiled, "Where is she?"

Ilda's smile dropped as she looked away slowly, "I don't know," she said. "I haven't been able to see her."

"What happened – was she taken from you?"

"She . . . It's a fate of my own design," Ilda said. "I did things that took me away from her."

"Was it worth it?" the child asked.

Ilda stared, unable to answer.

"If it's not, then maybe you shouldn't be away from her. I think you should find her," Ildawad said, "Because I believe some things aren't worth sacrificing."

Ilda gazed at the mother and child thoughtfully before she rose. "I should be on my way," she said.

Ildawad rose from her own seat as well. "I hope you find whatever it is you seek."

"I'm grateful, Ildawad. I wish I could repay your kindness."

"Don't worry about it. That you have merely kept your word shall be enough"

* * *

Gytha could never mistake that voice for someone else. It was Ilda. She was sure of it. But was she telling the truth? How Ilda could possibly have Olin? Gytha couldn't see how it could be so.

"Gytha?" Ariana said.

The grand sorceress turned to meet Queen Ariana's eyes with a frown, "My lady."

"Are you okay? You rather seemed carried away all of a sudden."

"Yes, of course. I apologize," Gytha said. "My mind is ravaged by thoughts."

"I understand."

"If my lady won't mind, I should like to be on my way now."

"Of course, you do what you must. Shall I ask – where do you turn now, if you have looked everywhere?" Ariana asked.

"I shall turn over mountains if I have to. I haven't looked hard enough. I must continue," Gytha said.

Ariana nodded, "I trust you will. I shall bid you good luck, even though it's hard and it might not mean so much kindness upon Ravinshore," she said. "And know, grand sorceress, that you have an ally here."

Gytha nodded as she bowed curtly and walked past the queen. It took all of her might to keep herself calm as she returned to the throne room to find William in the presence of the king and the atheling.

"Your Majesty, if you will allow it, we should like to take our leave now," she said.

William met Gytha's eyes and, though he couldn't tell what had happened, he knew something had changed; something was different.

"Very well. I should like to hope that the next time we see you there is less unease," the king said.

Gytha nodded.

"My lord," William bowed, "Atheling," he nodded to the heir before he turned and followed Gytha out of the throne room. A few steps away from the door he spoke without looking at her as they approached the main exit. "What has happened?"

Gytha said nothing.

"Gytha?"

"We shall get the horses and ride, as far out of sight as we can, and then we head north."

"Why? What has happened, Gytha? What have you discovered? What is north?"

"The watcher that knows where my son is," Gytha said.

*

"What do you mean a watcher knows where your son is?" A perplexed William asked in a hushed voice as they stood outside waiting for their horses to be delivered.

Gytha looked around and William quickly understood her hesitation. They were still in Ravinshore, and regardless of what the king had said about Olinander being treated fairly, he was a person of interest. If anyone else were to discover where he was, things might not go as smoothly as hoped in the palace. And if whoever didn't serve the king and crown, Olin would be in danger. Even if they were merely an enraged subject of the kingdom on the verge of war because of Olin's actions. And if anyone learned he was in the company of a watcher would all but damn Olinander, even in the face of the royal orders.

They rode hard away from the palace, past the gatehouse and further till they were surely out of sight and had left any lurking ears far behind. Only then did Gytha stop and turn to her accomplice.

"Will you explain now, for the love of the gods, what has happened?"

"You remember the watcher we were told escaped from the king's guards?" Gytha began.

"Yes, what of her?"

"Her name is Ilda. In a different life she was a friend, a trusted one. I was the one who captured her when the watchers attacked the palace. But while I was with the queen, I heard her voice. She managed to reach me via a medium. She said she knows where my son is, and that I should reach Leigesdom to find her,"

"What?" William said, surprise evident on his face, "Surely you don't believe it? You have to know that you can't."

"I have no choice, William."

"You do. You cannot take the word of an escaped watcher, someone who is probably desperate. Someone who's following the orders horrible plans. This could very well be a trap meant to lure you in."

"As much as it could be, I know it's not."

"How can you possibly know that, Gytha? She's a watcher! A mistress of deceit! It doesn't matter who she was in a different life, the order has her now and she does their bidding. And, if I'm not mistaken, the same order has tried to kill your son several times -- how does a watcher suddenly know where he is? And why is she telling you? Why?"

Gytha exhaled. Everything William said held sense. All the signs pointed to deceit. It could very well be a plot of the order, a way to get her in one place, to get revenge for foiling their plan for the king. They may not even have Olinander, and if they did, he certainly wouldn't be safe. Not with his magic – it would be chaos either way. But Gytha couldn't shake that part of her that wanted to believe.

"Wasn't it you who asked me to believe he's still alive and that I would find him?" She asked.

"This wasn't what I meant. This is the sky meeting earth kind of unlikely. *This* is madness."

"There's nowhere else I haven't looked, William. It's my son, I don't care what trap the order might have waiting for me, if there's half a chance, or even one-quarter of one, that someone knows where he is, then I have no business being anywhere else. I must try, even if it means that I have to kill a thousand watchers to find the truth," Gytha said. "And you really don't have come with me. The order isn't your fight."

William's face was twisted with displeasure, but he sighed. "I don't fear watchers, I merely hope that it won't take you further from your son. I'm not going anywhere," he said.

Gytha nodded.

"Did you ask how she knows where he is?"

Their conversation had been so brief that she hadn't asked – she'd been so relieved at the mere thought that someone knew something. "That's what I shall find out," the grand sorceress said as she kicked her horse into a gallop; William followed.

*

Ilda couldn't take him with her, even if he didn't have the look of death about him. She stared at Olin -- he didn't seem to have twitched since she left. She listened for a heartbeat in his chest again. All she heard was silence before she finally heard a thud. She couldn't understand how he could be living in this state. She didn't know if he even was. Whatever had come of killing the king hadn't been good.

Ilda rose to her feet and stared at the young man. With any luck, his mother would find him here, and she would at least have his body to bury, when he inevitably died in truth. But Ilda wouldn't risk Gytha's wrath after the last time they'd met, as the worst of adversaries and not the fondest friends they'd once been. But Gytha had spared her life, and no doubt that was part of the reason why Olin was in a cave with her.

Ilda sighed. She needed to see Gytha, and if the grand sorceress seemed unwilling to be reasonable a second time, then it was her son who would suffer for it.

Ilda left the cave and found the horse where she'd left it the night before. She mounted the beast and headed in the direction of Leigesdom; she was sure Gytha would be nearby.

NINETEEN

Ilda nudged the horse to a slow walk as they arrived at the small hillside overlooking the path that led north. Leigesdom. She scanned her surrounding, as she was now in the open. Gytha wasn't the only thing she had to worry about now – she was an escaped prisoner with chaos in her trail to freedom. And even that wasn't the end of it. She was a watcher unmasked, a ghost uncloaked. Ilda listened to every change in the landscape around her, clutching the only weapon she had – the dagger on the belt around her waist.

A moment passed. Ilda wondered if Gytha wouldn't show up. It was unthinkable, considering the wrath the grand sorceress had inflicted on the order when it had come to her son. Then a twig snapped to her left and Ilda swiftly pulled the dagger, only to find herself suddenly yanked to the side, off the horse and against the cliff wall. The dagger fell from her hand. Ilda quickly reached for it, but felt her body stiffen and her neck tighten, keeping her in place.

"Give me one good reason why I shouldn't finish it this time, Ilda!" Gytha appeared from behind a tree, eyes full of rage as she stared at the watcher struggling to breathe.

"Gytha," William said as appeared at her left. "She cannot say anything if she cannot breathe," he reminded the grand sorceress.

"Where's my son!" Gytha yelled, stepping forward and lifting Ilda against a tree, until her legs dangled in their air. Gytha watched impatiently, fingers spread wide at her side as she nailed Ilda to the tree with her magic.

"You need to let her breathe, Gytha. She needs to be able to talk," William pleaded with Gytha.

Gytha's eyes didn't leave Ilda, even as she eased her hold on the watcher's throat. Ilda gasped and coughed.

"Tell me where he is!"

"I shall! I shall!" Ilda yelled. "I didn't ask you to come here because I wish to die. I shall tell you where your son is. But only if you swear to let me go and tell me where you sent Ella."

"And what makes you think I will do that?" Gytha asked.

"Because I'm the only one who knows where Olin is."

"I can just pry it out of your head, then kill you," Gytha said.

Ilda's eyes widened, and she glanced at William, but knew he had no control over what happened to her.

"She will do it and I'll have to watch," William said. "Speak."

"I suppose you'll have to, then, because I won't say a word till you promise me that I can go and find my daughter," Ilda said.

Gytha took another step forward and Ilda pressed against the tree in panic.

"I saved his life!" Ilda yelled, managing to catch the grand sorceress's attention and stop Gytha's strike. "Had it not been for me, he would be dead or captured. I know what he did," she said, looking Gytha in the eyes and managing to find her voice. "I know he killed the king of Queen's Hill and the entire kingdom is looking for him, though I didn't know that when I picked him up where he collapsed."

"He collapsed?"

"Yes, on the road to Black Castle. I suppose that was where he was going. I escaped from the guards and saw him just as he collapsed. I risked my own life to drag him to safety. I risked being found and captured again when I chose not to leave him behind to allow myself to get away quicker. I should have abandoned him there, but I didn't. I did not, Gytha. Instead, I dragged him with me even when I didn't know what he'd done. He's where I left him. Safe. I shall tell you –"

"No, you will take me to him!"

That wouldn't favor her, Ilda knew. "No, you will have no reason not to kill me."

"I still have reason to."

It could become worse for her very quickly if the boy happened to be dead when they reached him. Ilda would have no escape -- she was already outmatched, even when she'd had her dagger, which was now in William's hands. Unless she wanted to die, to test just how desperate Gytha had grown since the last time they'd met – a mother whose child was at stake. Ilda realized her leverage was worth less than she thought. If Gytha could do as she said – rip the boy's location out of her head, something Ilda couldn't imagine would be pleasant – then she held no leverage at all. Whatever had caused Gytha to hold back before was gone, now that her son was concerned. Ilda had no choice.

"Fine, I shall take you there," she finally answered, "But we must hurry."

"Why?" William asked.

"He – He doesn't seem well."

"What have you done to him?!" Gytha asked.

"Nothing, I swear it! He has been so since I found him – hasn't opened his eyes or said a word. And, you must know that he breathes as though he does not," Ilda said.

*

Gytha rushed into the cave and dropped to her son's side. William stood behind her, watching Ilda. Gytha grabbed her son's shoulder, tyring to wake him as she called his name.

"Olinander! Olin!"

"He won't respond, no matter how much you scream or shake him. Something's wrong, and I don't know what. Look at his eyes," Ilda said.

Gytha peeled apart her son's eyelids, then gasped. They were as black as the bowels of dusk. Gytha stared at him as she held his face and then took his head in her hands. Trying to feel for his essence, but there was barely any sign of life, even though he was warm. She placed her hand on his chest, then her head to listen, and it was just as Ilda had said – the beat of his heart wasn't merely weak. It seemed as though it came in season. Gytha took Olin's hands and then turned to his legs. Something was certainly wrong.

"That doesn't look like something that would happen from his magic," William said.

"It's not," Gytha answered.

"How can you be certain?" Ilda asked.

Gytha was quiet as she searched her son's body, running her hands through his curly hair and then down to his chin, turning his head to check the back of his neck. She pulled his shirt up and checked his chest, his shoulders, his belly, his sides, and then his back.

"What are you looking for?" Ilda asked, stepping closer with William on her tail. She dropped to her knees as well.

"I will know when I find it," Gytha said as she turned Olin to his side to get a better look at his back.

Ilda pulled off the young man's boot and William took the other one. They checked his feet and worked up his legs. Ilda pulled Olin's trouser up over his right thigh and froze.

"Gytha," she said.

Gytha turned sharply and at once she saw what she had been looking for. It wasn't Olin's magic -- something else had gotten to him, something had gotten inside of him and this was how.

"He has been poisoned," Gytha said, staring at the mark on Olin's thigh. A wound, blackening his veins around the opening. It was clear the poison went much deeper. All the way through his blood and further into his body, so deep that it was blocking his very essence. Ilda hadn't been wrong when she'd said Olinander was dying.

"I haven't seen this kind of poison before," William said, looking at the watcher in their midst.

"I had nothing to do with this!" Ilda said, "I only just escaped, remember? And I found him this way."

"But someone did this to him," William said. "What kind of poison is it?" he asked Gytha.

"Step back," Gytha ordered. William and Ilda stepped away as his mother placed her hand over the wound. "Give me the dagger," she told William, who pulled the knife from his side and handed it over.

Gytha nicked her own palm and let her blood drip onto the wound.T hen she lowered both hands over the cut and shut her eyes. Luminous threads weaved from the grand sorceress's arms and wrapped around her son's leg, concentrating on his thigh as she muttered the words of the spell.

"Sevanios , beil arionas. Intentum – leleria."

William and Ilda watched silently. Gytha's hands glowed all the way up her arms as she held the spell over her son. She twisted her hands, as though she sought to pull at something with the threads of her spell. As she did, Olinander began to shake. Soon Gytha's hand were also trembling. It wasn't long before the ground around them trembled as well, spreading to the cave itself.

"This cannot be good," Ilda said, inching towards the exit.

William grabbed her arm and gave her a serious stare. "Gytha? Gytha!" he called, but the grand sorceress didn't seem to hear him.

"I won't die here!" Ilda said.

"No one is dying!" William yelled as the cave continued to shake. "Gytha!" he said again. When she didn't respond, he knew he had no choice. William clasped his own hands together then pulled them apart; threads crackled between them as he stepped next to Gytha and took the grand sorceress's arm.

Ilda ducked as William was thrown backwards against the wall. But whatever he had done had been enough to interrupt the spell, as the cave stopped shaking, and soon Gytha and her son quieted.

As Gytha's eyes opened, she looked at William, who groaned as he got to his feet. "What did you do?!" she yelled.

"He stopped you from killing us all," Ilda said.

"The cave was coming down. It wasn't working," William said.

"He's my son, William, I don't care about a cave!"

"And you can only save him if you're alive, Gytha," William got to his feet. "This isn't the place. We need to get him away from here and try again. Trust me," he said, taking a few steps closer.

Gytha looked back to her son, taking Olin's hand and then his face. "We have to take him to Duken."

"I agree," William said.

"What about me?" Ilda said, at the risk of inciting Gytha's rage. "I have kept my word. I have shown you your son. Where is my daughter?"

Gytha turned to her.

"Please, Gytha, tell me where Ella is."

* * *

"My lord, we should get you back to the palace quickly," the guard said.

"Soon enough, Larik. I came here for something, and I should like to have it before I leave."

"The king will have my head if he realizes you aren't in the palace," Larik said.

Prince Ulstan, the heir to the throne of Duken, chuckled, "If my father has your head, what will my mother have, then?"

The guard's face paled.

The atheling shook his head, "Don't fret, no one will know. We'll be back before anyone notices. And if they do, I shall tell them we went outside to practice."

"All of your lessons are supposed to happen within the walls of the Hadeburgh, at least until –"

"Don't say when I'm older, Larik. It makes you sound like a bore, and doesn't suit you," the atheling said as he craned his neck to look around. Ulstan spotted something in the distance and his smile widened, "Besides, what fun is being stuck inside the walls where everything I do is watched. This is how I'm able to manage," he stepped in the direction of the approaching figure.

Larik sighed at the sight of the girl falling into the prince's arms. The hood of her cloak slid off her head to reveal her blonde hair. She giggled as they kissed. The guard felt his face crease with worry; this was going to be his end if anyone found out.

"My Lord –"

"We won't be long, Larik, just take a few steps away. Unless you want to watch?" Ulstan said.

The guard frowned and turned, walking several paces away to put distance between himself and what was about to happen, but remaining close enough that he could hear if his name was called; he needed to be able to reach the prince in time if something happened.

Finding a tree to stand behind, Larik pulled down his breeches and relieved himself, pissing on the floor as he shook his head at the luxury the atheling enjoyed. Looking to his left, he could see the west wall and the top of the gatehouse of Hadeburgh that housed the palace of

Duekn. The gatehouse had guards watching every moment of every day, and he credited himself on his ability to sneak the prince out and back in before anyone noticed.

The lass giggled as they kissed and Ulstan touched her face, making no attempt to get her to lower her voice. Taking off his own cape, he laid it underneath a tree. The girl sat and the atheling kneeling between her legs, kissing her till she surrendered and laid back against the ground. The prince followed her down as she held his face, holding his weight on his arms as they continued to kiss. He nibbled at her earlobe and she giggled again.

Ulstan heard the sound of the twig breaking, but didn't lift his head, continuing to kiss the lass. A shadow fell across them, and the prince chuckled, "So you couldn't stay away after all, Larik. Decided to watch?" he said.

When response came, the atheling broke the kiss and looked up at the figure. It wasn't his guard. He opened his mouth to say something but was knocked hard in the back of the head. The blonde lass managed a whimper.

The smile vanished from Larik's face as he heard the scream. It didn't sound like something made in the heat of reckless passion. He turned sharply.

"My lord!" Larik yelled as he rushed to the prince. "My lord!" He stumbled across a hole. He pushed himself up quickly and drew his sword, rushing past the rest of the trees.

"No," Larik said when he saw the scene, dropping the sword to wrap his hands around the girl's throat. She gasped, choking on the blood from her punctured neck.

"No, no! Where is he?" he asked, "Who took him?" He looked around, frantic, but didn't see the prince anywhere.

"Who was it?" Larik asked, hoping to learn something useful from the dying girl, but her final breaths only offered him terrified gasps as she held onto his arm, her blue eyes locked on him till she went silent and still.

"No!" he screamed as he rose, hands covered in blood. He picked up his sword and turned on his heels and turned again, and again

"Ulstan!" he screamed into the woods and got nothing. Larik looked at the dead lass, then turned in the direction of the Hadeburgh and started to run.

* * *

"My lord, there's something you must see," the watcher said.

Otto turned from staring at the fire in the pit. "What is it?"

The watcher was quiet for a moment before he answered. "It's a horse, my lord, racing all the way to the gates."

"And what business do I have with a stray horse?"

"It's not the horse, but what it carries," the watcher said.

Otto rose and guestured to the watcher, "Show me."

The lord watcher of The Order of the Three followed the watcher to the front of the castle, where a black horse stood; a sack was on the ground nearby. Otto stepped fearlessly towards it, but he hesitated when he caught sight of the severed head of the prince of the kingdom of Duken.

TWENTY

The hidden room was as he had left it. Thorne looked around, but nothing had changed, not even the scrolls he'd left on the table before it had all gone to hell. This was where it had all started, both his plot against the king, and the undoing of it all by that useless boy. A sciff.

The lord watcher cracked his neck to the side, feelingt the pull of the Alzeibier, despite feeding it the essence of the demican. Despite the mover's power, he could still feel the ring reaching for his blood and his essence, especially as the mover's blood faded with time.

Thorne wasn't here to reminisce. He pushed the wall open from the inside and returned to the main room. The watchers sitting at the table spotted him immediately. They rose from their seats when they recognized him. Thorne didn't need to look beyond their masks to know he had taken them by surprise.

"Lord Thorne!" one voice called and another echoed.

"Watchers of Walrea," Thorne said as he slowly approached. There were six watchers at the table, half of whom bowed at once with two others following curtly. The last watcher to bow had been the last to rise, slowly from his seat at the head of the table – the seat that belonged to the lord watcher of the order. "It's good to see you again," Thorne said.

"We recieved no word, My Lord, we didn't know where you were or what happened to you," a watcher said.

"Some believed you were dead," a second said.

"Well, that's clearly not the case now, is it?" Thorne said. "I merely needed some time to regain my strength, return to the path, past the obstacles in our way," the lord watcher said.

"And we rejoice that you've returned," the watcher at the head of the table said.

Thorne nodded as his steps brought him to the table. "I can see you have been busy in my absence."

"Yes, we have. As you know, the order must move on in the case of the passing of the lord watcher."

"But I didn't pass, Diaro, I was merely absent," Thorne said.

Diaro, the watcher in the lord's seat, pulled down his mask, "Nevertheless, your absence needed to be addressed, considering the situation in which the order has found itself, after recent events."

"I see. So, this is how you address my absence?" the lord watcher asked. "By taking my place?"

"Lord Thorne, you must understand. I'm not after personal gain. No watcher in the order is. The circle is leading only until Walrea clarifies its stance with the crown, then I shall take charge."

"So, you are lord watcher now?"

Dairo's face was firm as he looked Thorne in the eyes, "Yes, I am."

"But I am lord watcher of Walrea. There cannot be two lords of the order," Thorne said as she stepped pensively towards the window. He peered down at the gates of the fortress of Walrea.

"Lord Thorne, you must understand that the order's actions against the throne have brought deep reflection upon many watchers. For in your absence we have needed to understand the order's goal of late and how they matched the principles held since Walrea was created centuries ago."

Thorne turned from the window, a look of attentiveness on his face s he asked, "Is this true?"

"It's one of the many reasons why the circle sits today – Lord Thorne, we understand the need for the order to be seen as more influential in the matters of the state, but does that respect really have to come from betraying the crown? Does it have to come to removing the king himself?" Diaro asked. "The events of a fortnight ago have left some watchers conflicted – the service to the order is supposed to be *for* the kingdom. But how does killing the king and taking the crown serve the kingdom, Lord Thorne?"

Thorne stared at Dairo, and then scanned the rest of the watchers. "Well, I suppose I can understand how it can be conflicting for some watchers. It takes a lot to see the entire picture, even for the circle," he said. "I will admit that I myself have had some time to think of how the order could have done better in reaching its goal, and how we might correct the mistakes of the past."

"Then perhaps, Lord Thorne, you can be part of the way forward. We must do all we can to return Walrea to where it belongs, in the light of the crown and the people of Ravinshore," Diaro said, confidence ringing through his voice.

Thorne regarded the watcher, as though his words might have struck something in him. Then he looked down at the ring on his left hand and clenched his fist.

"The order must make amends," Diaro said.

Thorne let out a breath. "Very well, and so it will be," Thorne said, looking at Diaro.

Diaro nodded and looked away from Thorne. The next second, he gasped at a sharp pain in his chest.

The circle stirred staring at Thorne holding Dario's heart in his hand as it beat in futility. Diaro simply blinked in shock as the lord watcher held his own heart; then he collapsed to the ground. Using the demican's power, Thorne had moved his fist through the man and plucked out his heart. The blood drained from the organ into the Alzeibier.

The lord watcher dropped the dried-out heart onto the dead man's body and looked to the rest of the circle.

"We should surely continue to make amends," he said.

The other watcher who'd been vocal about change took a step backwards. As Thorne turned to look at the body, he hurried towards the door, seeking escape. But he stopped as Thorne appeared in front of him. The watcher started to plead for his life, but his words were swiftly drowned in a gasp as the lord watcher stabbed a knife up into his jaw.

Thorne pulled the knife out and the blood spewed from the watcher's neck. The lord watcher took the dying man by the throat so the blood could seep into the Alzeiber. The rest of the circle watched, petrified as the watcher in Thorne's hand withered and he dropped what was left of the man to the ground.

"Cowardice stinks," Thorne said. "It shouldn't be in the blood of a watcher." He bent to wipe the blood off his dagger on the dead watcher's cape, before returning to the circle. "So, if there's no one else who wishes the order return to groveling at the feet of a king and his tiny little emissaries, I should like you to begin preparing yourself for true justice so Ravinshore is cleansed of those that stand in the way of the Order's right to rule."

The watchers all bowed at once, "Yes, lord watcher," They said in chorus.

"And while we prepare, let there be no word of my return to Ravinshore or Walrea outside the walls of this room," Thorne said, "For there is much to be done."

* * *

Ilda hadn't really thought Gytha would tell her. She had hoped, but a part of her had thought it would end in that cave once the grand sorceress discovered her son. Ilda couldn't have stopped her, if Gytha had wanted to kill or trap her in a spell to send her back to the dungeons, as she had once before.

But when Gytha had actually uttered the words and told her where her daughter was, Ilda had felt the heart in her mouth drop back to her chest. Gytha had also give a promise, that if anything were to happen to the family watching the child, she would hunt Ilda down and take her apart in every way.

Ilda hadn't for a moment thought there was a lie in what the grand sorceress's promise. Not after what she'd seen in the cave. She would have remembered that promise, even the family she sought wasn't one she too had been all too familiar with in a different life.

Ilda stood a fair distance from the house, watching from the shadows. Ilda had managed to convince William to return her dagger; it sat once again in the scabbard at her waist. She could feelt its weight, even without reaching for it. Though had told her that her daughter was here, and Ilda knew that grand sorceress had no reason to lie, when it would have been easier to kill her in the cave, Ilda couldn't stop the need to be certain that trouble wasn't lurking in the house.

She watched the house cautiously until she saw Old Ronolf return with aboy, who she guessed was his young son. Then the door opened and Ilda saw another familiar face as Sara stepped out of the house. Then Ilda's heart began to gallop when, not a few moments later, Ella stepped out after her.

Sara motioned for the child to take the bucket inside the house and turned to follow her back in, only to turn back around at the sound of the bucket falling to the ground. She gasped at the sight of the little girl captured in Ilda's arms.

"By the Gods!" Sara placed her hands over her chest and then over her mouth.

Ilda lifted her face from her child's shoulder to look at Sara. She hesitated, unsure of what would come next as Sara shouted for her husband, who rushed over.

The tension spun ideas through Ilda's head, none of which were pleasant. Then Old Ron approached slowly and raised his hand to touch her face. His hand felt warm but she didn't twitch.

"She's real. Sara, she's really here," Old Ron said.

Ilda looked at Sara, who was approaching to stand next to her husband; they stood inches away from her while she held Ella in her arms. She steadied her breath for what would follow -- she hoped dearly that she wouldn't have to use the dagger, not only because of Gytha's promise, but because she couldn't imagine harming these people, as she'd harmed so many others before.

Ilda's caution was proven uneccessary as Sara gently cupped her face and a film of tears appeared over the woman's eyes.

*

Ilda had been in Ravinshore often these past few years, but she had forced herself to keep her distance, so that her work with the Order could never affect them. It had been one of her conditions when she'd become a watcher. Hunter's Grove wasn't all that far from Walrea, but she needed to banish her memories of it regardless.

It was obvious to Ilda that Old Ron and his wife hadn't been told of her new life. For some reason, Gytha hadn't told them what she had become. Ilda didn't know why, but she was certainly grateful. Their welcome almost made her feel like a lost child returning home, and not a murderer and sworn watcher of the order. Though since her capture, she was no longer the latter. But the former would always be a part of her.

If they knew how many people had met their end by her hands, in her service to the order, Sara wouldn't sit by her side and Old Ron would have so much amazement in his eyes as he looked at her. If they knew the vile things she'd done, and the many gruesome ways she could take a man's life, she wouldn't be allowed to sit so peacefully in a house like this with a family that merely wished to know what had happened in a decade and a half.

Ilda sat on a chair, with her daughter in her lap resting her head on her chest. For once, her mind wasn't busy trying to achieve a mission goal. She wasn't feigning a smile or concern so she could get close enough to stick the man of the house with a poisoned needle, or his slip the wife something similar in her food. She wasn't thinking of how quickly or slowly they must die to aid her escape. Ilda wasn't sitting in the midst of this family, as a small flame burned in the fireplace and candles flickered on the stands, plotting the manner in which they would meet their doom at her hands. Instead, for once, she wished doom would stay away.

"To say that his heart broke when you disappeared wouldn't do enough justice to his pain," Old Ron said, sitting with his hands folded across his chest. "Wylie became a man lost for a long time. He searched for you – all over Ravinshore. He would have gone further had he the means to, and if he hadn't needed to be there for Olinander. He searched for days into new moons, and very soon into years, but you were simply gone. Eventually he stopped searching, stopped talking about you, and though he was doing it to protect himself, I don't believe Wylie ever stopped wondering what happened. I don't think he ever truly stopped thinking about you."

Ilda had been sworn to never return or seek any contact with her old life. Slowly she had let it all became a distant memory. The pain of the disconnection had soon been overshadowed by the deluge of the horror that came from her service to the order. It'd become easier to focus on only what she'd needed to do, when she'd known that merely thinking about the life she'd had before could put them at risk – the ones she still cared about.

Ilda knew it was only a matter of time before they asked the question that had been burning in their hearts for over a decade – why had she disappeared? She could see it in their eyes as they looked at her, and, if anything, she owed them an answer, as thanks for taking in her child without questions even when they hadn't heard from her in so long.

"Something from my past came back to hunt me. Something I did, and thought I had gotten away with, long before I returned to Ravinshore," Ilda began.

"And what could have been so bad, that you couldn't even tell Wylie?" Sara asked.

"Because the moment I realized it had returned, I couldn't bear to let it reach anyone I cared about," Ilda looked down at the child in her arms, who seemed to be slumbering peacefully, before she continued talking. "I killed a man, when I was a young lass in Edenborough living with my aunt. He visited the alehouse and couldn't control either his manners or his hands with a belly full of ale, and he came after me, trying to have his way. I fought back, though terrified, and I shoved him to his death. After, I dragged him down the street as far away as I could, hoping no one would connect his death with me.

"Not long after, I returned to Ravinshore and life was going good with Wylie and all of you, but one afternoon I met a man with a face just like the man I had killed. And he recognized me from the alehouse. Someone had seen me drag his brother's body down the street, and he had been hunting for me ever since. He was going to kill my family and everyone I cared for, and I believed him – he looked like someone who could follow through on the threat. But in that moment, I chose to offer myself to him instead. I told him that if he didn't kill me, then I would be his to do with as he pleased, if he would only spare those that I cared for. And he agreed. He took me away to Edenborough, and from then on . . .

"I only found my freedom in his death not long ago," Ilda said.

She hoped this story would answer their questions and keep them from prying further into her time away. The phrase 'used as he pleased' were words that held more meaning that one would want to imagine. Ilda told them what she'd wanted them to hear, all without lying. Not wholly.

Because she had indeed killed a man in Edenborough, only he hadn't been a merchant but a watcher of Order of Walrea. She hadn't shoved him to his death, but stabbed him with a butcher's knife behind the alehouse. And it hadn't been the man's brother that had came looking for her, but someone she would later realize would become the lord watcher of Walrea himself.

Thorne had made her swear her life to the order, to never return to her life before.

TWENTY-ONE

The watcher frowned as he saw the figures in the distance. He kept staring, to ensure he was correct before he sounded the alarm. A few more moments passed; they grew closer and he knew he was right. He couldn't believe it. Both what he was seeing, and where they were going. Eight riders approached the gates of Walrea. He would think these were just an insane bunch of bastards, foolish or seeking death, but the appearance of the convoy made him realize they couldn't be.

Even with sundown approaching, it was hard to miss the dark shapes of the horses, cloaked in the same black as the riders. Though the colour was significant, it was also the manner in which it was overwhelming; they wore no other colour. The riders looked like shadows sent onward from dusk itself.

Their fearlessness showed in the way they didn't stop until they the gatehouse.

The circle would know certainly, as he was only one of several others who would have spotted the advancement. In a matter of moments, the watcher could see the swift movements of other watchers below and all around, assuming positions, waiting for an order from the circle, if not the lord watcher. No bells had been bells rung to alert the fortress, but it seemed everyone knew already.

Out of nowhere, someone released an arrow from their crossbow, firing at the convoy. He didn't know what that watcher was thinking, or what was going on in their head. Perhaps it was a once-in-a-lifetime failed reflex that had sent the arrow flying, or the watcher had been out of their mind, but the arrow was stopped by a shield ensconcing the group. He could do nothing but watch as one of the rider's raised their hand, and the arrow spun around and darted back towards Walrea, striking the offending watcher in the chest and sending him tumbling over the wall.

A guesture like that was unimaginable, never seen by most of the watchers in the fortress in their lifetime, as Walrea wasn't the kind of place that suffered trespass, let alone an attack. The other watchers inevitably poised for battle, and it seemed as though the trespasser's shield would be tested with much more than a stray arrow.

Until the appearance of the circle at the front of the fortress and the sharp "Hold!" resonating within the walls, changing things.

Silence fell for a moment, the air thick with the suspense of a standoff as the cold winds whistled in from the east. The tension was strung so tight, that if a bird even flew near, it would be obliterated quicker than a heartbeat. The quiet was broken by a horse sighing. Soon after, a voice rang out.

"By the order of King Edmond, the wardens of Black Castel shall be passing into Walrea."

The circle watched from the top of the gatehouse, staring down on the shadowy presence. "This is the fortress of Walrea. None shall enter here, whoever they may be," a circle watcher said. He was maked, like the rest of the circle and every other watcher on the wall.

"These are wardens, watcher. The king has given Black Castle the power to take charge of the order of Walrea. That's why we've come."

The words caused a stir as, across the wall and from within the fortress, watchers began murmuring.

"As the order claims to seek redemption for its actions against the crown and the kingdom, this is what shall be," Abeni said as she urged her horse forward. "The Black Castle shall be taking charge of the order! As the king commands. To refuse is to declare your interest at repentance is false and name yourselves an enemy of the kingdom of Ravinshore!"

The four members of the circle glanced at each other, then swiftly back at the wardens. This was not some ambitious commander of the king's guards threatening war. The Black Castle stayed out of affairs of the state, but all knew what the wardens were capable of, and what had happened to those in the castle could never be forgotten. To say they were mages born and built for battle wouldn't do them justice. If the castle had been sent, this was the king's condition and his silence on the matter was over.

If the castle was involved, it would no longer mean war between Walrea and the king's guards seeking to protect the kingdom. It would mean Walrea against the hundreds of mages of the castle. And it wouldn't mean the dark cloaks and horses of the castle trotting to the front of Walrea's gates, it would mean assassins in the shadows, against what myth often called a fortress breathing mages of war.

"What shall it be?" the warden said.

Not a word came from the fortress.

"Open these gates, now!" Abeni demanded.

The circle watchers shared a glance one more time; no words passed between them, but they all knew what came next. A circle watcher nodde, and the watcher at his right gave the signal.

And so, the unconquered gates of Walrea were opened wide for the dusky presence of a convoy of the Black Castle, allowing the two rows of riders to make their way into the fortress with the wardens leading the way.

* * *

"You did this!" King Arthurid shouted in Otto Ragno's face as the lord watcher of the order of The Three stood in the throne room backed by two other watchers to deliver what had been brought to the order's door.

The head of the king's atheling and heir to the throne of the kingdom of Duken sat in a wooden box, pale and stray-eyed with the blood barely clotted around the bloody stump of a neck.

Dismay competed with rage and heartbreak saturating the room. The mother of the child wailed in the corner, where she was held back by two other women as she faced the unimaginable. Her sobbing rang below the level of the king's voice as he thundered with fury in his eyes.

Outside the throne room, the prince's guard knelt, spattered with blood and tears as he cried. His own tears were for the atheling who had been his responsibility and the lass who had died in his arms. Larik's one job had been to watch the atheling, night and day, and certainly not to indulge his shenanigans, like the one that had caused them to sneak out of the palace. The only piece of the heir to the throne that had been returned to Hadeburgh was his head -- his body nowhere to be found.

But failing his responsibility wasn't the only reason Larik was drowning in tears. After he had returned to the palace to raise the alarm of the atheling's disappearance, he had been captured and his hell had begun. Meanwhile, scores of guards had been sent to search the area. Larik no doubt had clung to the hope that the atheling would be still be alive, captive of someone who'd trade the heir for ransom. It had been his only hope; should the atheling still be alive, he would stand a chance at life. Larik's tears now meant he knew his doom was certain to be the same fate as his charge. His own head would part with the rest of his body by dusk.

The messengers who'd ridden to the den of the Three to bring news of the atheling's disappearance had arrived at the gates of the fortress, barely confessing a word before the gates were raised and the watchers rode out to meet them.

In response, the lord watcher himself led the group of four to deliver their package to the king.

"This was you -- this was the work of the order!" the king yelled now.

His accusation was fair – the order had conveniently brought his son's head just as the messengers had arrived. There was no one else to blame. Otto reported the heir had been delivered to the order's den and no one had seen anything, save for the riderless horse carrying the sack.

It was certainly all but impossible to believe someone other than the Order would dare. Who could possibly possess the guts to, not just take the atheling, but, as if seeking the wrath of the king wasn't enough, deliver his severed head to the one place that was feared, perhaps more than Hadeburgh itself? Counting the number of men who do such a thing would leave you with nothing. To think of the one that would *actually* do it was impossible. It was this made the king sure of the accuracy of his accusation.

"The order did not kill the atheling, my lord. It is unfortunate that you feel you need to assign blame so," Otto said.

"Assign blame? My son is dead!" the king barked. "You have brought me his head from *your* fortress! How mad do you think I am, that I don't assume this was you? If the order didn't do this, tell me who has! Tell me, lord watcher!"

Otto could not. "I cannot, my lord, for I do not know. But the order shall find out who did, and they will pay,"

"And if it was you?" the king asked, staring at the lord watcher as he stood in front of his throne. "I would have your head, lord watcher.

I would have your head, as I shall that of the useless guard, for letting something like this to happen in a kingdom with an order. Centuries since the order began, and decades in your reign as lord watcher, and nothing like this has ever happened before. You should offer your head for failing me, for failing my son, the crown, and the kingdom of Duken! If a watcher cannot prevent something like this from happening, then what use is The Three!" Arthurid yelled. "I know very well what your fellow lord watchers have been doing with their kings in Ravinshore and Queen's Hill. It's no secret. Yet you swore to me, and this kingdom, that the order shall not turn on the crown, and I believed you."

The king took a breath. "If you haven't done this, then I want the head of who did in front of me. I want the heads of all of his family, his keen as well. If he has a newborn, I want it yanked from its mother's tits and beheaded as well. I want his bloodline completely erased from existence, his lands cursed, and his houses razed to ashes!"

The king stepped towards the lord watcher, allowing the much taller Otto to look down to Arthurid's eyes. "And if the death of my son is your doing, Otto, you should know that I shall not be like the kings of the other two kingdoms waiting till their Order's could strike them. I shall fight, with every last drop of my blood, and I shall make sure that I have your head too. I promise you that,"

Otto forgave the words, as they came from grief. Any other day, and the king wouldn't have had the courage to threaten him so. Any other day, and Arthurid would regard the lord watcher with reverence. But the man had just faced the impossible – it wasn't simply his child that had died, it was his son, his heir and the succession of his line -- line that was now ended. For that, wrath would cause even an ordinary man to do the unthinkable.

The lord of The Three turned and marched out of the throne room with the rest of his masked watchers following as they left the palace. The king had ordered him to find the man fearless enough to do something like this. Such a man would be scarce in Duken.

Otto had told the king he didn't know who could have killed his son, but as the lord watcher mounted his horse and galloped out of Hadeburgh, he thought of how much of a lie that was. There was one man whose atrocity and vileness would be a match for that.

TWENTY-TWO

The faint hope of the morning had faded, as hour after hour passed without William's appearance. Isabelle had watched the girl's liveliness dwindle as the day drew on, and she knew very well what was wrong.

But the disappointment of the night faded as a heavy knock sounded at the door.

Isabelle, who was closest, glanced at Mary who was staring intently at the door. Holding her breath, Isabell unlatched the door, opening it to reveal Gytha, and behind her William, with a body slung over his shoulder.

Her heart jumped in her chest at the sight of him. And who he was with.

"Gytha . . ." Isabelle stepped aside as the grand sorceress entered and William followed. "Bring him inside," The sorceress guided the path as Olinander was moved into the bedchamber.

"You shall have to forgive me, Isabelle, I had to bring him here. I couldn't take the risk that someone has found my house and is waiting for him," Gytha said as her son was laid on the bed.

"You have done nothing wrong," Isabelle said. Indeed, Gytha's apology was a mere formality, as this was William's house, and he'd clearly thought it their best course of action. "What's wrong with him?"

"We fear he's been poisoned," William answered.

Isabelle's mouth fell open, "Poisoned? What with?"

"We don't know," he said.

"Surely you can heal him, Gytha, can you not?"

"She's tried, but it has proven challenging," William said.

"The thing inside him is something dark, darker than anything I have encountered in another human before."

"She'll try again," William added.

Gytha lowered herself on the bed to sit next to her son, taking his hand in both of hers. Olin lay still, unmoving.

Isabelle turned to see William embracing Mary as the girl quickly wrapped her arms around him. Despite the uncertainty of the young man lying unconscious on the bed, the sight of William and Mary eased the pain in her heart.

"You said they were looking for him at your house, did something happen?" Isabelle asked.

"Yes, but the most important thing right now is that he's here and we're going to do what we must to heal him of whatever has taken hold of him," William said.

Isabelle nodded, despite the concern in her eyes.

"There's no need to keep the news from her, William, she'll find out soon enough," Gytha said as she leaned over Olin's body and pulled his eye open; they were still the same as they had been in the cave.

Isabelle looked to William, "What news?" she asked.

"King Ranald of Queen's Hill is dead," he said.

Isabelle couldn't hide the surprise in her voice. "Dead?"

"Yes," William looked at Olin, "And all signs point to Olin as the killer – he was the one holding the knife over the king's dead body when we arrived in the throne room."

Isabelle gasped, pinching her brows over her eyes in confusion. Then fear ran in a faint chill down her body as she realized the urgency of Olinander's presence in Duken -- in a place where no one would think to find him. Kingkillers were not often given clemency, nor were they ever truly far from chaos. She glanced at Mary who stood firmly between her and William.

At the risk of assuming the worst, Isabelle asked, "But why would he do it?"

"He wouldn't," Gytha answered. "Olinander would not."

"Whatever reason there was – whatever caused him to do it – we think it must have had something to do with his magic," William answered. "We went to Kelegro and the seer's words all but said this would happen. It looks like Olin's magic is battling is magic – it may be consuming him, if it hasn't already. If that's true, we must find a way to help him."

"But now it looks as though the poison has done more harm to him than anything else," Isabelle pointed out.

"Which is why I must free him of it – I shall try again," Gytha looked back at William.

"And we will help you," Isabelle answered for him.

"It would be best for the girl to leave the room," Gytha said, "And your hands alone should be enough, Isabelle."

William stepped forward. "Why? I can help,"

"I know. I know you want to. But you have used more of your strength today than you might even remember."

"I'm not tired, Gytha."

"Please, I know what I am saying. Take the child to the other room. Isabelle and I shall be enough," the grand sorceress said.

William looked at Isabelle, who nodded at him. "We shall only be in the next room," he said, as he placed his hand on Mary's back to guide her out of the bedchamber.

Daylight was fading and Isabelle lit the candlesticks with a wave of her hand. She stepped to the opposite side of the bed. Isabelle had a feeling

that Gytha hadn't only sent William from the room because he was
too spent. Isabelle knew something of healing with magic, and even
more about mysterious poisons. Gytha knew better than to allow two
guardians of the same child in a room where there was a chance that
things could turn on its head.

"I'm going to try to rid him of the poison -- you wil do nothing more
than hold him in place," Gytha said.

"I'm a healer too, Gytha."

"I know that. But until I know what this is, you won't try to use your
magic to take hold of his essence, only his body. Promise me you will
do that and nothing more," Gytha said.

Isabelle was dissatisfied with the idea, but she knew she couldn't con-
test Gytha's order, not unless she wanted to be thrown out of the room
completely; she had no choice but to agree. She nodded, "Very well."

Pulling off her cloak, she placed it on a chair. Gytha swept her hair
backwards, using a twist of magic to weave the hair in place. Pushing
the sleeves of her gown up her arms, she then returned to her place by
her son's side.

Isabelle placed her hands on Olinander's right arm, noticing the un-
natural warmth of his skin. She gripped his leg as well, threads from
her hands encircling around his limbs.

Gytha pulled Olin's breeches up, exposing the injury on his thigh. She
placed her hand over the wound, as she had before, then slid another
hand beneath his head, cupping the nape of his neck.

Shutting her eyes, Gytha recanted the spell as she had in the cave. "Sevanios, beil arionas. Intentum – leleria."

As she said the words, the threads quickly sprung from her arms and wrapped around her son's thigh and head.

The grand sorceress felt nothing but resistance as she sought to pull at her son's essence within his body. Casting two spells at once, she reached for her son's essence while simultaneously trying to drain Olin of the poison in his body. Unlike how she'd fought the Egro in King Ranald, Gytha already knew this poison wasn't merely trying to steal Olin's life. In order to draw it out of him, she needed to use her own essence as the bait with which she could trap and then obliterate whatever it was attacking her son.

Isabelle's stared, wide-eyed, watching everything as the grand's sorceress's threads to entangled her son. And she felt it the moment Olin began to thrash in her grip and she tightened her grip. From Gytha's hand on her son's thigh, Isabelle saw the threads begin to darken towards the grand sorceress's arm, as though something was being pulled towards her. Isabelle frowned, fearing she knew what Gytha was going to do to free her son, but the spell allowed for no interruption or indecision. Once again Olin's trembled, trying to rip free from her spell.

William sat next to Mary outside the room. "Everything will going to be okay," he said as she wrapped her arm around his.

The girl nodded as though she shared in his confidence, even though the house had begun to tremble.

"If you want, we can get you to sleep," he said.

"I'm not tired," Mary shrugged. "I'm glad you're back," she said.

"As am I," William said, looking at her. He wasn't sure he was prepared for what would come of Gytha's attempt to heal her son -- judging from what he had seen in the cave, and now she had pushed him out of the room, it would be bad. A mage being consumed by his magic wouldn't be healed with a simple trick, and whatever had poisoned Olin looked to be a menace of its own.

Gytha refused to release the spell until she'd found her son's essence, but everything was inside of him was fighting back, despite her draw.

"Beil arionas. Intentum – leleria," her lips moved as she continued to force her own essence through, her threads writhing around her son, seeking to find what hadn't been taken over.

The boy continued to shake, and Isabelle was doing all that she could to dampen it, using her own body as a buffer and using her essence to absorb as much of the shock as she could. It was more than enough task for her. If holding Olin in place was this draining, then she knew that whatever Gytha was doing was surely a hundred times harder.

Gytha's threads had continued to darken, climbing slowly up her arms. It didn't look good, but still she held on, even as it seemed as though the worst was about to begin.

Olin's hands had been warm before, and perhaps the trembling had obscured it, but there was no denying now that something was changing. Isabelle frowned at the feeling. His hands were growing warmer. She looked at him, and saw she wasn't mistaken -- his hands were beginning to glow, but not the glow that meant a thread was about to emerge. A thread wouldn't threaten to burn the flesh off her own hands as she held him.

Isabelle glanced towards Gytha, but she didn't seem to even notice what was happening. She wouldn't, if her essence was concentrating on something else.

Isabelle couldn't continue to hold him, not if she wanted to keep Olin in place. She couldn't tame the power in his hands and hold him in place at the same time. He was getting hotter -- she could feel the burn on her palm, and yet Gytha still hadn't so much as twitched.

"Gytha," she said, but soon realized how futile it was. Isabelle couldn't let go, or she risked the trembling spreading to the rest of the house, but if she didn't release him, her hand would suffer, and she would be forced to disconnect, whether she liked it or not.

The door flung open, and Isabelle met William's eyes, defeat on her face.

William took in the scene immediately: her distress, her hands, Olin's hands and limbs. Gytha remained blind to what was going on. William saw at once he had one choice, one he was probably going to regret.

"You must let go," he said.

"If I do . . . he will break into pieces," Isabelle cried.

"You have no choice or he's going to burn your hands off!" William hurried to Gytha's side, but still she didn't hear a word they were saying, totally taken by her efforts for her son.

"When I say, you must let go!" William said to Isabelle.

"I can't. . ."

"Isabelle!" William yelled, fear clear in his voice. He offered no more words as he put his hands together, then pulled them apart to draw his threads. William rolled his hands around each other quickly, causing the threads to spin.

"Now!" he said.

Isabelle let go of Olin and tumbled away from the bed. William took hold of the grand sorceress's arm with his own threads, much as he had in the cave, and he yanked her away from her son's body. He knew what would come next and was prepared for it, but the force still threw him against the wall as the house shook to its roots.

Gytha exhaled as she slumped over her son's body. She slowly pulled herself up, looking at Olin whose eyes were still closed. She pulled her hands from his nape and leg and only then felt the burn on her palm.

"He was burning up," William said.

Gytha glanced hopelessly at the sorcerer, and then at Isabelle, who was also getting on her feet. Her silence weighed heavy in the room, pronouncing her heartbreak. The quiet broke with the unmistakable sound of a groan from Olin. Gytha's eyes snapped towards him, and she took his face in her hands.

"Olin!" she said.

"Olinander!" said a second voice from next to Gytha. Levyna appeared in the room.

TWENTY-THREE

Levyna needed to find Gytha. It had been too long -- the whole day passed and she didn't know anything more than she had when she'd told the grand sorceress that her son could be in Black Castle. Levyna wanted to believe if something had happened, she would know by now – she would feel it. That was what kept her her, but it was also why she couldn't stop thinking about it. If nothing had happened, then that meant Gytha hadn't found him at the castle, then something was still wrong.

Or he had been found and something unspeakable had happened.

It had become increasingly difficult for her to fight against the fear that the worst had befallen Olinander. With each moment that passed that the part of her mind usually occupied with Olin's thoughts was quiet, the strange weighty echo of nothingness haunted her. While silence rang through half of her mind, confusion lingered in the other part. Her thoughts often went astray, but always led back to Olinander.

And to her dreams, *the* dream – the phoenix. Guilt flayed at her for how she'd never once considered it could mean Olinander. She had failed him, just like she'd failed her father.

While Levyna could hear nothing from Olin inside her mind, outside the noise never stopped. As the court continued to meet, Levyna could feel the palace grow tighter. It was in the faces of the guards and the nattering voices of the maids in the corners of the hallways, even in the palatine's quarters of the castle. She didn't need to read their minds or stare them in the eyes and travel into their thoughts to know the subject of their chattering. All they were concerned with was conspiracy they were all sure existed between the palatine, her daughter, and the kingkiller they schemed with.

Surely they were thinking it, just as Aldith, who had been her friend, did. The walls of the palace were closing in as the air carried the poison of torment in the aftermath of her companion taking the king's life. Levyna needed to get away, to wander the corners of the three kingdoms, where the conspiratorial gazes wouldn't be thrown at her while she tried to find out what had happened to Olin. It would be much better than where she was now, Levyna thought. She needed to find Gytha.

She rested her back against the chair in her room, looking at the light from the candle. She looked till her eyelids grew heavy and she closed them. Levyna drifted off into slumber where she dreamed. She saw the image of an arm dripping blood. The arm fell, so she could see the inside of the arm, where the dripping blood revealed a mark on the skin: the symbol of a trident.

Her eyes flung open and she blinked hard, gasping at what she'd seen. The mark in the dream had been clear, but she didn't know what it had to do with Olinander. She held it in place on her chair, her hand raised to her forehead in thoughtfulness before, out of nothing at all, she sensed him.

Levyna traveled to his location in an instant.

"Olin!" Levyna called again as her spectre dropped to her knees on the bed beside him. "You found him!" she said to Gytha.

The grand sorceress turned to Levyna, the only other person who was more broken by what had happened than she was. "He's unwell," she said.

Olin groaned faintly again but still didn't move, not even to open his eyes. Gytha leaned over to check that his eyes were still the same.

"His eyes," Levyna said.

"They've been like that since …"

"Since?" Levyna's face pinched, "So you found him a while agon, and didn't think I would like to know?"

"We only just found him – in Ravinshore – and brought him here. Surely you understand why healing him first was a little more important than trying to reach you," William answered her. He wouldn't let the girl's hurt feeling blind them to the real problem.

"What has happened to him?" Levyna asked, voice much calmer than moments earlier as she looked between William and Gytha.

"He has been poisoned. We don't know what with," Gytha said.

Levyna gasped as the grand sorceress revealed the cut on Olin's leg where she believed the poison had found its way into his body. Levyna frowned again, reaching towards Olin's thigh. That cut was familiar. She had seen it before,

"I remember this," she said.

"You do?" Isabelle asked

"He was attacked by watchers – the Red Flame – not long before I was taken. He got away from them, but he was injured. They managed to cut him but Posdel tended to it when he came back home. Olin said it was nothing. He said he felt fine. Posdel called the blade a black dagger or something."

"A black blade," William said.

"Yes. He said it was usually used to carry dark magic and that Olin needed to be watched. But Olin was fine afterwards. It didn't seem like the blade had affected him."

"Well, it appears that it did. It probably didn't show sooner because his body was fighting it with his magic," Gytha said.

"So the Red Flame did this?" William said.

"They probably hoped it would kill him, just as Walrea had hoped the Egro would take King Edmond," Isabelle said.

"It was the best they could hope for when they couldn't beat him in a fight," William said.

Gytha stared at the blackened mark. The Red Flame had hoped the black blade would kill him, but what did that have to do with Olin's later actions – the death of King Ranald?

"Gytha – his lips," Isabelle said.

Gytha looked back at her son's face. Levyna stirred in concern. His lipe were moving. The words were inaudible.

"What is he saying?" Levyna asked. She couldn't hear it, couldn't hear his voice in her head.

Gytha leaned in, all but putting her ears to his lips, "I – I don't know what tongue this is," she said.

Levyna copied Gytha's actions, bending to listen.

"Ferie … adion… et pu…" the words were barely a whisper from his lips.

"I know what he says but not all of it. Some of the words were said to him by a watcher before his death, 'you cannot burn what is already afire', that's what it means. But there is another phrase I don't know."

"Who would?"

"A man who knows Yetrik tongue – Posdel," Levyna said.

Mary, standing silently behind the adults, was the first to see it as Levyna spoke. She moved closer to be sure. "William, look," she said.

Gytha followed the child's finger to Olin's hand and her heart nearly stopped in her chest as she saw her son's hands begin to scale.

* * *

Sundown approached the shores in Duken, bringing news of the atheling's passing. In a time where tension rose one the docks, where people from different parts of the three kingdoms plied their trade, the cascade of terrible news inevitably seeped its way into the affairs of the docks. Many had already made their way across the sea to Edenborough and beyond, most others were loudly thinking about it, and some couldn't afford to wonder their fate should the situation grow dire. There was nothing like fear to steam chaos from the nether. Merchants had begun to increase prices on their goods, claiming the risk docking to trade within the three kingdoms needed to be worth the cost.

"How much for two bags?" a man asked a merchant.

"Eight silvers," the merchant, a tall dark-skinned man with a patch over his right eye, answered.

"Eight silvers?" the man said.

"I believe that's what I said, was it not?"

"How can it cost that much? It was six silvers seven days ago, five three days before that."

"Eight silver is the price right now. Assuming you haven't been living under a rock, you should know that things aren't the same now as they were seven days ago, or a fortnight ago," the merchant folded his arms.

The man scoffed, "But what has changed? What's different that has brought about the extra two silvers? Has the maize become harder to harvest?" he demanded.

"I don't have to answer you, but look around, do you see people behaving the way they used to? Rumor is, war's on the horizon, and if I'm caught here when it comes, there'll be a big difference between eight silvers and six. And between six and five. Two silvers could save my life, so if you know you don't have it, move aside and get on your heels, let me sell to whoever has coins to spend," the merchant said.

The man's face seemed permanently pinched into a frown as he looked at his sciff, standing by the wagon. Behind him, the next in line didn't look surprised by the merchant's prices. The man shook his head, but reached into his pouch and counted eight silvers, handing them to the merchant.

The merchant counted the money and nodded as he pocketed it. He waved at his sciff who brought two bags of maize for the buyer to cart away.

"What will it be?" The merchant asked the next man.

"Three bags," the man answered.

The merchant frowned, staring at the man. "Where do you sell?"

"Does it matter?" he asked.

"It matters if you want to buy from my wagon," the merchant answered.

"I'm from Ravinshore. Please just sell me the bags so I may be on my way."

The merchant frowned even more, "Ravinshore, you say? Sadly, I'm out of grain."

"What? What do you mean out of grain? I can clearly see you have bags in your wagon!" the Ravinshore man said.

The merchant glanced back, "Those aren't meant to sell."

The man scoffed, "You must not be joking!"

"Do I look like a jester?" the merchant said. "I say they're not for sale."

"But I have coin -- I can pay fair price!"

The merchant shook his head, "I didn't think you deaf, but perhaps you are too much of a fool to understand what I mean, so let me say it again: I have nothing in my wagon, not a single grain, to sell to an easterner, so turn around and find your way back to where you and your kingkillers come from."

The buyer's mouth fell open. He looked at his son, standing beside him, but the boy shook his head, "You can't do this – you can't let families starve because of what one person did. We had nothing to do with what happened in Queen's Hill, nothing to do with your king's death. Why would you punish us?"

"I can do whatever I want. It's my grain to do with as I please, and I say that I don't wish to sell to an easterner or anyone related to them. No one can make me. Now turn around and get away from here!" the merchant said. "Move the wagon. If the onely ones here are easterners, then I shall no longer be selling tonight," he turned to his sciff.

"You mustn't do this," the man stepped forward and grabbed the merchant's arm.

The merchant turned sharply, staring at the man's on him, and his face twisted with rage. "Get off me!" he yelled, shoving the man backwards into the dirt.

"Father!" The man's son shouted as he tried to help his father. The boy released his father's arm and jumped for the merchant, swinging his arm wildly, but the merchant pushed him away too. The boy was unchained with rage as he came at the merchant again. This time, the merchant pulled a dagger from his belt and plunged it hard into the boy's belly.

The boy staggered backwards holding his gut.

"Thien!" his father yelled as he caught the boy just as he was about to fall to the ground.

The merchant quickly got on his horse and hurried his wagon away before the crowd watching the commotion could stop him.

"Son!" the Ravinshore man screamed as he held his son in his arms, his hand pressed over the boy's belly, where the blood continued to pool. The crowd gathered around them. Like flintstones scraped together in a barrel of oil, it seemed as though chaos would spark as their voices raised in commotion, but many were calling for a healer.

The Ravinshore man was sure his son would die. Then a man barreled through the crowd, shouting "Make way!" as he dropped to his knees beside the gasping boy.

"Lay him down!" he told the father, who obeyed as the healer pulled the boy's shirt away from the wound so he could place his hands on skin.

The man watched, panicky and anxious, as the healer's hands glowed, shaking slightly over his son's boy. over his son. Everyone watching held their breaths in anticipation as the healer took his hands off the boy. It was clear the bleeding had stopped, and soon the boy gasped deeply and opened his eyes.

A chorus of relieved voices followed the boy's breath of life, almost drowning the father's excited cry as he embraced his son. Chaos sounded in the distance, in the direction in which the merchant and his wagon had disappeared.

The boy's father took the healer's hand and drew him in an embrace. "Thank you!" he said.

He pulled away and made to dig out silvers from his pouch to hand to his son's savior, but the healer stopped him.

"That won't be necessary. I just hope you know that not all of Queen's Hill wishes Ravinshore ill," the healer said.

TWENTY-FOUR

Mathea's demise and the creation of the order had been the dawn of a new era in the three kingdoms. It had seemed like a perfect answer to the challenges that plagued the kingdoms. It meant that trouble makers would think twice before they attempt to stir chaos in the land.

The first years of the order's reign had seen many conflicting reactions amongst people. There were those asking who the orders were, to be judge and executioners of those acting agains the kingdom. Differing opinions divided the kingdoms, and unrest marred the land, and the Black River's banks were often littered with the bodies of those that came short in their arguments.

But there was nothing to be done -- the kings of the kingdoms had commanded that their orders would remain, and so would its watch-

ers, and they would continue to do all that was needed – and re-
tained the right to remove whoever would stand in the way of the
kingdoms. These proclamations by the crowns tamed the unrest and
the protests, though some still continued to scheme in secret, plotting
to undermine the order and stop them from assassinating subjects of
their kingdoms.

In this quest, these groups would find watchers of all orders, and then
kill them. Of course, they had only managed this due to a spy in order,
who delivered the secrets of the watcher's identities to them. But as
years passed, that problem was removed, ending with the spy's heads
displayed in front of the order's fortresses, and the groups themselves
decimated, their members hunted and killed, even long after they had
given up their efforts. Naysayers ultimately accepted that the orders
would stay, with the belief that any hand raised against the kingdom
would bring itself doom, not only for the individual, but often their
family as well.

One such man who put themselves in the path of the order's rage was
called Yemina. He had been unfortunate enough to lead a group of
bandits into attacking a royal envoy from Duken, robbing them of
their valuables. Yemina lasted two nights before he was found by the
order and slain. Yemina's blood, and that of every member of his gang
of bandits, painted the walls of the alehouse they'd camped in. Though
none had witnessed the deed, all the signs had pointed to the hands of
the Red Flame.

But Yemina's name wasn't the one everyone remembered. It was his
sister, the dark sorceress Rohesia. She returned from Maedro to the
news of her brother's death and fumed at the injustice. She didn't just
want justice, she wanted revenge. She sought carnage upon everyone

responsible for her brother's slaughter. She wanted the Order of the Red Flame's doom. This was three decades after the order had been created and watchers were never seen, and were thought of as little more than myth.

But the dark sorceress wouldn't let that stop her – she would have her revenge, even if no sorcerer she approached would help her in her scheme to rain destruction on the Red Flame, and no army she bought marched with her against the Den of the Flame.

Soon enough, the order learned of Rohesia's mission, and the sorceress was hunted. Though watchers caught up to her, she managed to escape by reducing two of the three watchers attacking her to ash.

Rohesia went into hiding, some claimed it was up in Crow Cave. It was from this refuge that she managed to buy herself another group of fighting men from Maedro, two scores of which, she possessed to force them to attack the order's den. These fighters fought valiantly for an impossible cause, and even managed to reach the den, but failed to so much as breach the walls before they were slaughtered.

Rohesia was furious. Surely I wasn't impossible to conquer the order, she thought, if not by men, then those who were beyond them. And so, the dark sorceress created a spell with which she did the unthinkable. Rohesia used her threads to rip through the fabric of the realms to create a portal to another realm, from which she summoned three demons, called seiglings.

With these demons, Rohesia marched on the Den of the Flame, hoping to fulfill her quest and bring carnage to the order.

And she did.

Unlike the humans before them – both of their own minds and those that had been compelled – the seiglings succeeded in conquering the walls of the fortress and entering the den. They ripped the watchers apart. The attack happened at twilight, and it was said that the dark sorceress and her seiglings hit the watchers in the walls first, allowing the demons to possess them, and giving them access to the rest of the fortress. They killed a dozen of the order's watchers before the invasion was ven noticed and the watchers began to fight back. And yet another dozen watchers – humans – died before the mage watchers could join the fight, the strongest of them recognizing the creatures in disguise and finally finding a way to shield themselves against the demons.

A furious and blood-thirsty Rohesia, whose own blood and spell had been controlling the watchers while still commanding the seiglings in the attack attack, even as they were being irritated by the spells of the mage watchers. But Rohesia overestimated her ability to control the otherworldly creatures, and, after she had riled the demons' bloodlust into a frenzy, the only prey they had was the human that had summoned them, the one still demanding of them even now.

The seiglings attacked the sorceress. Before a whispered spell could save her, she was ripped apart, and her bond to the creatures was broken, allowing the demons to abandon the fortress and spread across the rest of the kingdom.

For days, night brought terror to Queen's Hill, as the demons attacked homes and slaughtered anyone they could find. But soon, the mage watchers hunted these demons, finding them in a cave in which they held solace and slayed them, to end the torment that had ravaged the Red Flame and the kingdom.

"You can still hear Rohesia's cry, in the wailing of Urlyin wolves in Crows Cave, where many believe the dark sorceress's essence faded. Most assume the watchers killed all three of the seiglings, but there are rumors that one lived and was captured by the order instead. I thought it was possible -- I couldn't imagine it could have been kept a secret," Posdel said, finally looking away from the flame of the candle on the table in front of him, and glancing at Levyna, standing nearby. "Now I know. Red Flame kept the demon."

"They did?" Levyna asked, frowning.

"I'm certain now."

"But what does this have to do with Olinander?" Levyna asked the mage.

"The phrase you say he spoke, after *ferie adion et pu putet adiona,*"

"Diet un Seignelum?"

"Son of the seigling. That's what it means in the old tongue."

Levyna's face pinched, "Son of the seigling?"

"Yes."

"I – I don't understand, Posdel."

"The black blade Olin was stabbed with was indeed carrying something, and I fear I know what it might be. It's no simple poison. You say his eyes are black, he has clearly acted out of himself, and now he only speaks these phrases. Individually, these things wouldn't even make sense to someone like me, who knows the chronicles of the centuries, let alone an ordinary person, but together, they become the pieces of one single terrifying truth,"

"And what is that?" Fiona spoke up for the first time. She'd been sitting on the bed listening silently to Posdel's explanation.

"The watchers possessed by Rohesia's demons – one of the features that was common in all of them was the utter blackness of their eyes."

"Do you mean . . ." Levyna began.

"Assuming Olin didn't encounter a full seigling when he battled the watchers, then the only answer is the black blade held a seed of the demon. And now the seed of the seigling is taking over Olinander, rather than some lame poison," Posdel said.

"Olinander is possessed by a demon?" Levyna asked, voice panicky and brows furrowed. She rubbed nervously against her arms.

"Terrifying as it is to say out loud, it's a possibility that answers all of our questions– you haven't been able to sense him because he is, more or less, not in control of his own essence, let alone his body. It would explain his actions, many of which even I have wrongly aligned with him losing control of his magic. Most of all, it would answer the question that has been burning in all our minds: why would he kill the king?

"The answer becomes simple if we understand that the Olin we all know did not, in fact, kill the king. Instead it was a boy possessed by a demon sent by none other than the Red Flame."

Fiona's brows raised, "And the Red Flame has been after the king's life from the very beginning. They possess the one man the king would trust with a demon, one that would do their bidding and no one would even look their way," the palatine. "I would be impressed with such a scheme if I weren't horrified," she said.

Levyna's mind was on the brink of collapse. In a deluge of both the horror at what Olin had gone through and the relief that it had been demystified. Even in the horror, the knowledge that wasn't the evil incarnate he'd been accused, a fear her mind had indulged all too often, she felt some relief. Olinander hadn't done it. He wasn't some mindless killer. He wasn't some watcher or a servant of the Red Flame in disguise – at least not his true self.

"There's one thing I should like to know, Posdel: how do we free Olin of the demon?" Levyna said, not even daring to entertain the possibility that there could be no answer to her question, that Olinander's fate was sealed.

"It's a rare feat – to face a demon, let alone defeat one, but I would think that if the Siegling in Olin is to be conquered, then the original demon will need to be killed. That is where the piece of demon is coming from," Posdel answered. "To free Olin of the seed, the demon it's tethered to must be killed. It's the only way to remove the demon from him without harming the host. No matter what the grand sorceress does, if the original seigling continues to live, it will all be for nothing."

Levyna exhaled, "Then I must let the grand sorceress know that at once," she said.

"You should, but you are merely delivering a message. There is no need for you to leave – completely," her mother reminded her.

Levyna nodded, "I hear you, mother." She looked to Posdel, "And if they are to hunt for this seigling, where do you think it is?"

"I would say it resides in the one place the demons were sent in the first place – the den of the Flame," Posdel answered. "I wouldn't imagine the order has managed to hide a demon for centuries in any other place, beyond the one where no one would dare come looking."

"Then I shall let Gytha know their search doesn't end in Duken," Levyna said.

"If we told the court what we have learned, it would give them their answer as to who the true enemy of the kingdom is," Fiona said.

"Please, mother, you cannot, I beg you. I have sworn to Gytha that I wouldn't utter a word of Olinander's whereabouts to anyone beyond you and Posdel. And that only included you because I told her you could be trusted to defend Olin."

"And that hasn't change," Fiona said.

"Mother. I have given my word. You cannot tell them Olin has been found, no matter your intentions. You have to keep it yourself, at least until we've found a way to bring him back so he can defend himself, I beg you," Levyna said.

Fiona stared at her daughter and the urge to argue was quickly buried. It wasn't only because it was her daughter asking for her trust, and breaking that would mean causing Levyna heartbreak, but also because Fiona knew there was truth in the argument. Many might not believe so easily in the innocence of the young man they had tagged as kingkiller, and their actions could prevent Olinander from being healed of the demon possessing him, something that would be a bigger betrayal of her daughter's trust and cause Levyna an even greater heartbreak.

"I have to agree with Levyna, Lady Fiona. We must keep this away from the ears of the court. They might not believe you, as they aren't always keen on being rational. Olin needs to be healed at any cost, and that cannot be done if the court is demanding he be delivered," Posdel said.

"Very well," Fiona nodded. "I will do as you have asked and the court won't hear of this from my lips. But I will say that whatever your plan is to save him, it needs to be done quick, as there is an army camped on the border of the Red Flame's den itching for a fight, and it is only a matter of time before the court points them in the wrong direction and attacks Ravinshore," the palatine said.

* * *

It was impossible for one young man to disappear completely in the three kingdoms with no trace . He had to be somewhere. If he was still in the three kingdoms, which Prince Petr was convinced he was, the chances were he wasn't hiding in the house of some random stranger. The boy had to be somewhere he would be sure that his secret would be kept, somewhere he would believe he was safe.

"If I'm to believe Ravinshore's claims that they have searched their kingdom and haven't found the boy, and -- as all of Queen's Hill has been searched and the boy is not here -- then perhaps it's time to turn to the only other place he could have run," the prince said. "I believe the boy's mother is some sort of outlier. She lives in Duken. I want you to take two of your best men and set out to Duken. Find out what you can about the sorceress – where she lives and where she is now. Pay and plant men along the path to the kingdom if you have to. Someone has to know something, must have seen something. It's the rule of history: someone always does," the prince said.

The man standing behind him bowed and made his way out of the crypt, leaving the prince to stare at his brother's tomb.

TWENTY-FIVE

Ole felt the heat with every step he took. If he was being truthful, he had felt it from the moment he'd left the presence of the king with the knowledge of his task, one he could never deny. He had felt the heat, even as the wind beat against his face on his frantic ride.

He'd been aware of the urgency of the situation, even when he'd still stood in his homeland, and that urgency had only grown the moment he stepped foot in Queen's Hill. He'd almost felt the air change the moment he'd crossed the border – changing from a gentle wind carrying the promise of life to sharp enough to chill an old man's bones. And the cold wasn't merely from the harsh weather of the kingdom of hills. Because, despite the initial wind that had welcomed his presence here, the deeper he traveled into the kingdom, the hotter it got.

It was common knowledge what it would mean for Ravinshore folk traveling to this kingdom – the king of Queen's Hill dying at the hands of a Ravinshore. As Ole travelled, every encounter a local strung on a part of his heart at what would become of him, if he was stopped before he got the chance to deliver his message. He could see it in the eyes of those who'd noticed he was a stranger. He wore no sign on his person or his convoy as he travelled, for that would have put a dangerous target on his back, but he felt the target anyway.

Even as he climbed the steps that led to Queen's Hill's palace, he had to convince his feet to move, convince himself that he was here on a king's mission. And despite everything that had happened, he liked to think that would at least count for something.

Ole was led through the hallways, sandwiched between two guards walking ahead and behind as he was marched towards the throne room. The doors parted for him, and he walked through. He stood a few yards from the door, with the guards not ten steps away from him on either side as the occupants of the room turned to look at him. Of the three people not wearing a guard's uniform, he was only familiar with one, though he'd knew them all slightly. Palatine Fiona stood to the left of Petr, the brother of the dead king. Damiran, the king's cousin, stood a distance from the pair.

"My Lord Petr, Lady Fiona," Ole bowed.

"Lord Ole. Welcome to Queen's Hill. I apologize you weren't received at the gates, we had no idea that you were coming," Petr said.

Of course, they hadn't. And even if they had, Ole wouldn't have been expecting a royal welcome, considering the state of the country, and the part Ravinshore played with the empty throne behind the prince. Ole also noticed that they didn't seemed thrilled to see him.

"Of course, my lord, no apology is required, as you have said – there was no time to send word beforehand. His majesty demanded that it could not wait," the king's counsel said.

"How is King Edmond?" Fiona asked.

"The king is very well, my lady, he sends his utmost greetings to you and the rest of the court."

"And what message prompts your presence in the kingdom of hills?" Petr asked, "I am sure that it's not only the greetings of the king you have come all this way to deliver."

"No, my lord, it is not. King Edmond has asked me personally to, first of all, formally bring his condolence to Queen's Hill on the demise of King Ranald, who was a great leader, a great ally, and an even greater man. King Edmond wishes Queen's Hill to know that Ravinshore stands by her side in support at this trying time, as we always have," Ole said.

Damiran scoffed, "Lord Ole, King Ranald did not merely *depart*, he was murdered – slain – by a Ravinshore no less. It would be wise not to insult this court with patronizing words."

Ole swallowed and breathed deep; it was getting hotter. "I assure you, Lord Damiran, I did not mean insult – I have only delivered the words as King Edmond himself feels with his reverence of King Ranald."

"I believe, Lord Ole, that Lord Damiran is merely expressing a fraction of the apprehensiveness and petulance that all of Queen's Hill is feeling right now. You must understand how it is understandable. But regardless, you shouldn't let it stop you from delivering the rest of King Edmond's message, as I believe there is more?" the palatine said.

"Of course, my lady, there is. His Majesty, King Edmond, along with his assurance of solidarity, wishes to let Queen's Hill know that the Kingdom of Ravinshore has no quarrel of ill will towards her sister kingdom. Although the circumstance of King Ranald's . . . demise is most unfortunate for Ravinshore, as it is for Queen's Hill, King Edmond wishes this court be reminded formally that Ravinshore had no hand and played no part in the tragedy. But, as it is the unfortunate truth that a Ravinshore was nevertheless responsible –" he looked to the prince as he continued "—the king wishes me to personally bring his reassurances that Ravinshore shall be doing all it can to find the alleged kingkiller and spare no effort in seeing he answers for his crime," Ole said.

"Alleged? Did you just say *alleged*?" Prince Petr asked, face pinched.

"Ravinshore takes us for fools now, do they?" Damiran asked, "Because surely that's the only way someone who was seen clear as day, by no less than eight people, holding the knife over the king's dead body in that very spot –" he pointed to the infamous piece of floor by the window "— gets called an 'alleged' accused!"

"Certainly that's a terrible way to convey understanding," Fiona said.

Ole lowered his head at once, "You shall have to forgive my terrible choice of word, my lords and lady, I have erred."

"But you speak for the king, do you not? You carry *his* words. Is that not what you said?" Petr asked.

"It is, my lord. But I beg you to excuse the error as an indiscretion on my part,"

"So far, if your trip was really meant to act as reassurance, it leaves very little to be understood," Petr said and Ole remained quiet at risk of only repeating what he had said before.

The silence remained for a moment, reminding Ole of the heat. It was far from his very first mission as an emissary of the crown in this decade, let alone the length of the time he had been in service of the kingdom and he was no stranger to acting as the face of the king's message and the embodiment of the crown's presence on grounds both foreign and domestic. The king's counsel had been the buffer presented for dialogue in some very tricky situations before, but none of them had been as severe as this one – the murder of a leader by the subject of another kingdom. And it couldn't have happened at a worse time -- when the country was plagued with doubt in the aftermath of the orders' recent betrayals.

The words weren't as unbearable as they could be. But right now his role as a king's emissary didn't assuage his concern, not on this occasion, as Ole felt like a hen that had walked into a den of wolves; the predator's stares were heavy.

"Regardless of the circumstance, and the luckless consequences. I believe I speak for the court when I say that King Edmond's thoughtfulness and his offer of solidarity will not go unnoticed," Fiona said, glancing imperceptibly to the men at her right. "It's true that Queen's Hill faces a precarious time and challenges, but hearing king's words, we can't consider they mean nothing. And hopefully whatever resolution comes forth, won't lead to the total abandonment of the centuries of allyship the two kingdoms have shared before now," she said.

There was no outright appreciation to be expected from the king's message, but they would be considered when the time came that Ravinshore acted enough to break the peace. Centuries of allyship wouldn't mean anything then. Ole knew the message behind the words. The subtlety of the palatine's response wasn't lost to him.

"My lady, the kingdom of Ravinshore would hope for no more than that, as I assure you that a war is not something we want and we have no sensible cause to incite it."

"Very well, then. King Edmond should be informed that his words have been received," Prince Petr said. "The court expects the aldermen to be informed of your visit. You should stay to receive whatever additional message they may have for the king."

Fiona glanced at the prince, "Surely whatever the aldermen have to say cannot be more than we can relay, and we shouldn't like to keep Lord Ole from returning to Ravinshore, as I am sure he is eager to."

"But he has only just arrived. He carried word from the king. What gracious hosts would we be if we sent him back without even a chance to catch his breath from the long ride or rest his surely tired bones from the treacherous path it has endured? Lord Ole will stay as a guest of the court," Petr said.

Fiona's didn't look comforted at hearing the sudden kindness of the prince's words, nor his invitation to the Ravinshore emissary to remain in Queen's Hill. Instead, all she felt was concern as she looked worriedly from Petr to Ole.

There was more than kindness behind the invitation and Ole knew it, but there was hardly anything he could do now. The situation was already too precarious for him to refuse an offer to remain in the kingdom, regardless of how suspicious it looked. Old had expected the journey to get a little uncomfortable, that was nothing compared to what could be.

"And it would be an honor to spend even more time in Queen's Hill," he said.

*

"He knows what he's doing," Damiran said, as the emissary was excused from the throne room. "His wording was no mere indiscretion; he knows what he's doing, they all do. It's an insult that can't be allowed to go unreciprocated, considering what they've already done."

"Lord Ole has apologized for his words, Lord Damiran. I understand you aren't a fan of his presence here, but you don't have to keep poking at the mistake just to give reason for conflict," Fiona said.

Damiran shook his head, "You might be right, Lady Palatine, but I don't buy into the gesture. It feels terribly insincere."

"Yet the man is here regardless, and hasn't protested the request to longer when we both know he would rather remove himself from the situation. Whatever we think of Ravinshore, we shouldn't simply ignore the fact that King Edmond hasn't remained indifferent or blatantly supported his subject's action. He has already sent an emissary. We can justify nothing more, if we desire to remain rational and diplomatic," Fiona said.

"If I didn't know better, I would say you seem keen on making a case for the enemy, Lady Fiona," Petr said, turning to her.

"Then I shall gladly say you don't know me well enough, Lord Petr, as you continue to question my loyalty. My loyalty is, and will always be to Queen's Hill, my kingdom. Be assured that whatever it is that I say and do, regardless of how it may appear to you, I have nothing but the thought of this kingdom's goodness in mind. And, I should say, I don't appreciate that I have to keep defending myself to you, either of you, when it was the choice of His Majesty, King Ranald that I should take on the role of the palatine, something I don't believe he would do if he held any doubts about my loyalty to this kingdom," Palatine Fiona said, standing firm and looking both men in the eyes.

Damiran looked tempted to mention King Ranald's other decisions, the ones even she had argued were most usual for a man in his right wits, let alone a king. But he also knew that Fiona wasn't wrong. She had, more than often, been the voice of reason in the palace, even when Ranald had been at the peak of his madness. It wasn't unlike her to say what needed to be said, even if it wasn't pleasing to hear. Damiran would dare say that it wasn't unlike the palatine to see the pieces of the board moving before the players were even settled.

* * *

"I wish we had better leverage than a mere court's advisor, but I suppose he'll do. He should be kept in Queen's Hill until we have decided what to do about Ravinshore. It will send a message that we don't take what has been done to our king, and our kingdom, lightly," Alderman Benedikt said, as the aldermen gave their opinion on the Ravinshore emissary.

"I agree, I say we make a quick example of him in response to Ravinshore's actions. When the time comes, of course," Simoen agreed.

"And since when did we become savages, who would cut off the head of an emissary and a guest and send it back to make a point even at such a time as this?" Fiona asked the court, "Or did you have another manner of example in mind, alderman?"

Simeon's face twisted as he looked from the palatine to the prince. His brow twitched, "Well, I didn't say we should do that –"

"Then what do you mean? We have a man who has brought the word of his king, a man Prince Petr himself has called a guest of this court, yet you believe making an example of him is the best course of action. Do you want war and nothing more?" Fiona demanded.

"But a Ravinshore has killed our king, and one has just been sent to us, I don't see why it would be atrocious to consider making a statement," Simoen answered.

"A statement? Where does it end? Do you take a finger, or two? Do you take an arm? Or will you just have the man's head? Tell me, Alderman Simoen, if it were you sent to Ravinshore, would you agree to be the sacrifice? Or if the messenger dies, will you still want war against the kingdom?"

"Don't make me out to be a brainless savage, palatine, I only speak as someone who knows the toll this is taking on the kingdom. Unrest grows across Queen's Hill. The presence of the easterners is stirring a reaction from the people," Alderman Simeon said.

"But the easterners have been here all of these years and have stirred no trouble. It's the people of Queen's Hill who feel betrayed and are taking it out on their neighbors," Alderman Royo said, causing Simoen to glance at him with a disdainful expression.

"People want Ravinshore to answer for the crime. They want a response!" Simeon said.

"And what do you want, Alderman Simeon?" The palatine asked.

Simoen scoffed, "This isn't about me."

"But it is. It is about you, and you, Alderman Benedikt, and Alderman Royo. It is about you and me and all of us here in this room, as it is about every other Queen's Hill man, woman, and child who would have to face the consequences of war. Consequences that I don't think any of you have realy, truly grasped, despite how you clamor for it. For centuries, we have been protected by the order to protect us, and we have lost the memories of the brutality of war. You cannot complain about mere unrest in the corners of the kingdom and then roar for a battle in its place. Because if we truly seek war against Ravinshore, then we must be prepared for everything it will mean," Fiona said.

"Word is already spreading of merchants refusing trade and supply all the way back in Duken," Alderman Royo said.

Fiona looked to Petr and Damiran, "And that is hardly the beginning."

"But we cannot merely stand by and do nothing, which is the Aldermen's argument. That leaves far too much room for uncertainty to breed in the corners of the kingdom," the prince said.

"And we are not. I believe it needs to be said that if there had been no witnesses to a Ravinshore killing the king, then we would have no reason to consider animosity with them, and instead we might focus on the enemy within – the order. It's worth considering. Right now we have leverage against Ravinshore, at the very least. Leverage to allow us to consider how this might be resolved *by* Queen's Hill taking action. Now, if that action should be the war we once clamoured against when King Ranald wanted it with the order, I do not know."

TWENTY-SIX

"O lin?"

"Olin!"

Olin's ears perked. The voice echoed from a distance. It continued to ring even as its intensity dwindled after the last call. Olin opened his eyes, but saw only blurriness. He could sense light -- it was day -- but his eyes wouldn't focus on the image in front of him. It was the silhouette of a face, of a person standing over him. He closed his eyes and opened them again, blinking quickly as his sight refocused and he could see clearly.

"There he is! Welcome back. It's taken you long enough."

"Where –" Olin sat up slowly as a thundering headache threatened to pull him back into unconsciousness. His sight dimmed again. "Where am I?" he asked.

"You're awake, you're here!"

"What – Where is here?"

"What do you mean, where is here, silly sciff? You're home, remember?"

Olin frowned as he raised his eyes to look at Yondi's face.

"Yondi?" he said.

"You say my name as though you're surprised to see me. Were you really that far gone?" Yondi said, standing in front of him, arms crossed.

"I . . . you're here? Really here?"

Yondi tilted his head, "Course, I'm here. Where else would I be?" he dropped to the bed next to Olin, as the sciff swung his legs onto the floor. "It's clear you might have outdone yourself yesterday. Even I didn't know you could go that far. Certainly neither did your uncle."

"What did you say?"

"Wylie, he's –"

Yondi was cut short as the man walked into the room.

Olin swallowed hard as he stared at Wylie. His uncle wore a simple tunic with a belt around the waist. He regarded Olin before he came closer.

"How's your head?" Wylie asked.

"He sounds like he doesn't remember much. He might need a little help getting around."

"Wylie?" Olin said.

"He said my name the same way," Yondi said.

Wylie shook his head as he patted Olin on the back, "Get up, come on, we should get going, there's a lot to be done."

Yondi got on his feet and stepped away before he looked back at Olin. "Come on."

Olin finally got up, "Where're we going?"

"To see what's left – what remains of what you've done."

Yondi walked outside and Olin followed cautiously. A few steps away from the threshold, he frowned as he saw what they meant. Wylie stood, looking in the distance, and Yondi stood next to him, arms raised towards the smoke rising from the line of trees -- forests, fields, and houses all in ash. Everything around them had been burnt. Everything save for the house they'd just stepped out of.

Olin turned, shifting from side to side as watched, confused. "What is this? What happened here?" he asked.

"What do you mean 'what happened'? *You* happened -- you did this," Wylie answered.

"No, no!"

"You did, Olin, this was you, this is what happens when you needed to know just how far you could go – with your hands no less. I wonder if this is far enough," Yondi said.

Olin's breath stuttered in his throat and his heart began to beat rapidly, "No, that's not true," Olin said.

"Isn't it? But look around you, see it all. It *is* true, Olin," Yondi said.

"There's no way beyond this, but perhaps you'd still like to try again, to see how far you can really go?" Wylie asked.

"No! This wasn't me! I didn't do this!"

"It is you, Olin, look at your hands," Wylie said.

Olinander looked down at his hands. They were on fire. He looked up and turned sharply around to see the house crumbling into flames. "No!" he shouted.

"See, it is you. You went even further. Again. You never stop. You can never seem to just stop," Yondi said.

Olin looked over to see the apprentice's feet slowly catch fire, flames rising up his legs. Then Wyle began to burn as well.

"No – no!" Olin shook his head, "What's happening?"

"What's happening is your letting your guilt take charge. It's taking everything away, including her," Wylie said, nodding his head. Olin looked over to his left, inside the house, where he saw Levyna, trapped as the fire consumed the structure.

Olin shook his head, "No – no. This isn't true. I didn't do this. I don't want this!" he said as he hurried towards the house just as the rest of it fell. Olin turned back to Wylie and Yondi as they continued to burn. "I haven't done this! I don't want this!"

"You do, Olin, you do. This is your guilt, for seeing how far you can go and this is what it gives you – what you want," Yondi said as the flames consumed half his body. Still he didn't move.

"It is not. It is not!"

"Are you certain of that?" Wylie asked as the flame rose, and Olin dropped to his knees, trembling as he sobbed in horror.

*

Mary got up from the now-empty bed. She could hear the voices in the living chamber. As she got on her feet, she saw Olin, still laying motionless. The sheets beneath him had charred beneath his hands. She stepped closer, staring. He didn't move. He hadn't so much as twitched since the night before, when he'd been brought in. Then his lips had moved and he'd uttered something, but that was it. Nothing more had come from him since.

The little girl stared at the boy. She'd heard them say he'd killed the king, but they'd also said that it hadn't been him, but something else inside of him. She looked from his hands up to his face. He didn't look like he was breathing. His chest wasn't rising and falling at all.

Mary stepped closer, glancing back at his hands. They were covered in scales up to the knuckles, just like his feet were. She gently placed her own on Olin's scales. They felt rough against her fingers and then very warm, but it didn't burn her like it'd burned Isabelle.

Mary wondered what it felt like to him. Did his arms hurt, when they seemed to catch on fire and burned when he was touched. Suddenly, Mary's curiosity about Olin's hand went sour, as she saw the scales begin to grow further up his knuckles, to his wrist and even up his arm. She let go and stepped back.

*

"Olin!"

He opened his eyes. Once again, he saw only blurriness. But when he blinked, his sight quickly refocused. He looked at the figure standing at his bedside.

"You're awake. Welcome back," Yondi said.

Olin stared at the mage's apprentice as though looking at a stranger. He knew him, surely, but something seemed amiss as he stared, beyond the surprise of seeing him. "You're here."

"Of course I am. I've been waiting for you. Did you rest well?" Yondi asked.

"I –" Olin didn't get the chance to answer before the door opened and Wylie stepped through. Olin's brows raised as his uncle stepped closer.

"You're up," Wylie said, watching him.

The man wore a cloak over his tunic. Just like he'd stared at Yondi, Olin couldn't stop looking at him but still couldn't figure out what was amiss.

"Do you feel alright?" Wylie asked.

"I – I suppose," Olin said.

"Great. Come on, then," Wylie nodded, "There's much to show you," he placed his hand on the young man's shoulder and lead him towards the door.

Olin looked to Yondi, who waved him on. "Come along, you'd like to see this."

Olin followed them outside. His brows raised as he saw the green of fields spanning the landscape. They looked alive. Birds chirped in the air, and next to him, Wylie reached for a buck and pulled out something trapped before slapping the animal and sending it on its way. There seemed to be a sense of calm here. Olin wasn't sure why but, even as things still felt amiss, the calmness couldn't be denied.

"You like it, don't you?" Yondi asked.

"Of course, he does, he wants this. Deep down, he knows he does," Wylie said as he raised his arm level to his shoulder as a falcon-like bird landed and perched on him.

Olin regarded it all. Indeed, it seemed like a place that kindled tranquility. No chaos. He looked from the bird in Wylie's arm back to Yondi.

"So?' Yondi asked, expectantly.

"I like it here," Olin said.

"Good, then you should stay," Wylie said.

"You should," Yondi encouraged, "There's much more to show you."

"Soon enough. Soon as he brings her along," Wylie said, nodding behind Olin.

Olin turned and saw a girl whose back was turned standing on the other side of a small bridge. Then she turned around and he saw Levyna. She looked despondent.

"Levyna!" Olin called, but she merely stared at him with discomfort in her eyes. "Why – why does she look sad?"

"Because she doesn't want you to stay. But you have to bring her along so she won't bother you anymore, Olin," Wylie answered.

"Why doesn't she want me to stay?" Olin asked.

"It doesn't matter. You want to stay. So you go and bring her," Yondi said.

Olin glanced over at Levyna, taking a few steps towards her and then stopped, turning back, "Why doessn't she want me to stay?" he asked again

"You ask too many questions for your own good, just bring her already!" Wylie said.

Olin turned back towards Levyna and took a few more steps, "Levyna!" he called. She shook her head as he approached. She looked like she was about to cry. "Levyna!" he called again and she raised her hand to stop him.

"Bring her!" he heard Yondi's voice call from behind.

Olin reached the bridge. Water flowed beneath, and, as he stepped onto it, he stopped when Levyna yelled, "No, Olin. Open your eyes!"

"What?"

"Open your eyes, Olin!"

He frowned.

"What are you waiting for? Bring her over!" Wylie shouted.

A confused Olin looked from Levyna to the bridge beneath them.

"Open your eyes!" she said again.

He closed his eyes and opened them again to see the bridge suddenly change to bones. Beneath it the water turned to a river of blood. Olin trembled, hating the thought of losing his footing.

"Bring her!"

Olin spun to face the voice. The fields had turned brown with blood, the animals were dead and rotten, and the faces that beckoned him were suddenly no longer those of Wylie and Yondi. They had no eyes and no nose, and their mouths looked twice as big as that of a human's. Their arms stretched down tot ehri knees and they stood on thin legs. Olin's eyes widened with fear at the sight of the creatures.

* * *

Otto knew only one man who would commit such atrocity. He required no evidence to know that Thorne had been responsible for the atheling's death. The man had been unchained after his defeat, his failure to kill the king and take the throne and, as he had made the lord of The Three aware, Otto's betrayal for abandoning the plan to turn on the crown of Duken. The abduction of the atheling might have been a mystery the others -- any man with an axe to grind would have been capable of it, to kill the boy and his lass friend, sparking a wilder hunt by The Three. But, as his watchers scoured the kingdom for signs of a culprit, Otto was all but certain that the head of the prince was a message to him. A message sent by a rare maniac.

No sign of Thorne had been reported from any of his spies at the borders, not at the shores or the docks. If Thorne was back in the three kingdoms, which Otto was sure of more than anything, then he had managed to sneak past all measures that had been taken to stop his return. Or he'd never really left in the first place, though that was unlikely. Thorne wasn't the type of man to let word of his defeat fester where he could hear. If he had been in the kingdoms, they would have seen signs of it. From the last Otto had heard, Walrea had been quiet. Otto didn't believe Thorne was there. If he were, the silence wouldn't have continued. Though it was equally as unthinkable that the Walrea lord had used another's hand to do this from a distance.

The head hadn't been a message to the king -- it was meant for him, of that Otto needed no convincing. The lord of The Three couldn't declare to the king that an enemy from Walrea had been responsible, or that would cast blame on the entirety of the eastern kingdom, a blame that should be for one man alone, or, at the very most, the order itself. Otto didn't want to allow the entirety of Ravinshore to suffer the wrath of the king for Thorne's need for revenge.

The lord watcher stood by the window of the main chamber as the morning breeze blew across the land. Thorne had played his hand well. The Three's response would be fatal, should they choose, if Otto were to declare his suspect for the crime. In a room in the palace of Hadeburgh, the queen was inconsolable and the king was unplacatable. Both lost and expecting an answer that he couldn't provide, unless he wanted to damn all of Ravinshore.

Otto turned away from the window and walked to the corner, staring at the coals burning in the brazier. The flame was all but gone, as it had kept through the night, and all that was left was the depth of the coal struggling to breathe hot. Nevertheless, Otto could still see a wave of light as it rose and danced out. As he moved his hand to feel the heat, he felt a brief stir of air around the fire.

Lifting his head, Otto turned sharply to find Thorne, unmasked, standing in the middle of the room.

Otto shook, even as he kept his stance, a part of him wanting to ask how Thorne had made his way into the fortress. It seemed like the least of his concerns, when faced with the man who'd promised he would pay for his betrayal. The lord of The Three reached for his side and pulled two knives into his hands.

"Did you really have to kill the boy?" he said, stepping to the side into position to attack.

Thorne shrugged, his arms behind his back. "How else would you know you needed to prepare?"

"So you hide and cower and murder a child because that's all you can do – that's who you can get to?" Otto said, spinning the knives in his hands, his glowing threads twining from his wrist and around his blades.

Thorne chuckled, "I'm here, am I not?"

"Yes, and it shall be the greatest mistake of your existence!"

Otto threw a knife at Thorne, who dodged, vanishing and appearing feet away. Otto's threads pulled the blade back and he threw both of the knives the second time, missing as Thorne dogged them. The lord of The Three sent out the blades yet again, this time enchanting them. The blades glowed with his threads as they flew distances apart from where Thorne was, hopeing surely the lord watcher to be caught in at least one of them, but Thorne appeared to the far right side.

"All you had to do was what you were told," Thorne said, tone eerily determinant.

"And turn on my own kingdom," Otto pulled back the knives and ripped the gauntlets off his own arms, revealing the trident symbol burnt into his flesh, "I would rather die!" He yelled as he tightened his grip around his knives and his threads twined further up his wrist. Otto spun, to obscure the movement of his next attack as he let loose yet again at the seemingly still Thorne, who vanished and appeared on the other side of the room.

"Your death will be as slow as I promised," Thorne said.

Otto knew that so far Thorne as could continue escaping, he would stand no chance, and so he turned the blade of one of the knives and nicked his own palm.

Thorne watched, enthused, as Otto reached to his neck and pulled an Alzeiber ring from where it hung on a chain. Otto slid the ring on his finger, his bloody fist. The lord of The Three groaned as the ring absorbed his essence. At the same time, the door to the room opened, and a watcher stepped behind Thorne. The Walrea Lord vanished and appeared behind the watcher, snapping his neck before he could do anything.

Otto's eyes grew bloodshot as he stared at Thorne, whose smile disappeared as Otto unleashed the ring's power. There were suddenly two and then three and finally four replicas of Otto standing in the room, each wielding knives as they circled to entrap him. Only one was real, Thorne knew. The rest were illusions.

Thorne stood cautious as the Ottos released theeir daggers, and he began to dodge, only this time he appeared behind each one. Then Thorne stopped moving, allowing the enchanted knives to reach him this time. A fuious Otto let loose his own blades, then stood, frozen and shocked, as they returned, buried in his chest. The lord of The Three gasped, looking up from the knives to see Thorne holding a looking glass.

"You should have known the bane of a spell like. It always comes back when faced with its own reflection," Thorne said. He dropped the looking glass he'd yanked off the wall and the illusions vanished as Otto dropped to his knees.

Thorne stepped towards the man, kept alive only by the Alzeiber ring he wore. Otto grunted, raising his hand to reach the blades, but Thorne slowly knocked them away. Then he lifted the man, as blood streamed from the wounds in his chest and the Alzeibier drained more of his life.

Thorne tilted Otto's head and stared in his eyes. "How you thought crossing me wasn't choosing death should never be forgotten,"

He reached for Otto's right hand and broke his finger to remove the Alzeiber. Otto dropped to the ground at once, gasping with his eyes locked on the lord of Walrea, who stared at his last efforts for life.

Thorne wasn't done with him just yet. He grabbed the man by his shirt and dragged him across the room, all the way to the brazier with coal.

"I have always heard that you crave to be burnt," he held up a weakened Otto in front of the dimly burning heat, lifting his head and placing it inches from the brazier. Otto's face twitched for a man that had hundreds of scars he had melted in his own flesh.

"What a befitting end. Drowning in fire." Thorne said as he shoved Otto's head into the hot brazier, twisting his neck over the sharp, spiky rim of the metal furnace to ensure the lord of The Three remained in the fire.

Thorne looked down at the Alzeiber ring in his hand. He hadn't known a second existed. A flutter of thrill washed over him at the unplanned prize of his conquest. He took the ring and slid it onto the opposite finger of his other hand, and gasped, as it felt as though his guts had been sucked in before the ring began to burn around his finger, seeking blood.

"Soon enough," he said.

TWENTY-SEVEN

"I will admit it's still quite hard to believe," Isabelle said. "I haven't encountered demons since I became a healer."

"Neither have I. I don't believe the grand sorceress has either. They are things of myth. To have beings of other realms wandering around is one thing, to have them possess a human is another," William said.

"I don't think we would have ever known what it truly is, if we didn't have all of the pieces of the puzzel. And if Posdel hadn't been able to put them together. I would have continued trying to get the poison out of him, not knowing that it was all but impossible," Gytha added as she sat thoughtfully on a bench, covered by her cloak.

Levyna came out of the room and sat on the bench next to her, a specter still, as she had returned last night to deliver the news of

Posdel's revelation about Olin. They had listened to her explain how it was a demon that had taken over Olin, and not some lame poison, as Posdel had called it. Many considered the tale of the seigling demons a myth that had been spread by the order to instill fear and reverence. No evidence had been found, even after centuries, beyond the stories, and it had slowly faded in the minds of many. It sounded like a fictional tale, and they would have argued that it was, had the pieces not fit so perfectly.

The random watchers attacking Olin hadn't been random at all. The Red Flame hadn't sought to kill Olin for getting in their way of killing the king in the first place – they had used the attack to poison him with the seed. And after, all the times he'd seemed far from his usual self, he'd been battling the demon slowly growing inside him, while they'd assumed it was merely his magic. The time that had passed between when he'd been attacked and when he'd killed the king had been significant enough that no one had considered the possibility of the two being linked. And even if they had, to guess it was a demon would have been all but impossible.

Gytha had, for once, seemed winded, as she heard the details of how the Red Flame had managed to trick Olinander into their plot, using him to take out their greatest target. The Red Flame's seigling had possessed Olin, taking the wheels of his mind and doing exactly what the Order wanted.

But it could have been worse, Isabelle had pointed out. If the Red Flame had control of the seigling that possessed Olinander, they could very well have made him do more than just kill the king, despite that being their ultimate goal. Olin could have been forced to do even more harm, and it could have been difficult, if not impossible, to stop him from wrecking whatever havoc the order wanted. In fact, Olinander's essence could very well have forced him to become nearly dead, the state he remained in now, in a bid to keep the demon at bay. If his essence hadn't fought back, Olin could had done greater harm. It wasn't hard to believe that Olin's deathly unconsciousness was because the demon sought to take complete control, which could only happen if there was nothing left of Olin to fight back.

William knew the grand sorceress would have done just that -- she would have tried everything there was to wake him. He saw in her now, the unspoken words that must surely spark fear in her – she'd assumed the poison was something that needed to be conquered from the outside, and she would have persisted, possibly to the point that it caused him more harm.

William sat next to Isabelle, facing Gytha and Levyna's spectre. There had been very little slumber as the night stretched, as, though rest had been needed, the young man in the other room weighed heavy on their minds.

As a spectre, Levyna had returned after she'd reported what Posdel had said and spent the rest of the night next to Olinander. She hadn't been able to stay away, though finally knowing where he was should have brought some relief. But she still wasn't able to truly sense him, save for singular moments like the one between heartbeats. It ached. Returning to Queen's Hill was impossible. It helped that at least her mother wouldn't be worried when her body was safe in her bed.

"I must return to Queen's Hill," Gytha said. "I must find that demon and end it," Her words echoed what was no doubt in the minds of all of them. Waiting until now had been forced on her by William, on account that Olinander had at least been found and they now knew what was happening. It was perhaps the reason she hadn't decided to plunge towards Queen's Hill and the den of the Flame in the dead of the night.

She looked up from the nothingness she had been staring at towards William and Isabelle.

"I know what you're thinking, Gytha, and it's not going to happen," William said.

"For someone who is neither a seer nor a dreamer you seem confident of my thoughts," Gytha said.

"That's because I know you, and I told Isabelle last night that I half expected you would vanish in the night, alone, just like you're planning right now," William said.

Gytha glanced to Isabelle, who looked like she also knew what was on her mind. She glanced over through the open door to where Olinander lay on the bed.

"Both of you have been most kind, but you must know, of all of the many things I've done, facing a demon won't count as one. While I would break every bone in my body to free my son, you will understand why I simply cannot ask you to do the same," she said as she slowly turned back to William.

"Then it's a good thing you don't need to ask, because I'm coming either way and there will be no more talk of anything otherwise," William said.

"We'll watch him here," Isabelle said and Gytha nodded just as Mary stepped out of the room.

"The scales on his hands are growing," the little girl said.

* * *

"I confess that I don't remember what it looked like last time I was here," Ole said.

"You would be forgiven, it's been a while," Fiona answered.

The Ravinshore emissary nodded as he looked at the features of the yard in the middle of the Queen's Hill castle. "I do remember that there was once a Sigmon tree right there that smelled very terribly."

Fiona nodded. "That's probably the reason why it's no longer there,"

Ole turned to her, arms crossed behind his back, "Lady Fiona, I understand that my . . . stay here might end up being a little longer than I intended," he began.

"No, Lord Ole, it will not be," the palatine answered.

Ole glanced at the guard standing a few yards away, the one that had escorted him from his chamber to meet with the palatine. He and his envoy had been 'guests' in the palace, but couldn't so much as walk to the yard without a guard watching them. He swallowed as he glanced back to the palatine. Her words could easily hold a meaning that didn't conjur hope of him returning home.

"My lady, if something were to happen –"

"Nothing will be happening, Lord Ole. Not to you or the rest of your men. You will be returning to Ravinshore, and will be taken to the borders of the Queen's Hill with an escort."

Ole's brows rose and he slowly nodded, all but exhaling to show his relief, "That's most gracious news, my lady,"

"You will return home bearing the message that Queen's Hill, despite it all, is willing to be understanding enough to release you, though that does in no way say that all is completely well between us. The kingdom of hills insists that Ravinshore deliver the young man, Olin, and sooner rather than later. While that won't guarantee that Queen's Hill won't seek further penance, Ravinshore's claim of understanding will certainly be better heard when Olinander is here to answer for what happened."

Ole could read between the lines. His return home didn't mean war was completely off the table. Ole nodded again, "And I will make sure the king receives this message," he said.

Ole also hadn't missed the subtle fact that the palatine hadn't called the young man a kingkiller, and instead used his true name. The emissary glanced at the guard closest to them yet again.

Fiona got the message and glanced at the guard too, nodding at the sentry to give them privacy.

"I suppose the court wasn't quite willing to hear the other part of the king's message – the part that might suggest that Ravinshore believes there is more behind what the young man Olin has done than first appears," he said.

Fiona exhaled, "No, Lord Ole, the court has been reasonable enough to allow you to return on your way back home, but I don't think they are quite prepared for words like those. And it would save a lot of questions if they don't hear it," the palatine answered.

"Of course, Lady Fiona."

"That being said," she took a step forward, "The king should like to know that his thoughts are not completely . . . shocking," Fiona said.

Ole stared at the palatine long before he raised his head, brows creased momentarily and then he nodded yet again, "I shall make certain the king hears your words."

* * *

Levyna opened her eyes to see her mother standing by the window. "Have you been standing there long?" she asked.

Fiona looked back and shook her head, "No. I have only just entered. I tried to wake you but . . ."

"I haven't been asleep."

"You mean you weren't really here," Fiona said.

Levyna rose from her bed and walked to her mother.

"One would have thought I would have grown used to it by now, but I would be lying if I said a part of me doesn't hang in oblivion when you do that."

"I couldn't leave his side," Levyna said.

Not desiring to sound cruel, Fiona didn't say Olinander would hardly have been alone, not when she knew it meant more than that to her daughter. "How is he?" she asked.

"The only change is his hands. They continue to scale – a sign that time might not be on our side. Gytha and William will go hunting for the demon," Levyna said.

Fiona shook her head. That word would never sound normal to her, no matter how many times she heard it – a demon.

"And I should like to join them," Levyna said.

The palatine's eyes locked on her daughter's at once, face pulled into a frown, "Absolutely not," she shook her head.

"Mother –"

"No, Levyna! You are not to join them."

"But this is for Olin, I have to help him!"

"You have, and you can still, in any other way that doesn't involve you literally walking into the den of Red Flame to find a demon!" Fiona said, struggling to keep her voice down.

Levyna scoffed, "I can help, and I want to. I have to, mother."

"You don't *have* to do anything, Levyna."

Levyna frowned at her mother. "Would you say the same thing to Olin – would you have said the same thing to him before he came for me?"

"What – that isn't the same thing," Fiona said.

"How is it not?"

"Olin didn't go into the order's fortress to save you."

"But he would have," Levyna quickly said. "Olin would climb the walls into the order's den to save me if he had to, and you know it. Why should I not do the same for him? Please, mother, don't say you don't know it's true."

Fiona regarded her daughter. Deep down, she knew how true it was -- she had seen it herself when Levyna had been in danger. She had dared Olin to turn the world upside down to find her daughter, and he had been ready to. Ad if he'd heard Levyna had been in the order's den, he would have walked in without hesitation, Fiona couldn't deny that.

"Levyna, the entire palace has their eyes on you – on us. The court, they aren't comfortable with the fact that we know Olin, that he'd been our guest. They already assume we might have played some part. And for you to disappear at a time like this, to the order's den of all places. . ." Fiona shook her head.

"I could understand the need to stay here when I didn't know where Olin was, and his mother was searching -- there was little I could do and I accepted it. But now is the time that I can do something. I don't much care for what the palace or the castle or anyone else has to say, mother. In case you haven't noticed, it's as though they couldn't wait to turn their backs on us and didn't even hesitate to call for our hanging just for knowing Olin, even though he wasn't really responsible for the king's death.

"I don't much care for what they think, mother. I only care for what *you* think. Queen's Hill is my kingdom and my home, but I have since realized that I only feel at peace wherever Olinander is. I don't see a home without peace, mother. But I care what you think, which is why I would beg you not to make me choose."

Fiona sighed, staring in her daughter's eyes. The uncertainty in her own eyes barely shaking, even as she heard each word from Levyna. The palatine knew it would be an impossible choice for her daughter – to defy the court was one thing, to have to defy her mother would be something that would break both their hearts. To do as Fiona wanted, to stand by and watch, would be safe, but even if nothing went wrong and Olin was saved by the actions of the sorcerers, then Fiona would have forced her daughter to choose. Even if it was meant to make safe, the palatine would have made her do it regardless.

There was a healing scar over Fiona's heart from when she'd thought her daughter would slip away after Fredrik's death, and right now she felt it itch. Should she make her daughter choose, the choice would see Levyna sneaking away anyway, as Fiona couldn't stop her. And the next time Levyna might not so much as think to let her mother know.

"You've grown too smart, too fast, too –"

"Too much like *you?*" Levyna said.

Fiona's brows quivered and she shook her head. "I don't believe I have ever been so daring."

"Perhaps you haven't ever run into a battle against watchers in their own den, but it's your courage and your strength I have in my veins, mother. Yours and fathers," Levyna said, taking her mother's hand.

"You are kind, my love, but I'm not defeated to say that yours is a kind of fire that burns rare. If anything, it makes me the proudest of mothers."

"And the best one," Levyna added. "I shall be okay, mother. You have me now because Olin wouldn't let go when it mattered most, I should like to give him back to his mother, too. I'll be okay."

"Promise me."

"I promise. I will return and you will tire of me. But first, I must go."

Fiona exhaled deeply and she nodded. Then she pulled her daughter's hand and drew Levyna into a tight embrace.

It seemed that every conversation they had saw Levyna heading into wilder waters, and Fiona's chances of winning their arguments grew thinner. But she didn't mind, even with how precarious her heart felt as she released her baby to head into the wildest of dens, for no other reason than her heart. But Fiona couldn't deny that she was proud, and a wave of confidence in her child loomed over the anxiousness and the uncertainty.

TWENTY-EIGHT

I sabelle was carrying a bucket of water inside, but stopped as William stepped out of the house and their gazes locked. He saw the question in her eyes, the one she didn't want to ask: was it time?

William took the bucket and placed it on the floor by the door. Then he took her hand, leading her to the side of the house where they could see the other houses and farms in the distance.

"Mary isn't as anxious about me leaving again. If she is, she isn't showing it."

"She's a very clever child. She was used to seeing her father leave all the time, but he returned. I believe she struggles a little less when she knows there is hope for your return, and she knows you are going to help Gytha." Isabelle looked down at his waist and the sword t his side.

William followed her gaze, "I haven't had to use it a while, but then, I haven't had to be a warrior for a while either," he said. "I carry it only should there be a need for it."

"Gytha doesn't carry a blade."

"She does, just not a longsword, and I believe we both know why."

Isabelle nodded "I know what we have said, and I understand that you truly must help, but you must promise me that you shall return."

William took her hands and then reached up to cup her face, "I promise you, Isabelle. I shall do all that I must to return in one piece."

"I hope Mary won't have to wait by the window for long, for she won't be the only one you see –"

William leaned in and slowly kissed her. He pulled away, so he could plant another kiss on her forehead, "Don't be too worried, Isabelle, you aren't seeing the last of me. I'm only going to kill a demon in a watchers' den," he shrugged.

Isabelle grunted and she frowned, "I have faith in you, as I do Gytha, but speaking the words of your quest out loud doesn't cease to ruffle my heart,"

"I admit I do this largely because of my faith in Gytha, for anyone else except you and the little one, I wouldn't be so bold, even though I know I have the body of a god."

Isabelle chuckled and shook her head. Her eyes drifted to the floor. William took her chin and lifted it back up.

"Are there words that would calm your heart till I return?"

"Say them now," she said, quickly.

"I love you, Isabelle. You have my heart, woman, and I shall return to you. That, I swear."

*

Gytha sat next to Olinander, holding his scaly hand as she looked at his face. Her expression held the words she wanted to say, but couldn't quite bring herself to.

"He will know," Levyna said from behind her.

Gytha turned to her, brows pinched in the slightest manner. Levyna stepped closer.

"He will know all you are doing. He will know you care."

"I would hardly judge him if he didn't," Gytha said.

"You are about to do for him what only a mother could. I do not think anything else would matter to Olin."

"You have a great mother to say those words."

"I do," Levyna smiled, "And so does he."

Gytha didn't miss the fact that Levyna's attire was different from what she had been wearing earlier. Instead of a long dress, she now wore a tunic, pants, and a pair of long boots.

"It's not my specter. I shall be coming with you," Levyna said.

"I understand. But you should know this won't be like anything you have ever faced, Levyna. You will do things. See things."

"I am aware, and so is my mother. As much as I would like to sit by Olinander's side and watch him till he opens his eyes again, I need to be where I can do something – fight for him as he has for me."

* * *

They rode their horses watchfully through Duken, after journeying without rest through the night.

"Where shall we begin?" the first man said. Dressed in thick tunic and woolen cloaks, neither him nor the other men gave away who they truly were in their attires.

"I suppose the one place where the news would always come to," Mago, the second and larger of the men said as they rode through a village towards a tavern.

They arrived at the alehouse and dismounted their horses, securing the beasts and leaving the third man outside before they went in. It was early, but the tavern was fairly full, with about a dozen men sitting at the tables. Some only had a meal and others were already nursing a cup of ale. The diversity of the room was expected in Duken, which was more than just part of the three kingdoms, as its connection to the sea made certain it saw the presence beyond the locals. Travelers, merchants and continent explorers often found themselves roaming the corners of Duken. Hence, the two of them didn't stand out. Most eyes glanced at them and then returned to their own business.

"Who shall we ask first?" the taller man asked.

Mago's eyes scanned the room quickly, "We should start with him," he said, nodding in the direction of a table with two men, one of whom was the only one in the room still watching them.

They approached and sat themselves at the table as though familiar with the setting. The man they had targeted sucked at his teeth, then reached in with his hand as though to pull something out. He looked at his fingers afterwards, content with what he'd found.

"Travelers?" he asked.

"You could tell?" Mago said.

The man shrugged.

"What gave it away?" Mago asked.

"I suppose you have the look."

"I see. What about you?"

"Me? Duken, born and raised, been in the three kingdoms all my life."

"And what do they call you?" Mago's partner asked.

"Bjorn," he said.

Mago would have been interested in the man's father, had there not been a more pressing reason why they were sitting next to a man who picked at his teeth and then ate what he found. "So, Bjorn, would you know a lot about Duken, or does your knowledge stop at how to pick out travelers?"

"I don't think I'd be mistaken if I said I know more about Duken than anyone in the tavern."

The other man that had been sitting with Bjorn at the table scoffed, "The fool don't. I'd say I know better than he does."

Mago glanced at the man.

"You should like that, Leindor. But even though you're older, I'm twice as smart as you are."

"Of course, which is why I cannot tell your *travelers* here are from the north."

Mago's face went blank.

"You're from Queen's Hill, aren't you?" Leindor asked.

Mago glanced at his partner, "What makes you say that?"

"I have eyes and ears. The pitch in your tongue isn't as hidden as you think. You dress like Hillanders, and you walk like you're better than everyone else."

"How can you –"

Mago stopped his partner from saying anything. "Very well, Leindor. Since the two of you seem to know so much, I'd like to ask if you can help us with a little quest."

"Depends. What is it?" Leindor asked.

"Do either of you know the name Gytha? It belongs to a sorceress of some kind."

Leindor's face pinched as he shared a glance with Bjorn.

"We might have," Bjorn said.

"What business do you have with this woman?" Leindor asked.

"We're looking for her. We seek her help with something important," Mago's partner revealed.

"And what do you seek her help with?" Leindor said.

"That's something we'd like to discuss with her. Do you know where she lives?"

"We might –"

"No," Leindor quickly interrupted Bjorn. "We don't know where she lives."

Bjorn frowned, "What do you mean we don't?"

"I mean we don't, Bjorn," Leindor looked sternly to his friend.

"But we do," Bjorn answered.

"We do not. I know at least that I do not," Leindor said. "And if you aren't a fool eager for doom, you won't either," Leindor said. He turned to the strange men, "Hillanders, or whoever you are, I don't know who this person you speak of is," he stood up from his seat. "I've never heard of her."

"Leindor!" Bjorn called as the other man exited the tavern in a rush.

"What's his problem?" Mago asked.

"He's a coward, don't mind him."

"What about you?" the other man from Queen's Hill asked.

Bjorn scoffed, "Me? I'm no coward," he said, still glancing in the direction of the door. "As I was saying, I might know where this sorceress Gytha lives."

"Good, and are you willing to take us there?" Mago asked.

"It's not very close. A very long ride, you see."

"We have enough to make it worth your time," Mago said.

Bjorn glanced yet again at the back of the tavern, mind still perched on his friend bolting from the scene at the mention of Gytha. "I don't really know –"

He stopped short as Mago's hand landed on the table with a small pouch that sounded significantly filled with coins. Bjorn stared at it.

"It could really be worth your time," Mago said.

Bjorn's eyes stayed on the pouch. He reached to take the money, but Mago pulled away. "Not yet, you get some now and some when we find what we're looking for."

"How much do you have in there?"

"Ten silvers for you."

Bjorn shook his head, "She lives very, very far."

"Fifteen silvers. You get ten if we leave at once," Mago said.

Bjorn nodded and the men rose, heading outside.

"I'll need a horse too, won't I?"

"You know where to find one, don't you?" Mago tossed the pouch at the man. "Now you can pay for it." He nodded fpr the third man from Queen's Hill to accompany Bjorn to get the horse. "We don't have time to spare. If he tries to be smart, don't hesitate, kill him," he whispered.

The third Hillander nodded as he followed Bjorn, leaving Mago and his partner behind. Mago's eyes scanned the street till he saw Leindor, who stood in front of a house not a few yards away strapping a saddle to a horse. The pair stared at each other for a moment before Leindor mounted the horse and rode in the opposite direction from where they had come.

Leindor only knew of the sorceress because of a man who'd been unfortunate enough to find trouble at her house. Leindor wasn't the only person who would deny knowing Gytha, especially when it came to admitting it to strangers hiding who they truly were and thinking they were better than everyone else.

* * *

Hod brushed the back of his hand against his nose, then spat on the floor of the stable. He looked across the street. Obscured by the lone beast feeding on hay, he slowly ran his finger over the blade of the dagger in hand as he watched the man he had been waiting for appear to receive a barrel from a wagon. The man carried the barrel inside and the wagon left. Hod sniffled as he walked across the street.

The tavern was empty, and even though it was early, that was a little unusual. Hod walked slowly towards the front just as a man appeared from behind the counter. The man regarded him with a glance before he spoke.

"We're not selling yet."

"I'm not buying," Hod answered.

"What do you want then? There're no whores here, if that's what you're looking for."

"I have no desire for a whore either. I only wish to ask you a few questions."

"I have things to do – pigs to slaughter," the man pointed to the back.

"It will only take a short while."

"Then ask."

"Days ago, a beggar came to your tavern and handed you a coin, did he not?"

"What? What do you speak of?"

"Did you not hear me?" Hod stepped forward, to bring himself closer to the counter. "I said a beggar came to you and handed you a coin –"

"I own a tavern, idiot, I get handed coins all of the time."

"A watcher's coin," Hod said.

The tavern owner frowned and then chuckled, "Do you jest? What nonsense are you saying? What's a watcher's coin?"

"The man that brought it to you is dead, is he not? But he handed it to you. Where is it?"

"You're clearly out of your mind. You should get out of here before I throw you out with my own hands," The man turned to walk away.

"The man is dead. A watcher. He gave you a coin, which you recognized. Because you are one of them," Hod said.

The man stopped, his back still turned as his hand moved out of sight. Then he turned around and darted towards Hod, but Hod saw the blade in a flash of silver and quickly knocked the man's hand away. The watcher twisted out of Hod's hold, lunging to stab him again as he spun. Hod escaped the strike. The man's face had completely gone steely as the watcher spun around again to kick Hod in the chest. Hod caught the leg instead, stabbing quickly in the back of his knees.

The ghost watcher groaned as he landed on one leg and Hod wasted no time stabbing the man in the arm as the watcher tried to strike at him. He whimpered as Hod pulled the knife out and placed it against the watcher's throat,

"Where is the coin? Who did you give it to?" Hod demanded.

The watcher's face, though full of agony, remained steel as his nose flared. Hod wouldn't learn anything from his lips.

TWENTY-NINE

"**P**rince Petr, Lord Damiran," Fiona said as she saw the two men approaching the passageway to the palatine's quarters. "I was just about to make my way to the throne room,"

"We thought to come pay a visit to this part of the castle instead for a change," Petr said.

Fiona glanced at Damiran, whose face betrayed nothing but seriousness, "How thoughtful, Lord Prince. But I'm afraid there isn't much to look at beyond the usual." *Thoughtful*, she said, but she would have seen through the guesture even if she wasn't the palatine who knew everything going on in the palace.

"That may be, but it's still a part of the palace castle is it not?" Petr asked.

He wasn't king, at least not yet, but he already looked to remind her of her place. And there was something else, she could tell.

"Of course, Lord Prince, it is,"

This was her private quarters, surely they wouldn't dare rummage through her bedchamber and inspect her chamber pot just because it was part of the castle.

"Lady Fiona, I haven't seen your daughter all day, where is she?"

There it was – the reason they were here. "I'm sure she is in her room, resting. She is taking the events of the past days more seriously than I imagined she would. It weighs on her terribly,"

"Is that so?" Petr asked.

"Of course," Fiona said, calmly.

"I would like to see her. You say that she's in her room?"

Fiona's face pinched, "Yes, but Lord Prince she is quite indisposed and isn't in a fit state to receive guests."

"She won't be hosting, Lady Fiona, I merely seek to see her with my own eyes. Of course, only to see she is well."

"And you should merely take my word for it, Lord Prince. I don't feel very kindly at the fact you would impose. My daughter is in her room, and I would not have her disturbed for any reason. Recent events have challenged each of us in different ways, and she must be given time to recover. I should like that you respect this," Fiona said.

Petr glanced at Damiran, who looked to Fiona, "Lady Fiona, we don't intend to bother your family, which is why we have come all the way here. We only ask that you tell your daughter to show herself so that we may be sure."

"Why? What for? You didn't come here yesterday or the day before to demand to see her or seem concerned about her wellness. What has changed?"

The prince stepped forward, "Lady Fiona, tell your daughter she is summoned or my men will go to her, and the imposition you fear will happen."

"You surely will not." The palatine said.

"I will, Lady Fiona, don't test the court. You might be the palatine, but you and your daughter were known acquaintances of the kingkiller. The respect the court has for your role is, I believe, the reason you and your daughter walk free. But that is only acceptable when there is no reason to believe you or your daughter are involved in any further conspiracy."

"Conspiracy?" Fiona said, confused.

"Where is your daughter, Lady Fiona?" Petr asked.

"I don't appreciate that you keep asking me the same question even though I have answered you. She is –"

"You will step aside for your daughter to be fetched by guards," the prince said, nodding as the two guards who'd accompanied them marched further into the quarters. But they halted at the sight of another guard, standing in the middle of the passageway with his spear blocking the path. Behind the palatine's guard Posdel stepped slowly into view.

"Unless you're prepared to lose your hands, guard, you will step aside as well," the prince said.

The guard didn't move, watching Fiona for her orders. Fiona, fearing the situation could turn dire very quickly, looked back to Damiran and the prince before she finally turned to her guard and nodded. The guard stepped aside, withdrawing his weapon and was all but pushed aside by the palace guard marching into the quarters towards Levyna's chamber.

Posdel met the palatine's eye as he stepped closer.

A few moments later the guards returned. "Lady Levyna is not here, Lord Prince," one of them said.

Fiona didn't say anything as Petr's eyes turned on her.

"She is not here because she is in Pedina," Posdel said. "She has volunteered to help me retrieve something important from my house, as it has been made clear that I am not to leave the palace until Olinander is found.

Petr frowned, "Pedina?"

"That's where she was headed when she left," Posdel answered.

"When did she leave? How did she leave?" The prince demanded.

"She left this morning, of course. As for how she left well she . . . I didn't really see how. She took a horse perhaps."

"No one has seen Levyna ride through the gates of this castle. She didn't leave on the back of any horse."

"Well, I mean, the horse is only an option for her, my lord, she has more," Posdel answered, referring to Levyna's magic, one of which was common knowledge outside of her aquamot powers.

Prince Petr didn't at all look pleased with the news, nor with Posdel's hauty manner. He looked to the palatine, "Lady Fiona, your daughter is not in this palace, though her acquaintance with a kingkiller is still being investigated. She has left this palace without the court's knowledge."

"I was not of the opinion that she needed to keep the court informed of every errand she runs," Fiona said.

"And I am to believe that she wasn't supposed to inform you either," Petr asked.

"My daughter has a mind of her own, Lord Prince."

"Of course, she does, and what that mind has to do with the actions of a kingkiller, we shall find out. Lord Damiran?" he said.

"Lord Prince."

"Have men head to Pedina to bring back the palatine's daughter at once. Tell them they are to use force, if they must, to get her here."

"You will not have men do anything to my daughter!" Fiona shouted.

"Lady Fiona, you might be immune to much, but your daughter is not the palatine. She answers to the court and she is to be summoned. You should hope that Levyna is found in Pedina, as if she's not, you will answer for her mysterious absence at a time like this, and I'll tell you now that this doesn't appear to give any confidence to you and your family's ignorance of the kingkiller's actions," the prince said before he turned around and walked back the way he had come, Damiran and the guards following.

"I don't want to imagine what he means when he says you will answer for it," Posdel said.

"I shouldn't like to find out either, but we both know it's only a matter of time before the men return from Pedina and realize she's not there," Fiona said.

"How did they even know she left?"

"I wasn't naïve to think they wouldn't notice, I only thought it would take a little longer," Fiona answered.

She knew there was the chance the palatine's servants would see no reason not to inform on her and her daughter. If not to the court, then to the queen and the princess. Loyalty was hard to keep when they were suspected of plotting with a kingkiller. Fiona wasn't ignorant enough to think the castle's eyes on them wouldn't offer what they saw to someone else now.

Petr wasn't the king, but he surely held the ears of the court, including the aldermen who'd wanted him there in the first palace. No vote had been taken yet, but Fiona expected it was only a matter of time before she wouldn't be able to be so bold as to deny him entry into the palatine's quarters, even if for some reason she remained in the role of the king's right hand.

"I don't think we should wait till they find out she isn't in Pedina, Lady Fiona," Posdel said.

* * *

Ilda watched as Ella beamed a smile as the boy covered his face with his hands, pretending not to see where she wanted to hide the pebble. She looked at peace, comfortable. She looked happy, and a smile snuck onto the corner of Ilda's face as she sat on a bench in front of the house.

Ilda would stay. Had things been different, she would have stayed. She would have tried to build it all back again here, in Ravinshore, with friends that were like family. She would have liked to see her daughter grow up here, in the company of Ronolf and his family, whose doors and arms were always open no matter what. It would bring some relief to her heart, even joy, that she could have all of this. And it would be possible, if all she'd been running away from was a slaver in a foreign land, and not the order of Walrea and the fate that had been destined for her before she murdered her way to escape.

If Ilda stayed in Ravinshore, she would spend the rest of her life looking over her shoulders. She hadn't so much as closed her eyes in slumber all through the night -- her first night in the open since her escape and her unmasking. The fear that one or both of the plagues chasing her would find her into Ronolf's house while she laid next to her daughter wasn't something that would fade with time. She would continue to be watchful of everything around her – man, woman, and even child. She wouldn't know who to trust -- perhaps she would never trust anyone truly anyway, but if she stayed in Ravinshore, Ilda knew she would never stop questioning every thought in every person's head or the meaning of every gesture, every look, every glance. She would never stop.

If what she was running from was the story she'd told Old Ron and Sara, then perhaps she could have stood a chance. But after all that watchers had done, to them – to Olin and Wylie – after all she had done, she couldn't bring herself to imagine the looks on their faces when they realized the truth. She had started serving the order to keep her loved ones safe, but she had done unspeakable things, thinks they would never understand?

Ilda had lost herself in it. It had become who she was. She had been joyless, without anything that mattered. Until she'd stolen feelings for the little girl whose smiles she watched endlessly now. Even if, by some unimaginable turn of fate, she confessed to Old Ron and his wife and they didn't detest her to their souls, it still wouldn't remove the risks that would continue to plague her as an unmasked watcher and an escaped fugitive.

It was a twist Queen Ariana would never have seen coming -- that the words Ariana had said to her had forced a crack in the hold the order held over her. She had said there was nothing worth hoping for, for a watcher beyond blind loyalty to Thorne. Those words had spurred her into planning her escape at the first chance she'd got. That, plus the inescabable truth that the order would find her in whatever dungeon she'd been thrown in, and ensure she paid for her failure.

"She's happy here," Sara said from her seat next to Ilda.

Ilda turned to the woman, "I can see it."

"You can be happy here, too. You can find happiness here again."

If only it were that easy. If only the order stopped existing, if only Thorne wasn't hunting her. If only she hadn't had the murder of four more men to answer to. "I wish that were true, Sara, but things aren't the same as they were. I have. . . had experiences that make it very hard to remain in Ravinshore."

"Will we ever know all of it?" Sara asked.

Ilda frowned.

"Of course we know there is more to your disappearance. And though we'd like to know, we understand how hard it must be to talk about what happened. Not just the things you witnessed but perhaps even those you did. And to have all of that and remember Wylie . . ."

Ilda stiffened.

"I don't believe you should let the past hold onto you so much, Ilda. Ravinshore is your home and you shouldn't have to abandon it again."

"I'm not, I . . . I am not."

Sara stared at her before she looked away, back to the children. "You disappear and then Gytha disappears. And then she appears and you do, too. If only you would wait around long enough to find each other here."

Something Ilda was sure wouldn't be as pleasing as Sara was imagining.

"If you must go, at least promise you will return. That she will return," Sara said, looking at Ella. "It's not a good thing, to tease our hearts with happiness like this and then take it away. If anything, she should know that she, too, has a place here, should her mother grow weary of vanishing."

Ilda felt her heart ache.

"Perhaps, this time, you won't wait a decade," Sara said.

THIRTY

I f the order had rejected Black Castle from taking the fortress, it would have given them reason to attack Walrea.

Thorne couldn't have that, not when he still had other things to put in place before his plan was truly realigned. Risky as it was, he needed Ravinshore to continue to believe that he was far gone, and for Black Castle to think that they could indeed take Walrea from him. Let them all get comfortable in his absence, so that when he struck there would be no way out for any of them. To have the wardens of Black Castle within his own walls was a gift he hadn't been expecting. He would have in the single greatest antagonists of the order within his reach. And when the time came, he would right all of the wrongs that had been centuries in the making, and it was going to be him at the top of it all.

The Castle would never realize how tightly Thorne controlled Walrea. Gossie worshiped at his feet, and couldn't wait to hear words of his praise with Red Flame. Otto's death was more than just revenge, it was a message to the rest of The Three that the man had been undeserving of his title as the lord of the order. His demise paved the way for another man, one who, just like Gossie, understood the importance of what the Lord of Walrea was trying to accomplish. Thorne would have it all, take it right from under the noses of those who'd thought that he had scurried away with his tail between his legs.

Gossie had managed to remove Ranald where his predecessors had failed. Edmond was enduring the false relief that he had escaped death from the hands of the lord watcher and his men, and Arthurid wouldn't know what hit him when his own time came, just like his atheling hadn't seen the strike that had removed his head. Where one of the remaining two to fall, it would make the final king standing fearful and cautious. Hence it must happen at the same time, just like it had always been meant to, before the unforeseen circumstances befell the orders.

Things weren't going to happen like last time, Thorne thought, there would be no surprise interventions to thwart his plot to remove the kings and have the orders united under one rule. For them to serve under one kingdom.

The lord of Walrea looked at the rings on his hands, each of which pulsed around his fingers so tightly he could feel them in his chest. There would be no stopping him this time, and whoever tried would learn that fact the hard way.

* * *

"As much as I'd like to leave, Master Posdel, my presence here is important – I'm nearly the only one who has managed to keep the talks of a war at bay. Without me in court, there would be no rational voice. And they would see my absence as another indication of a betrayal, something that might just send them over the edge against Ravinshore." Fiona said.

Posdel stared at the palatine, "There is no doubt truth to that, Lady Fiona. But the court clearly distrusts already, and should the men return without your daughter in their midst, do you believe that you shall still have their ears? Would they even believe a word you say?"

"I have done nothing wrong."

"But your daughter has, and even though it was for the right reason, they won't understand that before it's too late. She has given them cause for suspicion. Personally I don't very much care for the court, not one that has failed to recognize your importance, the least of which was to help save Ranald's life before the Red Flame killed him. The only way they might listen to you again is for you to say something different, something they haven't heard. Something your daughter has trusted you not to utter to anyone, let alone members of the court. And even then, as we have said, it won't guarantee they will see everything for what it really is, or that they will believe you."

Fiona looked down at the palace grounds through the window. Every word he said was true. She had promised her daughter that no one would know of Olin's predicament, let alone his location. Fiona had considered that breaking that promise could only make things worse on each side. The court wouldn't believe her, as Posdel had said, and she would have betrayed her daughter for nothing.

"Perhaps there is a way I can manage to salvage some time," Fiona said.

"And how is that?"

"I shall have to speak after all, only not to the entire court, just one person," she said, her eyes still fixed on the ground of the palace.

Posdel stepped next to her to see who her eyes were fixed on. "And you believe he will listen? Do you trust him?"

"As for the chance to be heard, I believe I have earned it. As to whether trust still exists. Well, I suppose I shall have to find out. With this, I'm not betraying my daughter's promise, but I won't like to leave Queen's Hill without a voice of reason, or there'll be nothing to return to after all."

*

The door to the room opened and Fiona turned, releasing her hands that she'd been holding in an apprehensive manner.

"A part of me feared you wouldn't be bothered to show," Fiona said.

"It wasn't a terribly hard choice, Lady Fiona. But I will admit that this is dangerous, especially considering your daughter's actions."

"I understand your concern, but I should like to assure you that there is indeed no conflict."

"In light of recent events, I find that hard to believe."

"You once felt the need to speak as old friends, Lord Damiran, that is what I would like us to do now – that is why you are here, because I should like to burden an old friend," Fiona said.

Damiran stared at her, "What is this, Fiona? Where is your daughter? What do you know that you're not sharing?" he asked.

"Before I say any more, I should like to know if, deep in your heart, you share the belief that either I or my daughter would be part of a plot to kill the king."

"Fiona, you must –"

"Please, Damiran, answer me. Do you believe the suspicion as well?"

Her eyes did not stray from his. It seemed as though she wanted to see the truth in them herself regardless of what he said.

"No I do not, truly. But my faith is tested with every word you utter in defense of the boy, which is why I believe there is more going on."

"And you're right, there is," she looked away from his gaze. "I'll tell you now that the party to find my daughter in Pedina will return fruitless."

Damiran scoffed, "Of course. Where is she?"

"She is where she needs to be," Fiona answered. The palatine almost couldn't believe the words were hers, considering where her daughter was really headed.

"And where could possibly be more important than here, in the palace, where her loyalty to her kingdom needs to be reassured?" Damiran asked.

"You've just told me you don't believe the suspicions of treachery. But I'd still like to ask, Damiran, if you still trust me. I don't speak as a palatine and a member of the king's court, but as someone who was there twenty years ago when it mattered the most for you."

Damiran's face pinched. She hadn't so much as inferred it once since his return to Queen's Hill. It had been as though it had never happened and she had no memory of it. The sole soul who knew the truth of the reason why he'd left for Maedro on the back of a scandal. Almost twenty years and not a breath of it had escaped her, not even after they'd seemed to have taken opposite sides lately,

"Yes," he said. If a friend meant loyalty, she had earned the title.

"Then you must understand when I say that I cannot tell you what my daughter is doing for a good reason – I shouldn't like to put you at odds with the court and I should certainly not be looking to betray a promise. Whatever happens, Damiran, you must not allow the court to incite war, certainly not one against Ravinshore."

"Why? A Ravinshore killed the king. You said you weren't involved with the king's death so –"

"There is more to what we saw that day than you think. Far more. Though the boy may not be innocent of wielding the weapon, the will behind the act matters most, and that is something I cannot share, beyond the fact that Ravinshore had absolutely no part in it."

"Then who did?"

Fiona stared at him a moment before she answered, "I cannot tell you more. Simply that the Red Flame succeeded in their goal, and they achieved it in the most sacrilegious manner."

Damiran frowned. "Do not speak in riddles, Fiona."

"I do not, but there can be no proof of anything until their plot has been conquered. The court cannot know of the details, because they would certainly be too ignorant to believe the truth without proof. You must try to convince them against war by any means."

"They might be open to reason if you told them the truth."

"There is no time to have the court flay debate or try to get the prince to listen. Moreover, I made a promise I cannot betray."

Damiran shook his head slowly as he exhaled.

"There is one more thing I should like of you, Damiran."

"What is it?"

"I must leave the palace, and I must do so quickly," Fiona said.

*

Regardless of what Damiran knew, which he couldn't really share convincingly with the court, Fiona couldn't stay in the palace to find out how and if the prince and the court would hear her defense.

Perhaps even more importantly -- she couldn't merely remain in Queen's Hill. Her heart had been yearning from the moment she'd realized she couldn't dissuade Levyna to stay. Fiona would always want to be as close to her daughter as possible. Levyna had abandoned home for one reason only.

Fiona and Posdel turned towards the door as it opened slightly. Fiona took a deep breath at the sight of the man who, not long ago, had nearly died at her hands when she'd thought he'd had something to do with her daughter's abduction. Nari stepped cautiously towards them.

"My Lady Palatine," the shepherd greeted with a curt bow.

"Nari, thank you for coming," Fiona said. She'd doubted that Damiran would ignore her. Though this man would be in the right to not want to see her ever again, even though she had since apologized for her accusation.

"Of course, my lady."

"Did Lord Damiran deliver the message in full?" she asked.

"He did," Nari nodded, reaching for a pouch at his side and bringing out a folded piece of cloth he handed over to Posdel.

Fiona watched as Posdel unwrapped a feather of a bluebird -- ironically the same thing that had almost cost the shepherd his life.

"I cannot thank you enough, Nari."

"There should be no need to, my lady, my daughter is grateful for your kind gift. I believe this is for good, as you have been for this palace. I only ask that no one else learn of this," Nari said.

"And you can be assured of that," Fiona answered.

Nari bowed and carefully made his exit, helped by the palatine's loyal guard.

"Is that enough to get us there?" she asked Posdel.

"More than, my lady," Posdel answered.

"Then take us to Duken."

THIRTY-ONE

The wind whistled as the watcher strolled across the passageway and he slowed. The watcher turned around swiftly, but saw nothing behind him. He turned back ahead. Again nothing. He was alone in the corridor. He'd thought he felt something else, besides the wind teasing in from the balcony serval yards ahead -- perhaps steps or merely an oddness in the way the air had sounded -- but nothing prevailed on either end of the hallway.

He continued a few more steps before he felt the wind again; this time he was sure he heard something. He spun once again, drawing his blade, but his fingers suddenly twisted, relinquishing the weapon to his shock before he felt a force hit him, shoving him against the wall. The watcher groaned and choked as all he could do was struggle for breath while the intruders came into view.

Gytha walked ahead of Levyna and William as they approached the watcher. William reached for the man's mask and yanked it off so they could see his face.

"Where is the seigling?" the grand sorceress asked immediately.

"Wh – what – seig – ling?" the watcher struggled against the invisible force of the sorceress's magic crushing him.

"Shall I rip it out of your head?" Gytha asked.

Levyna regarded him. There was more than just fear in his face. It was more than dread and the panic at his likely fate. She saw only confusion behind his wavering eyes.

"I don't think he knows," Levyna said.

"Then he must know the whereabouts of someone who does. We need to find who leads the order," William said.

If the order had managed to keep a demon captive for centuries, it was unlikely they had succeeded in keeping it a secret for all that time, when just about any watcher would know of its existence and location. But if there would be one amongst the ranks who would know for sure, then it would be a member of the circle, or the lord of the order.

"Where is your lord watcher?" the grand sorceress demanded.

"Whoever you are, you will not leave – alive," the watcher said.

Gytha's nose flared, and she grabbed the watcher's head, ready to compel the words out of his head when two new watchers appeared at the end of the corridor. William jumped, appearing behind the approaching watchers, parting his clasped hands and pulling threads to life, stringing them around one watcher's neck and throwing him to the ground and punching him in the face.

The second watcher had a whip ready to catch William, but Levyna jumped to intercept, grabbing the whip. The watcher turned and pulled at the whip again, forcing Levyna to step closer as he pulled a dagger. He swung his other arm in a slash, but Levyna slid beneath his arm to wrap the whip around his neck and shove the watcher's head against the wall.

Spinning to recover, the watcher swung his knife wildly, but Levyna moved out of the blade's path. The watcher feinted left then spun to stab her, but Levyna vanished and appeared behind the watcher, yanking harder at the whip around his throat and choking him. Ignoring the pain, the watcher threw his weight backwards against Levyna, knocking them both to the ground as he tried to gain the advantage. But his face twisted with confusion as Levyna appeared above him, landing a kick against his head even as he could feel her body beneath his back. Levyna hit him in the head again before her body took over and she strangled him with his own whip.

Across the hall, the watcher facing William pulled a stiletto from his belt, stabbing at William's side, but William blocked it, then kneed the masked watcher in the face, sending his head jerking backwards. The sorcerer quickly picked up the stiletto and rammed it into the watcher's chest, just as a fourth watcher appeared from down the hall, darting a handful of knives towards William, who quickly raised his hand to form a shield, even as the watcher readied another set.

Suddenly, Levyna pushed her own dead watcher away and grabbed one of the knives he'd dropped, throwing it at the watcher aiming for

William. She only hit his arm, but it was just enough of a distraction for William to throw the man's own knives back at him. They sunk into his chest.

Levyna and William turned to the grand sorceress who was standing over the body of two other watchers, their ears and eyes leaking blood.

"He didn't know where their lord was, but the other one did," Gytha said. She looked from the bodies on the floor to William and then to Levyna. She seemed about to ask if Levyna was sure she wanted to continue, as she'd just killed a man, but the look on Levyna's face wasn't the look of a young woman who faced any confliction now.

"This way," Gytha said, turning as they followed her.

*

"There are two coming this way," Levyna announced as they approached another passage. William put out his arm in front of her, causing her to stop. The trio halted for a moment. Is the other passage, the oblivious watchers passed them by.

"We could have fought them," Levyna said.

"Maybe, but just because we can doesn't mean we have to. There's no point in making things unnecessarily challenging when we know what we came here for," William answered.

"Fighting takes a toll, even with magic," Gytha added, leading the way as they hurriedly continued to navigate the corridors of the fortress towards the lord watcher, aware that it was only a matter of time before the bodies they had left behind would be found.

A watcher appeared from a room, turning to see the intruders a few yards away from him. Gytha didn't wait for him to sound the alarm. She spread her fingers wide, then clasped them back into a fist, folding the skin of the watcher's face over his mouth and nose. The watcher raised his hand to his face, pulling his mask off to reveal horror in his eyes as he struggled to find air. He dropped to the floor, untouched, as they hurried past him. Levyna was the only one who gave the suffocating man a glance as they turned the corner.

Despite Gytha's quick action, a loud whistle sounded a few steps later, and almost in that instant two watchers appeared out of another room. Unlike the others, these were dressed differently and their stance was wary and ready.

Gytha didn't turn to check behind her, despite the steps she heard approaching from behind. She simply continued towards the watchers as one of them drew threads from his arms, lighting a spark he threw at the sorceress. Gytha didn't so much as blink as she raised her hand and the watcher's bolt sizzled against an invisible shield. She continued to advance. The watcher clasped his hands and raised them to try again while the other watcher pulled his knives, threw one and lunging, stepping off the wall as he swung the other. Gytha waved the knife he had thrown back at him, sending the blade into his throat and the watcher crashed to the ground. His partner soon followed suit, dropping to his knees as his the bones in his arms suddenly folded against him. Gytha walked past them.

Behind her, William slammed a watcher to the ground, took his own blade and plunged in the man's chest. Levyna pressed herself against another watcher, splitting her specter to kick him between the legs from behind, then returning to ram a knee into his face as he stumbled forward. She split again, slamming his head against the wall before she returned to her body.

They turned the next corner to find the hall flooded with a dozen watchers. Gossie stood amongst his men, as the fifth watcher led the attack,

"I only need the one with the red mask," the grand sorceress said.

William glanced at Gytha and nodded. Then Gytha vanished and so did the lord watcher. William appeared at Gytha's side with a dazed Gossie in his grip. The grand sorceress rooted herself in place before throwing her hands forward causing a pulse of power to rip through the watchers, sending them all crashing against the wall. Then she lifted her hands in the air, shattering a large column and bringing the roof down over their bodies..

Gossie's hands glowed as threw his arms open, sending both William and Levyna harshly against the walls. He quickly forced himself onto his feet just as Gytha turned around. Already aware of the sorceresses power, the lord of the Red Flame shot a pulse of power to knock her backwards as he drew his knife and turned to William. But William had got back to his feet, and had already raised an arm to block the onslaught, only to see the hand drop. Then the watcher in the red mask fell to his knees staring sightlessly. Levyna stood behind him, a hand on his head, with her own eyes rolled to the back of her head as she used her power.

"What – what is she doing?" William asked, face pinched with concern as Gytha drew closer.

"Something she's probably never done before – she's in his head," Gytha looked between the sightless watcher and Levyna. She grabbed Gossie by the vest. "The seigling demon – where is it?" she demanded.

Gossie groaned, his brows twitched, and he frowned before his lips parted, "In – the – cave," he stuttered.

"What cave? How do we get there?"

Gossie closed his mouth and clenched his jaw, trying hard as he could to fight Levyna's invasion of his mind. His head shook and he groaned even harder.

"What cave?" Gytha shouted.

The lord watcher's eyes began to bleed.

"Gytha. . ." William said, calling the grand sorceress's attention to the watchers approaching. "We have to hurry," he said as he turned, drawing his sword.

"Oomph . . . circle – cham – ber," Gossie cried. The lord watcher shook violently as Levyna released his head and he dropped to the floor, writhing.

Levyna gasped as she opened her eyes to find Gytha and William staring at her, anticipation fiery in their gazes.

"I know where it is," she said. She leaned in over a weakened Gossie, reaching for his neck, and yanked the key hanging around it off. Levyna turned to join her companions.

From where he lay on the floor, Gossie raised a glowing hand towards Levyna, but Gytha caught his movements, and the grand sorceress waved her hand, throwing the man several feet in the air, and bringing him down hard on a brazier that pierced into him as the trio vanished.

THIRTY-TWO

The horses came to a halt in front of the house and the riders dismounted at once, all except one. Mago and the second man waited for Bjorn who remained on his beast. "Do you need help getting off the horse?" Mago asked.

Bjorn shook his head, "No, of course not."

"Then why are you still on it?" Mago's second asked.

"Because I don't have reason to get off. This is the place –" he nodded towards the lone house with closed shutters "— you can pay me now so I may be on my way," Bjorn said.

"And was that the deal? I thought we agreed you get paid when we find what we're ooking for. We don't know whose house this is, what if it doesn't belong to the sorceress?" Mago asked.

"It does," Bjorn said.

"I won't be taking your word for it, not if you wish to get paid."

"I brought you here, have I not?"

"Get down and let us find out whose house this is. If it belongs to the sorceress, *then* you get paid," Mago said.

Bjorn's face twisted, buthe remained on the horse, weighing his options – if the money he would be forfeiting was worth the extra risk. He looked left and right into the fields surrounding them. He saw distant houses. Finally Bjorn looked back at the impatient Mago before he finally dismounted the horse and stumbled towards the front of the house, the supposed travelers following behind him. Bjorn looked back once as he approached the door, and Mago nodded him on.

Bjorn knocked and took a step back at once. A moment passed with no response and he stepped forward and landed another knock on the door. Nothing. He turned to Mago, who stepped up and remorselessly banged on the wood. Silence.

"I don't think anyone's inside," Mago's second said.

Mago grabbed the knob and forced the door open. The quiet of the empty house struck immediately, but Mago led the way around to confirm it was indeed empty.

"She's not home," Bjorn said.

"Or the house doesn't belong to her, and you lied," Mago said.

"I do not lie. This is her house."

Mago pulled his short sword and he grabbed Bjorn by the shirt, shoving the man against the wall and holding the blade inches from his neck.

"You've wasted my time, you bastard!"

"I have not, I swear it! This – this is her house! It is!"

"But she's not here, no one is – so you could very well be lying. You have wasted my time. I should spill your guts right now!"

"Please – please! I beg you! It's her house. I don't know where she has gone –" Mago pressed the dagger against his skin "— But – but there is a place, not far away, another sorcerer, they – they are acquaintances!" Bjorn said.

"Another lie?" Mago accused.

"I swear on my life, it's not – it is not! I have seen the sorceress there many times!" Bjorn begged.

Mago held the knife against his side of his neck, pressing his other arm across the man's chest and pinning him to the wall as Bjorn quivered. "Should we reach that house and find it unoccupied, or I discover that you are lying, I shall rip out your tongue from the back of your throat and tie it around your neck," Mago said.

"I haven't lied to you, I swear it on my life, this is where the sorceress lives," Bjorn said again.

"Then you had better hope that we find who we're looking for in that house, or you shall find out just how little we value your life," Mago's second answered.

Mago released him and Bjorn bent over to catch his breath before the Hillander shoved him towards the door as they headed back outside to the horses held by the fourth man.

Bjorn mounted his horse, even as his heart pounded in his chest.

"And should you be unfortunate enough to try and run, you will learn what a knife in your back feels like back before your throat is slit," Mago said as they prepared to ride.

As though he didn't have enough to be scared of. Bjorn stared at the terrifying man and then glanced back at the house before turning his horse around and leading them back in the direction that'd come from.

Bjorn wondered if there was half a chance he could make an escape for it. He hadn't lied about the house -- the grand sorceress lived here -- but he hadn't thought she would be absent. He thought of escape now, not because he had lied about the other house or the other sorcerer, but at the worry that the other sorcerer would be absent as well, and then what would stop the Hillander from killing him? Or what if they didn't find who they were looking for there?

Bjorn swallowed hard on the path to William's house, wondering what fate ten silvers had bought him.

***

They appeared in a circle chamber with Levyna's at the front. It was empty, but the sound of the chaos they'd started could be heard in the distance, approaching the large room. Levyna didn't wait to be asked as she quickly turned towards the east wall and turned an empty bracket, recalling the memory she'd seen in the lord watcher's mind.

William and Gytha stood behind her and watched as the wall fractured in a perfectly straight line and then caved forward. William stepped forward to help pull the handleless wall open.

Pitch darkness waited inside.

Levyna announced, "Through here, there' s a passage."

"Exonus," Gytha said as she snapped her fingers and one of the torches near the entrance suddenly lit, illuminating the passage. The grand sorceress took the torch, leading the way with Levyna right next to her and William trailing by a few steps as they advanced. It seemed as though the passage had no end as they walked on, the torch parting the darkness.

"There are steps and then the opening of the cave," Levyna said as they descended down the path, one after the other, till they arrived at the large opening and saw he narrow path leading to the other side of the cave.

"Careful," Levyna said.

Gytha led the way passed the cliff. The winds of the hill grew heavier and flirted terribly with the torch in Gytha's hand, but didn't extinguish the light till they made it to the other side.

"We go left. There's another passage," Levyna announced.

Gytha turned as she was told, plucking another torch from the wall and lighting it with the one in her hand, handing it over to Levyna to give to William. The three continued down the passage of dead walls. The walk seemed befitting for they were expecting to find at the end. None would willingly walk down this path and stumble on the demon, not unless they knew where it lead.

Their torches reflected off a door of Akearian silver.

"It's behind that," Levyna said, holding up the key for the door.

"No, I should be the one to do it," Gytha said.

Levyna looked at her steadily, before she handed the grand sorceress the key. Gytha slid the key into the lock and it clicked. She pushed through and led the way in.

Inside the case felt like the bowels of hell. Gytha slowly raised the light in her hand to scan the fissure. The smell alone would have been enough to warn away anyone else daring enough to wander here.

Just as William, the last in line, stepped in, the torches blew out.

"Exnonus!" Gytha yelled for the lights to come back on, but not before she felt a cold breath on her arm.

William's hands glowed with thin threads, but he froze at the feeling of cold slime on his skin.

Levyna stood frozen at the sight of an eyeless creature push its face towards her, breathing out its foul breath from the gape it had for a mouth. Its saliva splashed on her face, and, just like Gytha and William, she was wholly paralyzed, down to her essence, as their minds were plunged into darkness, makng way for the seigling to feed on them.

William was thrown into a memory. When he had opened his eyes and discovered that the woman he loved was gone. The pain of her abandonment took hold harder than that of her betrayal. He felt every inch of the heartbreak all over again, as though his heart was being ripped from his chest. When he opened his eyes again, he saw Isabelle on the floor, blood pooling from a hole in her chest. She was reaching towards something, and William turned his head to see, then stared in horror. Mary laid face down, scorched almost to ash. William dropped his knees as he screamed in pain, his hands on the floor as he crawled towards their bodies.

Gytha didn't fear anything, except to have the one person she cared about withering in her arms. When she opened her eyes, she saw Olinander laying pale on the bed. She reached towards him --his arms were no longer burning hot, and even his limbs were far from warm. Gytha grabbed her son's face, feeling his icy skin. She heard no heartbeat in his chest, not even the seasonal slow thud it had been. Finally she pulled his eyes apart to see the paled-out eyes of the dead. Gytha lifted her son's body in her arms and sound failed as she wailed out every bit of horror of beholding her greatest dread.

Levyna's father was dead. She snapped her eyes open, waking from the dream. Levyna jarred out of her bed towards her mother's room to find Fiona on the bloody bed, her throat slit open. Levyna screamed in soundless horror. Then someone called her name from behind her and Levyna turned to find Olinander. But soon blood began seeping through his shirt. He looked down, confusion on his face before he fell to his knees and she reached him in time to see him drop dead, a knife buried deep into his back. Levyna opened her eyes again to an utter quiet and blankness from yet another dream, this time of her own –

The demon lurked in the darkness, feeding on their greatest fears. But it snapped its head to the side just as Levyna's specter struck a sword over its head. The demon squealed as it fell to the ground, writhing towards the wall in search of an escape. But it failed, as Levyna darted after it and rammed the blade deep into its back and through its body.

THIRTY-THREE

Mary stood at the threshold of the door and stared at Olin. She wondered how long it would take before the scales took up his whole arm. It had grown again since the last time she'd seen it and was climbing up his forearms now. Isabelle had told her they believed the thing inside his body was making the scales. The more the scales it made, the further away Olin would be and the more of him the demon would have taken over for good.

Just then, Mary heard the sound of horses. She turned and hurried towards the window to see four horses approaching with strange riders. She frowned.

"Isabelle," she called. "Isabelle!" her voice came louder the second time and the sorceress stepped in from the other chamber.

"What is it, Mary?"

"Riders," the girl said. "Strangers," she added.

Isabelle moved towards the window and saw the figures. Indeed, the men were strangers, and three of the riders had an eerily distinctive dressing. She took Mary by the shoulders and pulled her away from the window. "Get inside the room, quickly," she said as she hurried Mary into the other room. "Stay inside, no matter what," she said.

"What's happening – who are they?" Mary asked.

"I don't yet know, but I shall have you safe first, so do as I say and don't come outside until I open the door. Do you hear me?"

Mary nodded and Isabelle closed the door. She hurried to Olin's chamber and closed that door as well. Then she drew a circle around the handle of the door as she said, "Invicatinus – ad muteros,"
The thread of the spell glowed from her hand as she quickly drew it around the frame just as the knock sounded at the door.

*

This house's shutters wereopen. It was a sign of life, and perhaps hope for Bjorn, who'd been considering taking his chances with an escape, rather that standing by when the Hillanders realized who they sought wasn't home, and remained convinced he'd conned them.

As with every step the horse had taken since a sword had been held to his neck, Bjorn wished he'd followed Leindor away from that table, or at least convinced him to stay so he wouldn't have been alone in this mess now. If only he had kept his mouth shut and picked his teeth in silence.

His heart continued to thump in his chest as he kept his eyes on the house, and his brows shot heavenward the moment he spotted a figure appear by the open shutters.

"There! There it is. That's the house!" he said, looking briskly at Mago.

Mago's face tightened, "You would be wise to make your choice very carefully, Bjorn."

"It's the house, I swear it! Look, there's someone inside already – it is not empty. You can ask them if what I've said is true," Bjorn answered.

Mago looked towards the house, spotting a child by the window and an adult figure behind her. He kicked his horse and hurried towards the house.

Bjorn stood no chance of escape. One of Mago's men took hold of his horse's reins as they followed Mago towards the house.

*

Isabelle waited for the harsh knock one more time before she stepped towards the door, opening it to see the pale face of a square-jawed man.

"Yes?" she said.

"Where is the sorcerer that owns this house?" Mago demanded.

"Who are you?" Isabelle answered, brows pinched.

"Someone who wants to see the man who lives in this house. Now, where is he?"

Isabelle behind Mago to the other men as they dismounted their horses.

"He's not home," she answered.

"And where has he gone?"

"On a trip."

"Where to?"

"Edenborough – why do you wish to see him?"

"It is not him I wish to see," Mago looked beyond her into the house, "It's who he knows – a grand sorceress named Gytha – and who she hides – a kingkiller son," Mago answered.

Isabelle shook her head, "Surely you knocked on the wrong door – there is no one else here."

"What about the child?"

"What child?"

"I saw the girl with my own eyes, woman," Mago said.

"What does she have to do with who you seek – I thought you were looking for a woman and her son?" Isabelle answered.

Mago stepped forward. "I will search the house to be sure no one else is hiding,"

Isabelle blocked his way, "On whose authority do you invade another man's house?" she demanded.

"On that of the king's court of Queen's Hill. Now, step aside, woman, or I will throw you aside!" Mago said.

Isabelle looked at the men standing behind him. It was like she couldn't take them on, she could right now reach three of them, if not all of them, but she absolutely could not afford to take any chances, lest they suspect something.

Isabelle stepped away from the door, letting Mago and a second man into the house, while the other two stayed outside. She noticed an apprehensive look on the face of the one dressed differently.

Mago walked to the first room – the one to the right – and opened the door to find the little girl sitting on the bed. Mary held her hands to her chest as the man stepped in and looked around the rest of the room. Then he walked back out and headed to the second room. His partner had already opened the door.

Isabelle stood at the threshold of Mary's room, the girl clutched to her side. Mary looked up into Isabelle's face as the men stepped out of the room, flushed with irritation.

"You see, no one else here. Now, you should leave, you're upsetting my daughter," Isabelle said.

Mago glanced at Mary, and then back up at Isabelle, "Where did you say the sorcerer has gone again?"

"Edenborough."

Mago stared at the woman for a long moment before he scoffed and marched out of the house, his man right on his heels.

Isabelle looked down at Mary as she quickly made to close the door.

"You failed!" Mago yelled at Bjorn.

"No – no, I didn't. I told you this was this sorcerer's house and it is. It's not my fault he isn't home as well." Bjorn said.

"But you wasted my time regardless."

"I did as you asked me – if anything you are the scoundrel!" Bjorn spurted and immediately regretted it as Mago's face grew red and he pulled out his sword. Bjorn yelled and made to run, but was held in place by the third Hillander. Bjorn screamed as Mago aimed his strike, only to freeze as a portal shimmered at his left and two people stepped out of thin air.

Mago tightened his grip on his blade, regarding the palatine of Queen's Hill and the mage.

Fiona gasped silently as she straightened, recovering from her escape from the palace. It had either been this, or to wait for the prince and the rest of the court to make a decision. Posdel had used a wand, and an extra source of magic, to get them out of the palace and this far to her daughter. Now they stood side by side as they stared at the scene they had appeared into.

"What's happening here?" Fiona demanded.

"Lady Palatine, such a surprise," Mago said, "We didn't know to expect you in Duken. We are on business of the court – we have reasons to believe that the kingkiller could be close by as this –" he turns to the house "— is a place where more acquaintances are to be found. That's why we're here – we seek the kingkiller of King Ranald. What purpose brings you here, Lady Fiona, and in such a . . . brash manner, of all ways?" he asked.

"I . . . I am here in search of someone as well – I was hoping that the sorcerer would be able to help with locating the young man I believe you are after."

"Is that so? But why is *he* here? I thought the court declared the mage couldn't leave the palace until the kingkiller is found and faces justice."

"He's here because I was able to convince the court to allow us to join the search for the young man," Fiona said.

"Truly? Even though you're under suspicious for being involved with the treacherous plot?"

"And who are you, to make such unfounded accusations – do you realize to whom you are speaking?"

"I certainly do, Lady Palatine, and as I am here on the order of the court –"

"I am part of the court, and I have no knowledge of this order," Fiona said.

"Yet it exists, regardless. As I am here on behalf of the court, I find your presence rather surprising and provoking of even more suspicion. I have no choice other than to escort you back to Queen's Hill."

Fiona gasped, "You shall do no such thing!" She stepped forward.

"I can, and I shall – I'd like to think this can be done quietly," he raised his sword, "But I won't shy away from doing whatever I need to."

*

Olinander's eyes snapped open and he gasped into consciousness. He blinked hard but the blurriness was gone. It had completely disappeared. And he could no longer feel the pull of the void. He placed his hand over his chest as he breathed. The last thing he remembered was his heart feeling like it was being ripped to a stop.

Olinsat up, looking at his fingers. He saw the scales. He ran his finger over them and they flaked away. Olinander looked around, but had no memory of where he was. He got on his feet and opened the door.

"Isabelle. . ." Mary tugged at the sorceress's clothes.

"What?"

The girl merely pointed behind them, and Isabelle turned away from the events transpiring outside. Isabelle's heart thumped as she saw who it was. She clutched hard at Mary and nudged the girl behind herself -- an instinct born of the knowledge of what could be controlling the young man.

"What's going on? Where am I?" Olinander asked.

Isabelle exhaled. He was awake. Gytha had done it.

"Where is –" He stopped short as he heard a voice outside. He frowned.

"Men are here looking for you from Queen's Hill. They want to take the palatine away," Isabelle said.

The palatine -- Levyna. Levyna! Olin marched towards the door and Isabelle placed her arm in the way.

"Are you sure?" she asked.

Olin nodded as he opened the door and stepped outside. A man was holding a sword against Fiona while a group of other stood watching. Everyone turned to face him, aghast.

Mago turned, seeing his men's reaction, and saw Olin, "You!" he shouted, as the rest of his men pulled their swords.

In the background, an attentive Bjorn took advantage of the distraction and jumped on his horse, taking his chance of escape with no mind for the rest of the pay he was leaving behind.

Mago wasted no time lunging towards Olinander, but Olin evaded and knocked away the man's sword-laden hand, grabbed him by the throat, and began to burn his skin. Mago screamed. From behind the window, Isabelle waved her hand and one of the men coming up behind tripped on a stone and stumbled into the other one.

"You draw your sword on her – do you know who she is?" Olinander demanded.

"Olin – no!" Fiona begged.

"Olinander!" Posdel said as Olin grabbed the man's sword and pointed it in the direction of the others even as Mago screamed as his throat burned.

"Olin, don't – please," Fiona begged.

Olin glanced at the palatine and Posdel, then shoved the man backwards into his comrades and took a hold of the sword's blade, his hand heating the metal, then bursting into flame as the steel melted in his hold. The melted sword quickly discouraged Mago's men.

Olin only had one thought on his mind as he stared at Fiona, "Where is Levyna?" he asked.

THIRTY-FOUR

The watcher lay on the floor, gasping for air as the hole in his chest spurted blood.

In the next hallway over, the fortress of the Red Flame was battling chaos the likes it had never faced before. Inches away from the dying watcher was another, who he'd just seen die. The watcher coughed. Their fate was soon to be the same. He was a watcher, prepared for the worst, prepared for death, as his life was meant to be ins service to the order. There was to be no remorse in the face of annihilation, no quivering when he stared doom in the face. He had learnt it all, and it had been what he'd lived by for the last five years. And in all that time he'd fought without every having to look doom in the eyes. He'd been the doom in the shadows many times, the unseen hand, but he'd never truly imagined what his end would look like.

Certainly he hadn't thought he would linger so long, that every moment would pass torturously, slowly dissolving all he had imagined his end would amount to. And surely he hadn't been expecting the dread of inexistence to choke him, despite the gallantness he'd believed had waited for him. It neared, quicker, in shorter, sanguineous breaths, the final destination as the man reached for the mask on his face.

A single moment passed before the watcher's eyes went pale. He lifted himself off the floor and cracked his neck to either side as he looked around. It wasn't hard to hear the direction of the battle. He walked towards the body of the watcher close by and yanked the blade from the dead man's throat, wiping it on the watcher's body as he followed the noise. Confident in his stride, he took his hand to his nose and brushed it, sniffing.

* * *

Levyna returned to her body, and was the first on her feet, after her specter wiped the seigling's venom off her face. She had needed a few moments to pull herself back to reality regardless, but she did soon enough and swiftly nudged the grand sorceress back awake, wiping the venom off her arm before Gytha could regain consciousness, and then helping William up.

Gytha and William looked at the dead demon. It had all but turned to a withered husk on the floor of the cave.

"How did you manage it?" William asked.

"Her specter," Gytha said, excitement in her voice.

"Yes," Levyna said. It had been a total turn of luck, and fate.

"I suppose we should be grateful we brought a spirit of our own, after all," Gytha said.

Levyna smiled. None of them spoke of what they'd seen. The fear the demon had tried to feed on till there was nothing left, was more than just a simple horror – it was something they wished to be far away from, and wouldn't want to imagine it happening, let alone remember visceral memories.

But despite the struggle of the fight, there was a question that begged an answer, even as they made it out of the cave sealed with Akearian silver to quench a demon's escape.

"Is he . . ." Gytha seemed too scared to voice the thought.

"I don't hear him yet," Levyna told her in a shaky voice. A moment passed as they stood in front of the cave in silence.

"It has only just been done, we cannot afford to assume the worst," William answered. "Olinander is strong," he added, seeking to answer the reason why the pertes bond hadn't reconnected at once.

"You're right, we should get out of this dungeon," Gytha said.

They had fought their way in to achieve what they'd come for -- there was no reason to break down in a panic when the odds had been in their favor all along. It must have been fate, that the specter would allow them to conquer the seigling, and if fate had shown them mercy thus far, what reason was there to let uncertainty fester?

They exited the passage with the dead walls, heading towards the thin opening of the cave. Just as they'd come down, Gytha lead the way back out, with Levyna behind her and William trailing them by a few steps. The cold winds of the hillside buffeted at them again, just as Gytha and Levyna turned briskly at the sound of the torch in William's hand dropping to the ground.

"No!" Gytha screamed as William's eyes bugged. He clutched a hand over his throat, tryin gin vain to stop the spurting blood. Then he toppled down the cliff. Allowing him to hit the bottom was unthinkable. Gytha sprung after him, vanishing in a heartbeat.

Levyna's gazed in horror at the scene. It had taken only a manner of moments to all come crashing down. She looked up as a figure emerged from the darkness a heartbeat before he plunged a knife into her belly.

But Levyna didn't give him the chance to throw her over the cliff, and used her power to vanish, following Gytha. The lord watcher stood at the edge of the cliff and looked down at the bottom of the hill, and a wry smile cracked on his face as he imagined the fate that had led him to his revenge so easily.

Gytha caught William in her arms moments before he hit the ground,

"No, William, no!" she screamed as she laid him on the ground and took his bloody neck in her hands. Her threads shot out, wrapping around the wound. Gytha looked sharply away from her dying friend as Levyna appeared next to her, dropping to her knees as she clutched the wound in her belly fearfully.

"No!" Gytha screamed again, holding tighter to William and struggling to hold his withering life steady. She would use all of her strength if she must.

Just then, Thorne appeared at the bottom of the hill and guestured at her with bloody hands, severing her healing spell as his red threads pulsed from one of the Alzeibier rings around his finger. He sent the grand sorceress crashing against the rock wall.

Thorne did the same with Levyna, and seemed poised to let them watch as the man bled out his last breath on the harsh bottom of the hill behind the den of the Red Flame. Until his triumphant stare was thwarted by the sound of an explosion coming from the fortress above.

* * *

Masked as a watcher, he walked through the passage in the direction of the source of the attack within the wall. The one speaking did so with command. He didn't have the air of the lord watcher, but he looked to have some hold in the order -- a circle watcher of the Red Flame most likely. He sent men in the direction to which they would find and eliminate the intruders, or meet their own doom.

When he'd heard enough of the watcher's rambling explanations, the last two after a handful had been sent away, he plunged his knife deep into the unsuspecting circle watcher's side, then quickly stabbed the man again in the neck. The second watcher looked confused, pulling out his own dagger and lurching forward only for his arm to be caught as he was spun and the blade was turned into his neck.

The watcher dropped to the ground, and the man who'd taken his life continued on, brushing his hand against his nose, thinking it was still wasn't enough.

* * *

Olinander appeared in the circle chamber in the presence of three Red Flame watchers.

One of them darted a blade at him, and he dodged, vanishing and then appearing behind the attacker and tugging the man's arm, swinging him in the path of his partner's next attack, burying him on a swinging blade.

Olin turned away as the third watcher who grabbed him by the arm Olin placed his hand over the watcher's arm. Olinander's hand glowed hot and the watcher screamed as his arm caught fire, even as he tried to stab Olin, but he took hold of the second hand as well, setting both the watcher's arms on fire before taking him by the scruff of his neck and shoving him against the wall, burning his neck and setting fire to the mask on his face.

He relinquished the watcher, still screaming, and turned to catch another watcher lunging towards him, stepping off the wall to pounce. Olin shielded his face from the watcher's strike with his arm before kicking the watcher a few yards back. The watcher was joined by a handful more and –

Olin heard Levyna cry.

His face twisted in rage. He turned towards the sound. He could sense her again. Olinander's blood slid down his arms as he furled his hands into fists, his hands and his forearms glowing with heat. Then the heat spread, and it was the entirety of his arms afire as Olin thrust his hands forward, sending a fiery pulse that blew the advancing watchers away with a loud explosion, caving in the walls of the circle chamber of the fortress of the Red Flame.

*

Olinander appeared at the bottom of the hill, arms afire, determined to make Thorne feel the burn of his flames.

The lord watcher aimed a pulse of power at Olin, just as he had just done to the others, but Olin raised a shield, blocking the strike before lunging at the Walrea lord and shoving him into the ground before Thorne could react. Olin landed a punch on Thorne's face and blood spilled from his nose. Thorne tried to vanish, but found himself slammed back into the ground – the Alzeibier had consumed the demican's essence and the lord watcher could no longer used the mover's magic. It couldn't have happened at a worse time, but the mover's magic had hardly been the last of his strength. Thorne landed a strike of his own as threads pulsed against Olin's side, sending him backwards.

Gytha peeled herself from the rock, feeling the ache deep in her bones and in her head. She ignored the blood streaming down the side of her face as she jumped back to William's side and clasped her hands around his throat. Her threads sprang to life at once. She found what seemed to be his last breath. It wouldn't be, not if she could help it, not after all he had done. Gytha would squander every bit of her own essence to keep the man alive.

William's eyes betrayed his terror as he held the grand sorceress in his gaze. He raised his hand to her arm, looking as though he wanted to speak.

"Hold on, William!" She cried. "Do you hear me? Do not let go! I forbid it, you wild man!"

Gytha could feel the life of her friend slipping in her hold, an end that would come swift if she moved. Seeing her son up against the monster she had failed to end, the grand sorceress turned to the side of the rock to bring Olinander hope from the only place she could.

"Levyna!" Gytha yelled.

There was no answer.

"Levyna!" Gytha shouted again, loud enough to reverberate against the mountain behind them, shaking down stones. And it worked. Levyna opened her eyes.

The pain was the first thing that greeted her -- a sharp stab of fire into her belly caused her to whimper. She remembered what was happening. Olin was facing Thorne, Gytha trying to save William.

"You must heal yourself!" Gytha said to her, knowing she couldn't do it herself, not if she ever hoped to see William alive again. "Focus! That's all you need to do – force as much essence as you can towards your pain!"

Levyna looked down at her bleeding gut and tried to do as she was told, her hand glowing slowly with her threads.

Olin darted back at the lord watcher as he got on his feet. Thorne stretched his arm to catch the boy with the threads of the ring on his right hand. The threads clutched at Olin's side and the lord watcher tried to rip at it with a pulse, missing as the arm burst into flames, breaking Thorne's hold.

Olin retaliated, grabbing the lord of Walrea by the neck, but Thorne caught his arm just before it lit on fire, his touch pressing the Alzeibier ring on his finger into the line of blood on Olinander's cut.

Olin's eyes contorted as he felt ring take hold, drawing at his essence. The ring drew so much that his arms began to lose their flames and he was soon falling to his knees. Thorne rose taller as he took the power, quite literally gaining an upper hand as he dug his finger deeper into Olin's blood.

"I have imagined this happening more than I should, to be thwarted by nothing but a flame bug like you! Undoing a plan that is beyond you – no more!" The lord watcher yelled as he consumed Olin's magic.

Levyna rose from her knees, clutching her now-healing gut as she eyed Thorne and Olin. Even if she wasn't next to him to see it with her own eyes, now more than ever, she could finally sense her companion again. She felt every bit of what he was going through, felt the agony louder than Olin's face betrayed. Whatever Thorne was doing was more than torture, and torture she had realized she was capable of.

Levyna fixed her gaze on the lord watcher, looking beyond his eyes and into his body. She focused, clutching her hand into a fist and watching what it did to Thorne.

An instant frown grew on Thorne's face as he felt the pain. He tried to ignore it, but couldn't as his body began to tingle violently. Thorne was forced to let go of Olin as he staggered back, looking as his arms as the pain tore through his insides, as if his blood was frozen and his heart was growing calloused, sending a shock that would cause his body to collapse. He fell further, eyes full of anger as he lifted his head to see who was responsible. The palatine's daughter's gaze was damning, but it was the aquamot's magic that was turning his blood to ice.

Levyna maintained her gaze on Thorne even as she called for her part-ner to get back on his feet. Olin seemed drained as he pulled himself up. The pertes shared a mind again. They knew what needed to happen.

Levyna walked towards Olin, and together they approached the lord watcher, who was fighting to get back on his feet using what little power the Alzeiber had stolen from Olin's essence to counter the aquamot's hold. He could see as the pair came together and held hands threads sizzled around their bodies. Thorne knew he couldn't allow whatever it was they were going to do. He could not be stopped. Not again.

Lacking his blade, Thorne took his hand to his mouth and bit into his own palm till he tasted blood. The lord watcher clutched the hand into a fist to squeeze the blood onto the Alzeiber rings as he clasped his hands together. He would give everything it took. The lord watcher felt the rings take hold of him. His eyes grew stained with blood. He rose to his feet.

The sky sizzled with thunderclaps, then lightning. The pertes felt the jolt ten times more than the first time they'd joined their magics. The quivering was inconsequential this time as the threads took hold of them completely. With the same mind, they turned to Thorne and opened their clenched fists, sending a pulse that would have obliter-ated the lord watcher, had he not ensconced himself in a shield formed with the two Alzeibier rings. The force of the attack pushed him across the ground, but he rooted his feet. But his shield couldn't protect him from what came next. A bolt of lightning shot down, striking the Walrea lord and flinging him hard against the coarse rock.

The threads faded. The pertes still held hands, and Levyna dropped to her knees just as her companion did, both breathing heavily and shaking as they held each other's gazes.

Thorne's body shook where he lay. His head jerked and then raised off the ground. His entire body writhed, strugging to force himself back on his feet. It seemed as though he might manage it, until William's eyes snapped open and Gytha watched in confusion as he vanished from her arms.

William appeared behind Thorne's writing body, taking off the lord watcher's head with a violent swing of his sword.

Levyna's brows raised. She saw William raise his left hand to his nose and brush it, sniffing before he dropped to his knees and collapsed next to Thorne's headless body.

* * *

If he had known this was the plan all along, he would have perhaps listened to what Levyna had tried to tell him when he'd had her captured. But how could he have? To take the pain of years and squander it on the hope that someone else understood, and would do whatever needed to be done. To carry all that he had, and then risk it on someone else's plan. It wasn't something he could stand. Had he known the future, perhaps adversity could have been shelved so they could all get what they wanted. But fate had held a different path for him to take.

It had almost ended in the cabin when the sciff had come to save his companion. He had seen a rage in the boy's eyes, and it seemed as though the boy held the kind of fire that would burn the Red Flame to the ground. The leihcon had seen that fire in flashes as the young man had sought to end him with his fists. And he had – the strikes had been enough to make his body succumb. His old body that is – his truest form. The one the Red Flame had left behind to perish in the fire.

Leaving the body of the dead young woman and finding a debtor on the brink of ruin hadn't been his original plan. When he'd taken hold of Hod's body, there had been nothing more natural than putting a man who thought it all ended when he said so on the ground and then in the ground. The creditor had been on the receiving end of the rage he had carried from being dispossessed of the one way he had that would allow him to finally obliterate the Red Flame.

The tavern owner hadn't revealed anything about the coin he had been given, at least not willingly. Taking a hold of his essence before the watcher expired had been enough for him to know there was at least one more. He knew who the coin had ended up with. That one died as well, but not until he'd learned the coin was heading back to the den of the flame.

That had been his chance – a chance to get inside and bring it all down. But, when he'd approached, he'd begun to smell the stench of death, of souls expiring and essences vacating bodies agonizingly. Of all the things that he had imagined, once he finally reached the den of the Red Flame, he hadn't thought he would find this much destruction. But it had only been better for him.

The gates of the fortress would hold firm or be too alert, but there was already an invitation waiting for him -- there were already multiple bodies. All he had do was take hold of the nearest one. He choose a watcher impatient by the wait, who'd sought to take off his mask.

From then on, it had been as easy as he could have dreamed. He'd taken them one by one, after he'd allowed himself to recover from the awe that this was indeed happening. He killed them all as he strolled through the passages like the master of death, the master they'd believed they were. While they scurried like chickens without heads, he slit their throats, stabbed their guts, and plunged his knife into their hearts, all while setting fire to anything he could.

None of them knew he was there. Something else was paving the way for him, of course, he knew that, he heard it in the chaos as, part by part, the fortress was defeated. He hadn't known what it was at the time, and even if he never learned their identity, he would have been grateful regardless. He lost count of how many he had slain. Three or so circle watchers it must have been, and each of them had felt better than the last. When he heard the loud explosion, it had thrilled his heart so much that he laughed like a maniac even as he slit the throat of yet another watcher.

But that had been the sign that had told him he needed to find out who he owed this chance to deliver his reckoning on Red Flame. He had made his way to the cliff in time to see the lightning strike the man, the watcher, and watched as he was thrown against the wall. He'd thought the deed had been done. Then he'd noticed notice the bastard twitch again.

He had all he needed in the drying sorcerer, and hardly anything could have made for a more satisfactory conclusion of this reckoning than taking the head of a lord watcher as vile as the one called Thorne.

He couldn't remain in the sorcerer, but he'd gotten just what he wanted.

Eusa pulled the mask off his face as he walked through the passage of a burning Red Flame. He brushed his hand against his nose. A tear rolled down his face as he thought of his wife and child.

This was for them.

THIRTY-FIVE

"Are you certain this is what you want to do?" Posdel asked.

Olinander looked down at his hands.

"If it's not, we'll be out of here. There are countless places we can go. A hundred homes of common folk who would gladly hide you – from Ravinshore down to Duken."

"He's right, Olin."

Olin looked up to his right where Levyna stood. He knew why, more than Posdel, she would support the idea. He scoffed dryly, "So you two would have me become a fugitive?"

"We would rather have you safe, and not test the graciousness of the Queen's Hill court, something I have ominous feelings about," Posdel answered.

Olin shook his head. "You have ominous feelings about everything, Posdel,"

"And it has worked for me so far. I also know what it feels like when I ignore it," Posdel said.

He didn't add anything to the words, but there was an understanding between him and Olin, who'd strayed into his home not so long ago and ended up being one of the things Posdel regretted. They both knew who it was he held the regret over.

"I won't deceive myself and say I'm not worried. I don't know what will happen. But I want this to end the right way, and that won't happen if I remain in hiding – I have to answer for what I have done, even if I had no say in why or how it happened, that will be left for fate to decide," Olin said.

"I happen to know something or two about fate being a terrible judge in my lifetime," Posdel said.

"Be that as it may, I cannot deny it has favored me," Olin answered, looking over to meet Levyna's eyes. The words he didn't say out loud, she surely heard. "Whatever happens, I found reasons to be grateful for where fate ended me," he said, still looking in her eyes.

"Whatever happens, I shall have bags packed," Posdel said, looking away from the pertes as he stepped towards the window and stared at the portrait of the sunset across the hills.

*

Mago's face tightened as his eyes as he caught sight of the boy who'd given him a flash of horror like he'd never before felt in his life.

Olinander climbed up the stairs leading to the palace of Queen's Hill. The guard's gaze was hardly the only one that followed the Ravinshore as he made his way through the gate towards the throne room. There was no one else who sparked a greater topic of discussion than this young man in all the three kingdoms. No doubt wondering if a moment like this would come, a crowd was quick to form even as the gates of the palace grounds parted.

Olin looked back at his mother once. There was both fear and reverence in her eyes as she trailed him by a few steps with Posdel. As they approached the doors of the throne room, two guards took Olin by the arms, escorting him as the doors parted and they entered the throne room to the already waiting court.

Olin saw hope in Fiona, who stood at the head of the room. He quickly found Levyna next to her, who would be one of the few people who were not members of the court to witness his trial. Then he saw another two faces, one he wasn't sure were on his side: Queen Katina and her daughter Aldith. The rest of the room held firm gazes, especially Damiran and Prince Petr, which was perhaps understandable, considering what had happened the last time they'd set their eyes on him. The aldermen flanked the prince right, a couple of yards away from the palatine.

Olin stopped in the center of the room.

"You are Olinander of Ravinshore," Prince Petr began.

"Yes, I am, my lord." He had to remember to remain respectful no matter what was said or how it was said. If indeed a fair trial was what he wanted, he couldn't grant any more reason for outcry against him.

"And you have been accused of taking the life of the ruler of Queen's Hill, my brother, King Ranald. What do you say in your own defense?"

He looked to the palatine, who nodded subtly.

"I do not deny wielding the weapon that took the king's life, Lord Prince."

"So you confess you are a kingkiller?" Petr asked.

"My lord, to confess would mean to say that I did something out of a reason or a purpose," Olinander answered.

"You admitted to wielding the weapon, to slaying the king. The question isn't about what purpose it served you, it's about the ultimate offense you have committed.

"Then perhaps it should be," a voice said from the door to the throne room, causing a stir and drawing everyone's attention.

Olin turned around, frowning, to see none other than the king of his own kingdom, King Edmond, walk into the throne room, accompanied by Ole and the woman warden of Black Castle – now that of Walrea.

"Your Highness, King Edmond," Petr said, "We were not expecting your presence here today.

"That would be my fault for not making it known I would be joining you. You shall have to forgive my intrusion, but as this is a matter of significance and a trial of a subject of my kingdom no less, I thought it best to be in attendance. Lord Prince, Lady Palatine," he greeted, "Lord Damiran and aldermen of Queen's Hill. I do not aim at insolence and neither am I here to take over your court, I merely speak for the sake of a fair hearing when I ask that perhaps Olinander here should be tried on the reason rather than the actual action of the offense," The king said.

"Your Majesty, Olinander is being tried for the murder of a king – our king – and by law, there is no reason great enough to bring death to a crowned king of Queen's Hill, certainly not for an outlander," Petr answered.

"He killed my husband, he murdered him in his own court. It doesn't matter what came over him, he must pay!" Queen Katina shouted. Her daughter seemed to agree.

Olinander's eyes found his pertes. Levyna held her hands together, brushing her left arm slowly. *She is in pain,* she said.

She is right, Olinander answered.

Murmurs sounded from the side of the Aldermen and King Edmond broke the disquiet, "Lady Katina, I should like to say again that your husband's death is a great tragedy and you have my condolence," he said.

"I have already received your condolence, Lord King, what I seek now is justice."

"Which is why I am here," Edmond answered, "In person. Not to give justice, but for this young man, Olinander. I have deemed it fit to be his advocate because of what he has done far surpasses even himself. His actions led to saving my life and, dare I say, my kingdom, too. The same actions cost him the life of his loved ones, one of which was a man who raised him as a father. It was his actions against the treacherous and evil plot of the orders of three kingdoms, speared by one man who today is finally no longer a problem, largely, once again, because of the actions of this young man.

"It wasn't hidden that Olinander saved King Ranald's life, and he alerted him of the plot of the Queen's Hill order. I ask that he be tried on the reason for this crime, not just because he is a young man who has gone through hell to save his kingdom and yours, but because no one here in this room can claim they could have managed a different fate, let alone survive what he endured – to be possessed by a demon, something the three kingdoms believed to not have existed for centuries. Who here, in this court, can rightfully say they would have been able to survive a demon taking hold of their body, when no one in recorded history managed it?"

Whispers broke through the room. Petr looked around, glanced at Olin and then ended his gaze on Edmond.

"Lord Prince, if this is intended to be a fair trial, then should it not be indeed on what we as humans perceive as fair? For anyone else in this room, including you, the aldermen, and myself, could have easily been the one called a kingkiller, if your Order of The Red Flame had decided it would be so. The only difference being that we may not be left standing to defend ourselves, as Olinander is now.

"I couldn't be more proud to claim Olinander as a Ravinshore subject, and many more share in my sentiment. The kingdom of Ravinshore should like to beseech her sister kingdom of the great Queen's Hill and this court to not ignore reason. Because of this young man, the root of all our problems is gone and there is no longer a reason to dread war. I say that I and my kingdom shall be eager to show gratitude, should you show mercy and let Olinander be spared,"

It couldn't be denied that it wasn't at all common for a king to present himself as a personal advocate, let alone something to be taken for granted. To have the ruler of the kingdom was to have the entire kingdom, so much authority and power come to plead one's case. No man, either in the court or anywhere else, could have claimed to expect it. If there was ever to be a fair advocate for the trial of a king's death, it didn't get much better than having another king.

*

Time seemed to tick much slower into oblivion as they stood in the yard. Levyna remained next to him as Olinander watched his mother talk with King Edmond, his envoy flanking him on either side.

"You should tell her," Levyna said.

Olinander turned to his companion. "Tell her what?"

"That you forgive her," Levyna answered.

"I believe she knows."

"You assume she knows, Olinander. It's not the same. To think she knows isn't the same as hearing the words from you. I can feel the panic ravaging her body still, panic that she almost lost you – she blames herself for more than you and I can understand. So you should tell her you forgive her."

Olinander looked back to his mother, just as she turned to look at him.

With the air heavy with uncertainty, Gytha's eyes held her son's for a moment, but whatever words needed to be said seemed doomed to come after certainty. Gytha's heart thudded at the sight of Posdel approaching from the throne room. She turned stiffly and everyone else followed her gaze.

"It's time," Posdel said.

Olin heard Levyna's breath stutter quietly. He looked back at her, the pair carrying each other in their eyes, her brows shaking. Their hands quickly found each other and held on tight, the jolt they felt not rare, yet still possessive.

"Whatever happens..." he started to say.

No, she stopped him, shaking her head. The rest of the yard merely watched as they stared silently at each other. *Don't say anything, please. I only want to hold onto your hand the rest of the way.*

Posdel nodded as he stepped aside, allowing Olinander to walk towards his fate, hand-in-hand with his companion.

EPILOGUE

William opened his eyes, feeling like a giant rock sat inside his head. He swallowed hard, his entire throat coarse and painful. He felt a warmth around his right hand, and then a fair weight against his right side and he looked over. William gave the little hand a gentle squeeze and it was enough to spring her awake.

"Has someone taken the bed again?" he asked.

Mary gasped, "Isabelle!" she shouted as she threw her arms around William. "You're awake!"

"Of course, I am, why wouldn't I be?" he said.

Isabelle rushed into the room and stopped short as she took in the sight of William alive. Her face went still before it morphed as the feeling slowly overwhelmed her.

"What?" William asked. "Has something happened to my face? Do I look different?" he frowned.

Isabelle chuckled, shaking her head as she moved to the bed, "Nothing has happened to your face, silly man."

"Oh, alright. I was beginning to worry I grew a horn or something," he said as he slowly sat up.

"Do you feel like you'll grow a horn?" Mary asked.

"I don't know, maybe," he joked and the child giggled. He looked at Isabelle, "How long was I out?"

Isabelle looked to Mary, "It has been five –"

"Seven days!" Mary announced.

William's face contorted as he stared at the two of them. "Seven – You know, if the two of you had planned a better lie, you might have just been convincing," he said.

"And what makes you think we're lie?" Mary asked.

"Because you don't look like I've been asleep for seven days," he said.

Isabelle shook her head. "You're a very proud man, William,"

"I am. I promised I would to return, and I did," he said, even though he suspected she knew just how close he had come to not being able to keep that promise. "I'm also proud because I have you," he turned to Mary, "And you, too," he said.

The girl smiled.

He took Isabelle's hand and pulled her down next to him. "Now, tell me, how long have you been waiting?"

"It has been one very long night," Isabelle said.

*

Fiona watched as Petr took his seat on the throne and the crown was placed on his head. There had never been any doubt as to who would take the throne. Though King Ranald had a son, he was much too young to wear the crown, let alone take charge of a kingdom recovering from a period of great instability. Conflicted as they may have been, even she couldn't have thought of a better person to take charge of the kingdom.

"I should like to wish you years of good reign, Your Majesty," she said, bowing curtly as it was now just the two of them left in the throne room.

"Thank you, Lady Fiona. I appreciate all you have done."

"I have only served my kingdom, my lord."

"And I shall ask how you'd like to continue serving – this kingdom," the king said.

"My lord?"

"I wouldn't make for a very wise king, or man, if I refused to admit that your efforts are largely the reason why Queen's Hill is still standing. Your presence in this court brought, as you say, a voice of reason."

"My lord, I was of the opinion that you would find my presence in the court something you'd want to be rid of."

"Not if I want to be a wise king," Petr answered. "You bring something not many leaders would like to admit is necessary – sometimes a challenging voice is important. I should like to keep you in my court, to keep me on my toes. Of all of my brother's flaws in the short time of his affliction, you were one decision he made that saved his kingdom and I should like to know that I will enjoy the same grace with you as my palatine."

Fiona stared at the king. Not long ago, she'd wanted to be as far from this palace as she could get with her daughter, but it seemed the palace wasn't done with her yet.

* * *

Olinander stood on the balcony, staring down at the view of Queen's Hill from the walls of its palace fortress. Levyna walked up to join him.

"I'll have to get used to this," he said.

"You should, five years is a very long time," she answered.

"It is, to be in service to the king," he said. "Or in service to the kingdom alone, it's a long time." He turned towards her, and stared his companion deep in the eyes. Olinander took her hand, "But I suppose it's not the king or Queen's Hill alone that I should have to serve, and that shall surely make five years feel like nothing."

Levyna smiled, "Tell me."

"What would you like to know?"

"The words you would have said before you knew your fate."

"You know them already."

"I should like to hear them still."

Olinander smiled, "Whatever happens, Levyna, you shall forever have my heart,"

Levyna smiled, "I'd like to kiss you now."

Olin let go of her hand to take her face, holding her still as he pressed his lips gently against hers.